Until the lights come back on
A cyber thriller

Lilly Setterdahl

NORDSTJERNAN
Förlag, New York

Nordstjernan Förlag, New York 2022

Until the lights come back on
Copyright © Lilly Setterdahl, 2022
Cover photo: iStockphoto
Cover design: Nadia Marks Wojcik
ISBN: 978-0-9968460-0-4
First Edition, June 2022
Printed in the USA

This book is a work of fiction. Names, characters, places, institutions, and incidents either are the product of the author's imagination or are used fictitiously.

All rights reserved. No part of this publication may be reproduced, stored in a retrieval system or transmitted in any form or by any means, electronic, mechanical, and digital, except for brief quotations in printed reviews, without the prior permission of the author or publisher

Nordstjernan Förlag
Book Services
PO Box 680
Minneola FL 34755
www.nordstjernan.com

Acknowledgments

Before this book goes to press, I wish to thank the following people for invaluable assistance and encouragement: Misty Urban for editing the manuscript and for expert advice; Dan Moore for technical direction; John E. Norton and my daughter-in-law, Jacqueline Setterdahl, for proofreading drafts, and my grandson Tristan for writing a trailer. As always, I appreciated many kind pointers from the Midwest Writing Center's critique group.

Finally, my sincere thanks go to Nordstjernan Förlag for publishing the book and especially its publisher, Ulf Barslund Mårtensson, for turning the manuscript into an attractive publication. My earlier books published by Nordstjernan, are *Not my time to die: Titanic and the Swedes on board*, *Katrin, almost American*, and *Titanic Sailing Again*.

About the author

For some 30 years, Lilly Setterdahl has specialized in writing about the Titanic and subjects pertaining to the Swedish emigration and Swedes residing in America. Much of her expertise comes from working closely with her emigration researcher husband, Lennart. Through the years, her activities have expanded to writing five novels. The book you are holding in your hand is a thriller about a cyber attack that severely affects Setterdahl's native Sweden.

Lilly Setterdahl

A word from the hacker

As a hacker, I love to observe the havoc I cause. One of the great benefits of working for a large government is that I can zoom in on people and see how they react to my cyber attack. There is a Swedish family that fascinates me. The eldest of three brothers, Toby, is a well-spoken, good-looking fellow who likes to be in charge. He has a degree in geology and enjoys a good position at University of Gothenburg on Sweden's west coast. He is married to a nurse and they have two children. His brother, Alex, is a married electrical engineer who works for the power company in the same city. The youngest brother, Kurt, is single and a doctoral candidate in computer science in Uppsala on the eastern seaboard. You will meet him first, because I believe he will have a huge impact on how this story ends.

The brothers' parents are farmers and not active on social media, but I can still find pictures of them posted by family members. Their medical records tell me they have been healthy so far. Anders looks strong and sturdy, but his wife Lena's body seems too frail for the work that awaits her. I'm trained not to have feelings for my victims, but I sympathize with Lena. She is going to need help.

Sweden's welfare system guarantees a secure cradle-to-grave life. The Swedes enjoy a high standard of living and six weeks of paid vacation, which they use to travel the world. They are in for a rude awakening. It was easy for me to shut down Sweden's large power grid that unfortunately includes Finland. Let's see how our Swedish family reacts to my handiwork.

Lilly Setterdahl

Chapter 1

Kurt Almåker has finished his studies in computer science at Uppsala University and is ready to start writing his doctoral dissertation. But first, he wants to take a few days off to relax in Tallinn, Estonia. Tallinn is located 380 kilometers across the Baltic Sea from Stockholm. It's closer to the Swedish capital than Gothenburg.

While Kurt takes a nap on the ferry, he is unaware of what has happened to Sweden and Finland, but when he checks in at his hotel in Tallinn, he hears other Swedes talking about something in hushed and frightened voices.

"Is what you are saying true? he asks.

"It is. Look at the TV." A large group of new arrivals has gathered in front of the television in the lobby. Like all the other Swedes, Kurt tries to call home but can't get through. After watching more televised reports saying in English that the power outage is expected to last a long time, he fears he may have to stay in Tallinn longer than expected. In a way, Kurt is lucky to have landed there. Estonia is considered the number one IT country in the world. It even exports internet services. All households are equipped with broadband, and every citizen can vote by using electronic ID cards. The country has only 1.3 million inhabitants but is amazingly advanced.

International corporations and European universities are well informed about Tallinn University of Technology, TTU, or TalTek, where students can study cyber safety and large-scale IT systems.

Kurt has heard of it, and after he has stayed at a hotel a few days, he considers contacting TalTek. He's afraid his Swedish credit card will be canceled, and he still can't call Sweden.

Kurt has been told that he looks more like his mother than his father and brothers. He stands in front of the mirror and combs his short, light hair and rubs his thin nose while wondering when he will be able to go back to Uppsala.

Growing up with two older brothers, Kurt always had to compete with them. They had used him to run errands for them and embarrassed him when he was too slow. Toby used to say, "See if you can get this for me while I count to 25?" Kurt feels like the race is still on with his brothers. He has set his sights at earning a PhD in computer science. His brothers Toby and Alex have not advanced that far in their academic studies.

After a few days of lounging, Kurt straightens up to his full 6'2" height. He has to do something while being stuck in Tallinn. Luckily, he has brought his laptop that contains all his important documents. The October wind blows hard from the Baltic Sea as he walks toward the new main building at TalTek, carrying his computer bag. He has an appointment with the president, Dr. Hagner. Kurt has begun to introduce himself in English when Dr. Hagner interrupts him and surprises him by speaking fluent Swedish.

"I understand you're Swedish, young man," he says with a kind smile, extending his hand for a shake. "Welcome to Tallinn, Kurtis Almåker. I'm sorry about what has happened to Sweden." Kurt was taken by surprise by the sudden switch in language.

"I didn't know I could speak Swedish here."

"My mother came to Sweden as a refugee during the war and married a Swedish man. I studied at Uppsala University but was curious about Estonia, so after I graduated, I came over here and got a position at the university. Estonia was a poor country then. It was held back as long as it belonged to the Soviet Union, but now it's catching up with the rest of Europe."

Kurt nods and notes that the president appears to be in his 60s, has gray, thinning hair, and wears an old-fashioned beige cardigan. *If I had met him on the street, I couldn't have guessed he was the president of a university.*

"So, you're finished with your studies but still have a dissertation to write." Dr. Hagner looks impressed.

"That's correct, but since I can't be in contact with my professor in Uppsala, I thought I should be looking for an advisor here."

"I don't know anything about data and can hardly handle a computer," Dr. Hagner says with a laugh. "But I can recommend Professor Hall, who's an expert on the subject. Would you be interested in teaching a course? We happen to have an opening."

"Of course. I need an income until I can return to Sweden, and I fear it won't happen any time soon."

"You're probably right." Dr. Hagner places a call to Professor Hall while Kurt waits in the outer room. When he returns, Dr. Hagner says, "Professor Hall will see you now. Good luck. Hope to see you again on campus."

The professor sits in front of a large computer screen. His shirtsleeves are rolled up and his coat hangs on the back of his chair. He sports a well-maintained beard and speaks English.

"Dr. Hagner was impressed by you," he says.

After the professor has read Kurt's short resume, he accepts the role of advisor and offers Kurt the opportunity to teach a class as a guest adjunct. No work visa is needed as both Estonia and Sweden are members of the European Union.

After a few days, Kurt moves from the hotel to a small furnished apartment. He worries about his family in Sweden. His parents will have to work hard to manage without electricity, and it will be difficult for his brothers to survive in Gothenburg.

Kurt stands in front of his first students and writes his name on the blackboard.

"You can call me Kurt," he says. "I'm from Uppsala University in Sweden, and I'm sure you all know that Sweden has lost power."

A young man holds up his hand and asks, "If a hacker has used the internet to shut off the power, couldn't it be restored with the help of data?"

"Maybe, but then we have to be smarter than the hacker."

"Is there anything else that can be done?"

"I'm not sure, but I talked to an electrical engineer yesterday, and he believes the power can be restored manually on a local level, but it would take too long to power up the entire country that way."

"So, it would be best to do it digitally. Our data experts should get together and find a way. If not, the same thing could happen here."

"Yes, that's true."

A young woman suggests that the power outage is caused by a terrorist attack. Everyone agrees, saying that hackers in either Russia or China are responsible. Another student says it's impossible to prove who has done it.

"Are you able to call Sweden, Kurt?"

"I can make the call, but I don't get an answer. Telephones and computers don't work in Sweden, and I presume it's the same in Finland. There's no postal service either. I can't contact my family at all. Our technology doesn't mean anything if we don't have power."

"Can Swedes drive their cars?"

"As long as they have gas or diesel in the tank. The trains can't run without power and the airports are closed. All communications inside Sweden are shut off, and I assume, also with the outside world."

"I heard on the news that grocery stores are almost empty."

"I'm not surprised. What do you think we should do to avoid cyberattacks?"

"We should get another system without passwords. We already

use voice, and we're experimenting with fingerprints and eye recognition," one student says.

"But the hackers can steal those controls and use them illegally. What do you think it was that motivated the attacker? What can be gained by making a country helpless?"

"It could be a way to take over a nation without traditional weapons," a young woman said. Kurt pointed to her and said, "I want you to write a paper about that. But, considering the current circumstances in Sweden with no working computers, you should write it in longhand to get the feel of what it would be like to be without power."

"I don't have any paper. I write everything on the computer."

"But you must have paper in your printer. Use that. Then I expect you to read your essay tomorrow in class. But you're not the only one. I want all of you to select a subject about the cyberattack. If you had a way to get to work, would you still go there? Do you think you would get paid? Would you stay home, hoping the power would be restored in a few days, or would you flee to another country? Consider the difficulty of fleeing when there are no planes, busses, or trains in service, and you can't pump gas." Kurt observed the reaction of his students and continued.

"I also want you to consider how we can prepare ourselves for a long period without electricity. Should we hoard food and water? How would we cook the food without power? How would we stay warm in cold weather? The central heating won't work. What would happen to people who live in high-rises? Here is yet another subject. How can we safe-keep medicine and distribute it when the pharmacies are closed? Insulin, for instance, has to be kept cold and cannot be stored for long. My roommate in Uppsala has diabetes. If he can't get insulin, he could die."

Before Kurt dismisses his class, all his students have accepted a subject and are willing to write the essay in longhand. It's obvious they like their new teacher.

Kurt feels inspired to work out a program that could undo the hacker's destruction.

The hacker: *So that is what Kurt thinks he can do! Be my guest, young man!*

Chapter 2

On an ordinary Thursday evening in Gothenburg, Toby Almåker is on his way home from work. The rainy and cloudy days of autumn are gone and the air feels crisp and refreshing. He turns on the car radio and listens to the forecast that predicts a beautiful October weekend. His good mood comes to an abrupt end when the city turns pitch dark around him and the traffic lights stop working.

What the hell? What could have caused this when there are no storms in sight? The traffic moves slower and slower before coming to a complete stop. Toby grabs his cellphone, but it's completely dead. After about 20 minutes of stop-and-go driving, he follows the example of other drivers and exits the main route to get away from the stalled traffic. His brother Alex works for the power company, and he should have an explanation for the power outage.

Alex lives in a typical Swedish five-story apartment building with built-in balconies. The building is dark except for candles in some of the windows. Toby parks and grabs his cellphone again but it still won't light up. Alex drives up beside him and they both get out of their cars.

"Hi bro, are you guys working on the power lines?" Toby asks.

"No, we're not. Our electric grid may have been hacked. I listened to the car radio, and one station said that Finland is just as dark as Sweden, and we're on the same grid. It could be very serious. Battery operated radios might be our only source of news."

"Is your phone working?"

"No, it's not. A normal power outage would not take out the cell phones right away. The cell towers must be affected."

"What do you think we should do? Get the hell out of the city?"

"We might have to. Mia should be home by now." Alex scans the windows above. "Yes, she's home. I can see a lit candle in our living room window."

More people arrive by car or bus and gather together in the parking lot. Everyone wants to know why the power is out. One man catches their attention when he says in a loud voice: "Listen to me. I'm a computer specialist guarding against hackers. This is a cyber attack on Sweden and Finland. We have received warnings and now it has happened. We failed to stop it. Our usual backup systems aren't working. Be prepared to be without power for a long time."

Sounds of protest can be heard. Someone asks if planes can still fly. "They can take off and land thanks to strong generators, but if the internal circuits are affected, the airports will close," Alex says.

Residents come out on their balconies and yell to the people on the ground, "The elevators don't work."

Someone on the ground yells back, "Open the doors! The keypad doesn't work." A resident opens the entrance to the building from the inside and holds the door open.

"Wait here, Toby. I'm going to run up the stairs and talk to Mia. We have to decide what to do."

More people gather in the parking lot, and they all have different ideas about what to do.

"We don't have much choice," Toby says. "Trains can't run without electricity. The buses need fuel. We can't pump gas. We'll run out of food and clean water."

"I'll try to catch a ferry to Denmark," one guy says. "I don't need a full tank for that."

Several people agree.

A woman with an accent says in a low shaky voice, "I have nowhere to go. It's worse where I come from."

When Alex returns, he says to Toby, "I'll go to the plant in the morning and see if there's anything I can do. I can't just take off and leave. But tomorrow night, if we still don't have power, Mia and I will drive to the farm. Pappa and Mamma need help, and we can't stay here."

"It's a good solution for you two, but I've got kids, and they need to attend school. If Ella agrees, I think we should go to her sister's in Oslo. I have enough gas to take us to Norway."

"If the phones don't come back online, we won't be able to keep in touch, so I wish you the best, bro."

"Please tell Mamma and Pappa not to worry about us. We'll be fine. I can continue my research in Norway." The two brothers hug each other. As Toby drives out of the parking lot and heads for home, he wonders how Ella will react when he tells her about his plan. He turns on the car radio and listens to a newscast saying that Norway and Denmark have power. It's a ray of hope.

When Toby drives into the garage next to the three-bedroom home where he lives with his wife, Ella, and their two children, Ella meets him with a flashlight in her hand. "I'm glad you are home, honey," she says. "What do you know about the power outage?"

Toby pulls down the garage door, and they stand in the dark and talk. He tells Ella what he has heard and what he suspects. Ella says she had just finished her shift at the hospital when the power went out and the generators turned on with dimmed lights.

"When I looked out the window, I saw that everything was strangely dark. We didn't know what had happened. But like everyone else, I thought it was temporary."

"How're the kids?"

"Of course they're disappointed they can't watch TV and use their cellphones. They don't know what to do."

"Was it hard for you to get home?"

"It was dark when I went to my car, and I was scared, but I knew where I parked. With the traffic lights out, I chose a different route home. I turned on the car radio and heard the special report. Did you hear it?"

"Yes, but I drove to Alex's place and found out more from him and a computer specialist. It seems like our entire electric grid has been hacked."

"Oh, no. Who could have done it?"

"We don't know, but I have an idea. Alex and Mia have decided to go home to the farm."

"That's good, but what about your brother, Kurt?"

"We don't know what he will do, but we can't stay here. The toilets won't flush. My office and the schools will be closed. Everything will close down."

"Not the hospital. It has generators."

"I know, but most of the staff wouldn't be able to get to work. We must think of the children and drive to Norway tonight. Tomorrow, a lot of people will head to the border. We can go to your sister's in Oslo."

"This is happening too fast. Couldn't we go to the summer house? The power might come back in a few days."

"It will be too cold. It's not winterized. And the kids would be bored. No skiing this time of the year and no swimming."

"We could go to one of the shelters. They must have some kind of toilets."

"You can't mean that. I don't want to bring our children into a crowded shelter. We'll take our camper with us to Norway and both cars. Is your electric car fully charged?"

"It was this morning."

Toby puts his large hands around Ella's waist and assures her they will be fine. In her mind, Ella already plans what to bring to Norway. She always likes to visit her sister.

"I'll empty the fridge and take the food with us. Hope we'll be back soon."

"It depends on what happens." Ella turns on the flashlight and Toby keeps one arm around her as they walk into the house. Their towheaded kids sit on the couch with flickering candles on the table. Emil is 15 and Lynn is 13.

"When will the power be back, Pappa?" Emil asks.

"I don't know, Emil, but it might be gone for a long time."

Toby sits down between them and wraps his arms around them. "How'd you like to visit your cousins in Norway?"

"Do they have electricity there?"

"Yes."

"Then let's go," Emil says and Lynn agrees. They are already on their feet.

"Pack your clothes, your laptops, and your schoolbooks."

"Here's a flashlight," Ella says. "I don't want you to carry live candles."

Toby turns to Ella, standing in the doorway, looking at him in the dim light from the candles. The kids are already upstairs.

"That was easier than I thought," he says.

"You will have a lot of explaining to do later on."

"I know."

"It will be so hard to leave everything here. I love this house."

"Hopefully, we'll be back soon. I have a few 100-kronor bills and smaller bills. It won't go far. How much do you have?"

"About the same. I seldom use cash. If worse comes to worst, perhaps I can sell my jewelry." She opens her purse, takes up a comb, and pulls it through her reddish-brown hair.

"You don't have to worry about your looks in this light, honey." Toby's runs one hand through his dark brown, wavy hair and messes it up even more.

He goes through the jar where they keep all foreign currencies from their travels and sorts out a lot of Norwegian 20-kroner coins. "I'll need these for the toll road when we approach Oslo," he says and pockets them along with a few euros. "If you have any euros, Ella, bring them."

"I think I do."

"I can pack the TV screen and all electronic equipment. It makes no sense to leave it here."

As a geologist in charge of a research project at the university, Toby is used to being the boss at work and takes charge of organizing the family's unexpected move. When they are ready to leave and the house is locked, Toby tells Emil to ride with him. "Lynn can ride with Mamma. That way, you can't fight with each other for space. I found this old Walkie Talkie in my closet, and I think we can use it to communicate on the trip."

"Ella over," he says, remembering how to use them from when he was a kid.

Ella smiles as she clicks on her unit and says, "Ella here, over."

"This is something you kids can do." Toby gives his Walkie Talkie to Emil. "You can follow me, Ella."

"Pappa," Emil says, "why doesn't my cell phone work when it's charged?"

"We have lost the reception. When we come to Norway, I'm sure our phones will work. Let's hit the road."

As soon as they are on their way, the children begin to play with their Walkie Talkies, but they soon fall asleep in their backseats. Ella thinks about the patients at the hospital, about the seriously ill who need surgery, about her colleagues, pregnant women, and newborn babies. What will happen to them? She thinks about her parents in Skåne, and wonders if they will leave for Denmark. She thinks about her grandparents and her great-grandmother confined to a wheelchair and living in a home for the elderly.

After about two hours of driving on E-6, they approach the Norwegian border. The horizon reflects the lights from all the lit streets and buildings. The border is usually unguarded, but now the many cars waiting to cross are stopped by a guard. Toby waits impatiently until it's his turn.

"Good evening. I'm a geologist. My son Emil is in the backseat. My wife and daughter are in the car behind me. We're coming to stay with my sister-in-law in Oslo. We don't know how long we'll be here. Do you need to see our ID cards?"

"Not right now. Drive to the side while you fill out this form. Then leave it at the next window and show your IDs."

Toby takes the form and parks on the side of the road. As soon as Ella is parked, she runs up to him and asks, "Did you have any problems?"

"No, but I need your sister's address for this form."

"My cell phone works," Emil croaks. His changing voice is either too low or too high. Lynn waves her lit cell phone. "Look, it's working." All four are happy to be in a country with electricity.

"I can call Malena," Ella says. Her sister answers at once. She knows what has happened in Sweden and has tried to call Ella. "Where are you, sis?"

"We just passed the border. We're driving both cars and we have the camper with us. We'll sleep in the camper tonight, but can we come and visit you tomorrow?"

"Of course. You have our address."

"Yes. This will not be a regular visit, and it feels strange."

"I know, but it will be fun to have you here." They chat a little longer before Ella turns off her cell phone and sighs with relief.

"They'll do everything they can for us. We can stay with them."

"When can we see our cousins?" Lynn is impatient.

"Tomorrow."

When Toby has finished filling out the form, he drives up to the next guard and hands it to him along with their IDs.

"Looks like everything is in order. Welcome to Norway."

"Do you know where we can find a camping place?"

"Straight ahead. You can't miss it."

"I'm hungry." Emil is always hungry.

"We can eat as soon as we come to the camping place," Ella says.

It's late when they arrive at the camping and no one is there to check them in. Almost all the sites are empty. They wear their jackets while eating their sandwiches at a picnic table.

"Thanks for bringing hot cocoa, Mamma," Lynn says.

"Now, it's time to go to the service house. Don't forget your toothbrushes."

The camper is damp and cold, but once they are snug in their sleeping bags, they feel warm.

"The worst part is over, thank goodness," Ella says. "Goodnight, my darlings." Three more goodnights are heard before it is quiet.

Toby thinks about how his ordinary Thursday has turned into anything but ordinary.

In the morning, the manager comes and knocks on their door.

"Do you have an ATM? Toby asks.

"Yes, it's over there."

Toby dresses quickly. He inserts his Swedish debit card, but it's denied. He inserts another card with the same result.

"My cards don't work," he tells the manager, but I have Swedish money."

"I'll take it."

As Toby puts his wallet back in the pocket, he feels his keys and remembers something.

The hacker: *In the rush of leaving, Toby forgot to give his spare key to his neighbor and ask him to look after his house.*

Chapter 3

Alex Almåker drives into the yard of his childhood farm in Västergötland, the home of his parents, Anders and Lena. His wife Mia sits beside him. Their car lights up the red painted farmhouse, and Alex lets the engine run for a while. The front door opens and Anders comes out to see who has arrived so late in the evening.

"Hi, Pappa. It's only Mia and me."

"What a nice surprise." When Lena hears who it is, she comes out on the porch.

"Hi, Mamma. You're sitting in the dark like everyone else."

"Yes, do you know what has happened? We don't know anything."

"Oh, all of Sweden is in the dark, and Finland too. We thought you could use some help, so we'll stay for a while—until the power is restored, I mean. We packed the food we had, and it will stay fresh in the car," Alex says.

Anders, dressed in a plaid shirt and baggy jeans, welcomes Alex and Mia with bear hugs. Alex is almost a head taller than his father. Lena pulls her red cardigan closer around her and accepts hugs and kisses from her tall son and slim, blonde daughter-in-law.

Alex hefts two large suitcases from his car and brings them into the hallway. When he turns off the car engine, it gets dark around him.

"Come inside. I'm so glad you came," Lena says. "Take off your jackets and come to the kitchen. It's the only warm place in the house."

Alex and Mia hang up their black leather jackets before entering the kitchen. They wear sweaters and designer jeans. The four of them sit down at the table and look at each other in the faint candlelight. Mia notices that Anders and Alex have the same square jaws and brown hair, although Anders has lost some hair.

"I brought as many candles as I had," she says.

Anders's eyes dart to his son. "Do you think the power will be out for a long time, Alex?"

"I'm afraid so. There might be a ransom request."

"In that case, it's good that we still have the old cooking stove. The electric appliances are useless now. Mamma and I are hand-milking the cows, but the milk hasn't been picked up."

"We can make cheese," Mia says. She is a domestic-life-skills teacher and knows how.

"Hm, if I have any rennet," says Lena. "I'm forgetting my manners. You must be hungry. I baked cinnamon buns this morning."

"I thought I could smell cinnamon buns when I came in," Alex says.

"A bun with a cup of tea sounds good." Mia gets up to set the table. Lena scoops up water from a pail and pours it into a kettle standing on the wood burning stove, checks the fire, and adds more wood.

"I can't understand why we lost the power when we didn't have a storm?" Anders says to his son across the table.

"Something else has caused it. I was on my way home from work when it happened. We couldn't stay in our apartment because nothing works there. It was best to leave the city. We are lucky to have a farm to go to. Before we left, I talked to Toby. He and Ella are driving to Norway for the sake of the children. They will stay with Malena and Svenung in Oslo."

"Oh? I hope they'll be back. Have you heard anything from Kurt?"

"No, but the last time I called him, he said he was going to Tallinn for a few days. I wonder if he made it before the power outage."

"I hope he's alright. I know he was almost finished with his computer studies," Lena says.

"That's true, and we need data experts right now. I fear that a hacker has sabotaged our electric grid. It's a new way to fight wars without weapons and bombs," Alex says.

Lena shakes her head and wraps her hands in her apron.

"I think I know why just Finland and Sweden lost power. Norway and Denmark are members of NATO. Finland and Sweden are not." Alex stops when he sees how frightened his mother looks. Lena sighs deeply, looking at Anders. "What will happen to us?"

"Don't worry. It will be alright. We have everything we need to survive," Anders says as he touches Lena's shoulder. "Our forefathers lived without electricity and so can we."

Nothing is said for a while as they enjoy the tea and cinnamon buns. They can hear the ticking of the clock on the wall.

Anders breaks the silence. "It was nice of you to come, but you should have gone to Norway, too."

"We don't want to leave without you," Alex says.

"But we can't leave the livestock." Alex understands. "Tomorrow morning, we must drive into town and see if any stores are open and buy what we can. We need cash." Alex opens his wallet to see how much he has and shrugs.

"I doubt the banks will be open. If you'd help me with the milking in the morning, Alex, Mamma won't have to. It's hard on her back. Well, it's bedtime for me," Anders adds while checking his watch.

"Of course. It's good that you still have your wristwatch, Pappa. I don't. I always checked the time on my cell phone."

"We also have the old kitchen clock on the wall that I wind once a week. But why doesn't the landline work, Alex? It usually does during a power outage."

"That's one of the reasons I think this is not an ordinary power outage. It might have something to do with cyber."

"I don't know anything about that," Anders says, scratching his head.

It's chilly in the guestroom when Alex and Mia cuddle together under the duvet and a woolen blanket, with one extra blanket beside the bed. It takes a long time before they can relax and go to sleep.

"Without electricity, we can't shower or take baths," Mia says.

"But we can fire up the old sauna."

Mia is confident that her mild-tempered Alex will come up with solutions. As the middle child, he had learned to adjust and compromise.

At daybreak, Anders and Alex walk together to the red barn and let the mooing cows in through the backdoor. Each cow knows its place in the barn, and Anders points out the ones Alex can milk. He recognizes their pungent odor. Anders climbs the ladder to the loft and pulls down hay that Alex spreads out to feed the cows. Everything has to be done manually. The men have only the faint morning light to guide them.

He thought about how he and Toby had helped with the evening milking after they came home from school while their mother took their place in the morning. Kurt didn't have to learn because by the time he was old enough, a milking machine did the work. If there had been girls in the family, us boys wouldn't have learned to milk, because in Sweden it was considered women's work.

"I haven't milked cows since I was a kid, but hopefully, it's like riding a bike: You don't forget," says Alex. "Speaking of bikes, we should start using them again to save on fuel."

"As long as I have diesel in the tank, I can drive my car," Anders says.

Alex begins to milk. The cows chew hay and are warm to the touch. After a while, he strikes up a conversation.

"When I couldn't go to sleep last night, I was thinking that maybe we could sell the milk in town on market days. It should be alright when all the milk is gone in the stores."

"It's a good idea. The city people can bring their bottles. I can take out the separator from the storage, so we can have cream, too. The grain farmers will buy milk from us, I'm sure."

"I'm glad you still have the cows, Pappa, and it's great that you have saved the old relics from the past. They can come to good use." Alex had always liked to work with his hands and tinker with everything mechanical, and now he has the chance to do it again.

Anders pours the milk through a filter placed over a large can in the milk room. "We can chill the milk outside," he says. When the men are finished with the milking, they let the cows outside again.

"You can feed the calves, Alex, while I mix feed for the pigs," Anders says. The barn cat meows while waiting for his milk.

When Anders and Alex come into the kitchen after their morning chores, Lena has the oatmeal ready, and they eat it with honey and milk. Every little chore has become a major task. By habit, they turn the faucet before they realize there is no running water and flip the light switches. Water for washing dishes has to be heated on the wood-fired stove, but first, it has to be pumped up from the well outside and carried into the house. The toilets don't flush. Everyone has to go to the outhouse and then wash their hands in a barrel used for rainwater.

"I wonder how people could live like this years ago, but they were not used to anything else," Mia says. "Now, we're spoiled with all the conveniences." Alex knows that his kind and unselfish wife will have no trouble working side by side with his mother. Thanks to the food and water available on the farm, they would not go hungry.

"I'll go and change before we go into town," he says.

Anders drives his car as the four of them head to town while it's still dark. Lena is bringing fresh eggs that she will trade for groceries. The fields slope gently toward the road, and spruce and pine stand thick and dark behind the farms. There are only a few cars on the road and they all drive in the same direction, toward the town with headlights on. Outside the bank, a line has already formed. Anders joins it at the end of the line. Alex goes to the hardware store and Lena and Mia to the ICA food market.

While the supermarkets in the cities have generators, ICA in their small town is lit only by daylight through the windows. The customers are grim-faced as they hurry to grab milk from the shelves. All the milk cartons are soon gone. People scurry back and forth and snap up what they need the most. Lena and Mia collide with other carts as they grab as much coffee, tea, sugar, and yeast as they can. Lena asks a clerk for rennet. "It's for making cheese," she explains. The clerk disappears behind a door and comes back with a small bottle.

Mia puts salt in the cart, both regular and sea salt. She adds oatmeal, pasta, and canned food. Lena picks up a dish brush and liquid detergent for dishwashing and laundry. There isn't much left on the shelves. Mia takes a basket and grabs a bottle of vitamins, toothpaste, shampoo, liquid soap, and other things for her personal needs.

At the checkout, the cashier adds up the items on a hand calculator. The eggs that Lena has brought pay only for a small part of the bill. Mia opens her wallet which seems to have a lot of cash and pays the difference. Yesterday, while Alex was at work, she had gone to two banks and withdrawn cash.

Anders has not been able to withdraw more than a few thousand crowns at his bank. As expected, the ATM doesn't work. Alex comes to the car carrying a bag and a can. "I found kerosene," he says, "and a few other things that can come in handy, like disposable razors, but all the battery-operated radios were gone."

While driving home, Anders reminds the others about the Great Depression.

"I have what I need, except enough cash. I should've put the money under the mattress. The banks could crash as they did in America in 1929. My grandpa was over there at the time, and he said it was awful how people suffered. The hard times continued for many years. Luckily, Grandpa had withdrawn his savings before the banks closed. He came home and bought the family farm. He was the one who changed the surname from Andersson to Almåker because he thought there were too many Anderssons."

"Now, we're responsible for the farm." Anders's voice fades as he looks at Lena sitting beside him.

"We'll manage with the help of Alex and Mia," Lena says while touching her husband's hand.

Over the next few days, they all work hard during the day, and after dark, the evenings seem long. Anders has cleaned an old lamp and fills it with the kerosene from the can Alex had bought. He cuts the wick to make it burn cleaner.

"It smells, but it gives much better light than the candles," Lena says.

Their neighbors, Lennart and Lisa, come to visit and they talk about how everything has changed. They are all in the same situation. Stories from the past lift everyone's mood. If it hadn't been for the power outage, they would've all been watching television.

Alex taps his forehead as if to find an answer to who is responsible for the power outage and why it has happened and assumes there will be a ransom request.

The hacker: *As far as I know, there is not going to be a ransom request. The stakes are higher than that.*

Chapter 4

Toby, Ella, and the children were anxious to get to Oslo. But where could they park a camper? Luckily, Toby found a shopping center where they could leave his car and the camper temporarily. "Come on, Emil. We're going in Mamma's car," he said.

When Ella rang the doorbell to her sister's house in the suburbs, Malena opened the door and hugged them all.

"Welcome, welcome, I'm so glad you are safe. Thorsten and Hedda aren't home from school yet. Come on inside and make yourselves at home. Lunch is almost ready. Svenung is flying reconnaissance for NATO. I talked to him about Sweden, and he thinks it's a terrorist attack and that the power outage will last a long time."

"Alex and I came to the same conclusion," Toby said.

The two sisters were the same height and had the same slender bodies. Malena wore her light brown hair short. They spoke the Scanian dialect typical for Sweden's southwestern province where they were born.

"Do you know anything about Alex and Mia? Malena asked.

"They were going to the farm."

"That's good. Alex is so handy with everything, and Anders and Lena will need a lot of help to run the farm without electricity."

Toby voiced his frustration with not being able to call his parents, leaving his job, and having to start over. The children were quiet until Emil looked up from his soup plate. "But we're going back home, aren't we?" Toby and Ella assured him that they would, but for now, they would have to adjust to living in Oslo.

"I want you to relax," Malena said. "It's Friday and you can take it easy over the weekend, but if the power isn't back in Sweden on Monday, you might want to start looking for jobs." Turning to her sister, she said, "I know you can get a job as a nurse where I work, Ella. I've already inquired. As you know, we have a shortage of nurses here in Norway."

"What about me?" Toby asked. "I have research to do, but I won't get paid for it."

"As a geologist, you may be able to get a job at one of the oil companies. They offer furnished apartments to new employees from other countries."

"I heard about it."

"It sounds too good to be true," Ella said. "We're practically immigrants."

"You're svenskar and your occupations are needed here."

When Toby said they had parked his car and the camper at a shopping center, Malena said, "You'll get a ticket. I'll get you an address to a storage place for campers."

"My charge cards didn't work this morning, and we don't have much Swedish cash," Toby said.

"We can lend you money if you need it. You have a home here with us. You can stay in your usual rooms in the basement." Toby and Ella felt like guests, but they worried about their future. They didn't want to impose on their relatives longer than necessary.

The children's cousins, Hedda, 16, and Thorsten, 14, came home from school in the afternoon, and the four teenagers went to the basement to compete in video games. They knew each other well since their families had visited back and forth for as long as they could remember. They had no problem communicating.

Toby and Ella drove to a bank to exchange their Swedish kronor and Euros for Norwegian currency. Then they went to the parking lot to get their other car and the camper and moved the camper to a storage place. They paid for one month's storage and put a "For Sale" sign on it and a phone number. Selling it would give them much-needed cash.

"Hope I'll get a job at S-oil," Toby said. "I'd like the chance of getting a furnished apartment."

"But if you don't, there're other oil companies that might have the same benefits."

"It will be interesting to hear what Svenung has to say."

"But tonight, I want to go to bed early. I'm tired after all the driving and excitement. It will be good to sleep indoors."

As they settled down for the night, Toby and Ella said goodnight to their children—Lynn in her small room and Emil on the sofa bed in the computer room. Emil didn't want a goodnight kiss, but Lynn accepted a peck on the cheek. When Ella and Toby were alone, they found comfort in each other's arms.

"So much has already happened, and we might have to make life-altering decisions," Toby said, pulling Ella close.

"As long as we can be together, everything will be alright," Ella mumbled and yawned.

Over the weekend, Toby asked Svenung many questions about NATO, and they discussed all the possible reasons why Sweden's and Finland's grid had been hacked.

"Because without electricity they're helpless and can easily be conquered," Svenung said. "The attacker can hold out indefinitely, but two small nations cannot survive without electricity for an extensive period. I assume that the backup systems were destroyed."

"That's why I think we have to be prepared to stay here in Oslo at least over Christmas."

Just to make sure the power wasn't back in Sweden, Toby tried to call his parents several times but couldn't get through.

On Monday morning, Ella went with Malena to the hospital to apply for a nursing job. When Toby called S-oil, he got an appointment for an interview the next day. He stayed with the children, read the newspaper and watched the news on TV. He and the kids took a walk in the neighborhood. All the vertically-sided wood-framed homes stood on narrow lots with high hedges between them. Pavers covered the driveways leading to one-car garages. A second car was often parked in the driveway. Narrow streets meandered up and down the hilly area. The intersecting wider street had a bus stop at the corner.

When Malena and Ella came home, a jubilant Ella declared, "I've got a job, and I can start tomorrow. My salary will be higher than in Sweden."

At S-oil, Toby was told he was over-qualified for the only open position. Normally, the company would hire a new college graduate for the job, and it didn't come with the salary Toby could expect. He wondered if he should accept, or try his luck at another oil company, but when he learned of the benefits that came with the job, he realized the apartment that would be available in a few days was more important than a higher salary. He was in a desperate situation and accepted the entry level position.

"I got a company cell phone," he said and waved it in his hand to show Ella and the kids. "But I'll keep the old one as long as it works." He pressed the number to Kurt and was surprised when he answered.

"Where are you, Kurt?"

"In Tallinn. Where are you?"

"In Oslo. My cellphone didn't work in Sweden. Nothing works there. Alex and Mia went home to Mamma and Pappa. How're you doing, Kurt?"

"I have obtained an advisor at Tallinn University of Technology, and I'm teaching one class, but I can't support myself on that alone. If I don't get more work, I will have to take out a loan. I know I can't go back to Uppsala right now."

"Ella and I both got jobs here in Oslo. Do you think the power outage will last a long time?"

"It will take months. The hackers are probably monitoring everything that is done to defeat them, and they are certain to counter it."

"Then we did the right thing by coming to Norway, and you did the right thing staying in Tallinn, Kurt."

The two brothers talked long enough for Toby to tell Kurt about his and Ella's new jobs and the apartment they could use. His job was nothing to brag about, but he couldn't afford to be choosy. They agreed to call each other every few days.

That evening during dinner in Malena's cozy kitchen, Toby summed up the family's first experience in Norway for his children. "We're very lucky to be here. Everyone is kind and willing to help us. Just think, it's almost a miracle that both Mamma and I have jobs already. Now you can get allowances again, but it won't be as much as in Sweden."

Lynn blurted out, "How much longer do we have to stay here? I miss my friends in Sweden. I wish I could send text messages to them." She was close to tears.

"We might not be able to return home until next summer, so you kids need to start school. You'll get new friends and you already know your cousins. I don't want to hear any complaints."

When Toby was alone with Ella, he said, "You've been fantastic. I'm so proud of you, honey. You'll make more money than I will."

"I'm proud of you, too. You have made more money than me for years, and I'm sure you will again. Thanks to you, we'll get an apartment."

"I was told that as soon as a more suitable position becomes available, I can apply for it."

"No matter, we must always stay together. I appreciate you and the children more than ever. I think we'll like it here in Oslo, but I'll miss our home in Gothenburg every day until we can return. It will be hard to get used to living close to other people and booking laundry time in the basement, but it's much better than living in Sweden at the moment. By the way, what did Svenung say about Sweden?"

"He was not optimistic, but he said that NATO might help Sweden if there's a war."

"Could it go that far? I wish I could call my family in Skåne," Ella said, sighing deeply.

Malena, Ella, and Toby drove together to look at the promised apartment. When Malena spotted another resident with children, she asked her where the schools were located. Toby signed up for utility service at the apartment, and at the end of the week, they could move in. The children experienced their first day at the Norwegian school, but only to listen and pick up textbooks. Ella had started to work at the hospital. She was thankful for the furnished apartment and tried not to think about their home in Sweden. Toby wished he could contact his neighbor. If the power was gone for a long time, their home might be ransacked.

The hacker: *I find it hard to stay away from my victims. It is like a good book you don't want to put down. There will be many drawbacks to the decision Toby and Ella have made, and I expect it to be a strain on their marriage.*

Chapter 5

Kurt enjoyed teaching computer science at TalTek. The subject could be applied to many other things. The students were attentive, and he appreciated their interesting essays about the cyber attack and their ideas of how to restore power. He phoned Toby at least once a week and kept informed about what was happening in Norway and Sweden. He planned to fly to Oslo for a visit as soon as he could.

His own social life was limited to the university. He met with Professor Hall and got his advice about the dissertation. Dr. Hagner had taken an interest in Kurt and invited him to dinner at his house. He was a widower and introduced his two daughters to him. Kurt suspected Dr. Hagner wished he would date his elder daughter, Heldi, who taught history at Tallinn University and had prepared the delicious meal. She was okay, but not Kurt's type. She talked endlessly about Estonia's and Sweden's common 130-year history and how the Vikings had raided their coastland in the 8th century.

"We have evidence to prove it. I remember when archeologists discovered a Viking ship in a burial mound on the island of Salme a few years ago. Inside the ship were 40 dismembered Viking warriors. The survivors of the raid had buried them in the ship," she said.

Kurt preferred the company of Heldi's younger sister, Sofia, who worked on her dissertation in computer science, and was delighted when she suggested they meet professionally to exchange ideas.

Many Swedes had arrived in Tallinn, and when Kurt heard them speaking Swedish, he conversed with them and found out Estonia ferried food to Stockholm and brought back refugees on the return trip. From them Kurt learned how serious the situation was in Sweden. The refugees said they had fled as soon as they had a chance but expected to return home when things were back to normal in Sweden.

Kurt told Sofia he wanted to free Sweden from the hacker's grip.

"It will not be easy," she said. "Estonia was hit by a cyber attack in 2007. Our government was forced to go offline. Many banks were affected. The blackout lasted three weeks. With assistance from our allies, we managed to restore our internet. Kremlin denied any involvement."

"It must have been a scary situation."

"Yes, I was only 14 years old when it happened, but the attack gave me an incentive to study computer science."

Kurt accompanied Sofia to a play she wanted to see. The actors spoke Estonian and Kurt understood very little. Sofia described the play to him afterward.

"I should learn your language," he said.

"There're classes online if you have time. I can help you."

The two met often during the spring semester, and Kurt learned a few useful sentences. Sofia could make him laugh and forget he was far from home. When they became intimate, he appreciated her even more. Both considered it temporary.

"If your father knew what we were doing, he would send me packing," Kurt said.

"He would probably prefer you dated Heldi. She doesn't seem to have any boyfriends."

"As you know, I'm not staying, but I'm glad for the opportunity to teach here and work on my dissertation. Thanks to a scholarship from TalTek I can complete my doctorate."

"I'm not going to stay here either. I want to see the world. Perhaps I'll go to Australia or Canada."

They talked about the pros and cons of the two countries. "They are both former United Kingdom countries. Winters are cold in Canada, but the weather in Australia is warm all year round," Sofia said.

"You could compromise and move to London and teach at Oxford."

"Perhaps, but I'm not sure I'd like that."

"This summer, I'll fly to Oslo and visit my family. Then I'll teach here for one more year," Kurt said. "If everything goes well, I hope to get my doctorate next year. But first I would like to visit Helsinki and meet the computer experts who have restored the power to Finland."

"As soon as I have my doctorate, I'm leaving. I don't intend to write a teaching contract with TalTek for next year." Sofia decided to make London her first stop on her two-year excursion around the world. Kurt said goodbye to her at the end of the semester and didn't stay for her doctoral ceremony. Instead, he flew to Oslo.

When his family had thoroughly welcomed Kurt, he accompanied Alex to his job and took the opportunity to visit the Oslo museums. Kurt found the Kon-Tiki Museum to be especially interesting. Thor Heyerdahl was a name Kurt remembered from TV shows he had seen. Now, he could see the balsa raft that Heyerdahl had sailed from Peru to Polynesia, and he marveled at the thought of such a small and fragile raft making it across the ocean.

One day, Kurt met a young attractive woman he liked. Mette worked with computers and seemed advanced in her field. The two of them dated at least once a week. She asked if Kurt had seen the Roald Amundsen Museum.

"No, I haven't seen that one yet."

"I can take you there." Proudly, Mette told the story of the adventurous Norwegian who was the first to reach the South Pole. "It was, of course, a very dangerous expedition, but he reached his goal 34 days before the British explorer Robert Falcon Scott."

"Yes, I know that. It was an amazing accomplishment."

Kurt found it both relaxing and enjoyable to be with Mette. They talked about the current Norwegian Olympic champions. The Norwegians excelled in endurance sports and were especially successful in decathlon races and cross-country skiing. Kurt admired them for training so hard. Norway was a country filled with fit and active people. Rain or shine, they all seemed to go on hikes on weekends. Kurt got to test his endurance when he accompanied Mette on long hikes in hilly terrain. They went to Oslo's beautiful lake Maridalsvannet and the Ekeberg Sculpture Park, filled with sculptures created by international artists, where they could admire the view of the city and the Oslo Fjord. Kurt didn't see any overweight people anywhere. He imagined what it would be like to live in Oslo when he was finished with his education.

At his farewell party a few weeks later at Toby and Ella's place, Kurt once again met Svenung and Malena. As always when Svenung was around, the talk turned to NATO. The men went out on the patio to be out of earshot of the children.

"It looks like the Baltic states are preparing for war," Svenung said. "They belong to NATO, and the alliance is strengthening its presence in the Baltic after Russia annexed Crimea and invaded parts of Ukraine."

Svenung and Toby continued the conversation while the others listened.

"Sometimes, I fly to the NATO base in Rukla, Lithuania. It's only 100 kilometers from the Russian border. Germany will lead a NATO contingent to Rukla. The contingent will include troops from Belgium, the Netherlands, Norway, and Luxemburg," Svenung said.

"But didn't Sweden take part in NATO exercises in Spain and Portugal?" Toby asked.

"Yes, but as you know, Sweden cannot be sure of a common defense. Only the member countries can count on that."

Toby agreed but doubted that one thousand troops in Rukla would make a difference.

"Do you think NATO would defend the Baltic states if they were attacked by Russia?" Kurt asked, looking a little worried. He had thought he would be safe in Estonia.

"We'd have to, but to be honest, I think the presence of NATO troops is more to show solidarity than strength," Svenung said. "The air defense is more important. Do you know that there's a center for cyber defense in Tallinn?"

"I've heard about it but I haven't been there yet," Kurt said.

"It was founded in 2010 and has 21 member countries from NATO and other countries. Look into it?"

"Will do. Thanks for the heads-up."

"You're safer in Estonia than in Sweden. I think it's only a matter of time before the Ruskey invades Stockholm. It's like an open door." Svenung marked his words by stretching out his arms. The scenario made Toby and Kurt shudder.

The hacker: *Svenung understands that Stockholm is vulnerable. Kurt thinks that a Finnish computer specialist restored the power to Finland, but they did get an assist from me. Why? Because Finland was not supposed to lose power in the first place.*

Chapter 6

Without electricity, life on the farm had become time consuming and primitive. For the men, it meant hand-milking morning and night. Water and firewood had to be carried into the house. Every day, they chopped wood. When the logs were almost gone, they hauled more from the woods. To go from effortless electric heat to woodburning presented a challenge. A lot of hard work would be required just to stay warm during the upcoming winter.

Anders and Alex shaved only once a week. Mia stood by the sink and washed her hair. She heated water on the stove and poured it over her head until it was clean. Lena did the same. The women cooked the food on top of the wood-burning stove. Without running hot and cold water, every chore had become a major task.

For their laundry, Anders brought out the old boiler and placed it beside the well. He pumped up water, filled the boiler with water, and lit a fire in the burner. The women came with the first load of laundry and detergent. Everything that could be washed in hot water was placed in the boiler. For the dark clothes, Lena used the old washboard. They rinsed the clothes in large tubs. It had become natural to divide the work by gender.

They all worked hard but had no income. Anders and Alex mounted a trailer on the tractor, loaded it with firewood and milk cans, and drove into town. The need was great, but most of the customers had no money. They came with things they wanted to trade, like a knife, a watch, a ring, or a sewing basket. Anders and Alex preferred cash, but sometimes they felt sorry for the hungry people and accepted an item in trade. Bartering had become common.

Anders suggested that Lena and Mia bake extra bread to sell in town. Lena had an old-fashioned baking oven built into the basement chimney. She mixed a big batch of dough, and Mia helped with the kneading. First, the dough had to rise, then it had to be kneaded again and flattened into rounds that were about one inch thick. While the individual rounds were set to rise again, Lena started a fire on one side of the oven and gradually added long pieces of firewood. When the stone surface was hot enough, she used a long-handled flat spade to place the bread in the oven and take it out when it was done. The heavy iron door stood open so she could watch. It was like baking pizza, and it took only a few minutes for the bread to get golden brown. Mia went up and down the stairs to bring down more bread.

If the two women were to bake enough bread to sell, they must bake almost every day, and they would run out of flour. They still had a sack each of rye flour and wheat flour, but if more grain couldn't be milled, they would run out of flour for their own needs. Their customers always asked for bread. The farmers also sold eggs, milk, potatoes, and firewood.

When the meat began to thaw in the freezer, it had to be cooked. Alex put the steaks on the grill and invited neighbors to share in their bounty, but the smell of meat attracted too many beggars. When the family couldn't eat the meat as fast as it thawed, Lena gave some of the cooked beef to people who came to their door. They needed protein and were delighted to get meat for a change.

"If you continue to give away meat, there will be no end to the beggars who come here," Anders said.

"Then I have to resort to the old canning method," Lena replied. "Mia, can you help me carry up the canning jars from the basement?"

"Of course." Having washed and sterilized the jars, the two women began to fill them with cooked meat and place the jars in a big kettle filled with water. The conservation method consisted of boiling the water until the submerged cans were sealed.

Sweden had lots of wind turbines, but Alex had no way of accessing power from them. He decided to build a small windmill that would bring light to the house. First, he brought out the old diesel-powered generator and cleaned it. Then he visited the museum park to study how the old gristmill was made. The next step was to select planks for the wings. Anders polished and oiled them while Alex rummaged among all the things his father had saved and came up with a wheel and other things he needed. He went to a junk dealer to get the rest.

The men raised tall pine logs on the highest point of the farm to get the most wind. The tractor came to good use. Curious neighbors came to help. Finally, Alex went to the power plant where he used to work to get power lines.

He chose a windy day to test the windmill. Would it work? All eyes turned to the house as they waited. When a wind gust turned the wings faster, a faint light became visible through the windows.

Lena came outside and yelled, "It's working."

Alex said that building the windmill was the most gratifying work he had done as an electrical engineer.

As the weather turned colder, Alex decided to install stoves in the bedrooms on the second floor. Luckily, Anders had saved the pipes needed to connect them to the chimney flue. He helped Alex carry the small stoves called kaminer to the second floor. After they were lit, smoke came into the house, but it soon subsided and the parents' bedroom began to get warm. Next, they installed a kamin in the room where Alex and Mia slept. They would light the stoves in the evening to get the chill out of the rooms but let the fire die down before morning.

The living room had a kakelugn, a beautiful ceramic fireplace that was seldom used. In the old days, the family had used the room mostly as a dining room for big parties. Now, it was furnished with a comfortable sofa and chairs, and, of course, a large television that wasn't working.

Alex enjoyed building a fire in the kakelugn. When the room began to get warm, he invited the family to come and enjoy it. He sat down in a comfortable chair, stretched out his long legs, and felt good about what he had accomplished. Lena came and closed the drapes. For the first time since the cyber attack, the family relaxed and felt comfortable. The most important rooms in the house were warm. But much work remained to be done.

If Alex could get hold of another generator, it could be used to power the milking machine. No one wanted to think about what would happen if the power was not restored before the spring planting. One of the neighbors had a horse, but it would be much in demand. They talked about the most feared scenario—war and occupation by Russian soldiers.

Everyone agreed that Sweden had a poor defense. Most of the former military barracks had been demolished or were used for something else. Where were the recruits going to sleep? Thousands of young men were being drafted before the army had accommodations for them. The soldiers were used mostly to transport supplies, and temporary quarters had to be found for them. Alex could be called up if needed. The military had diesel and gasoline, but rumors circulated that gengas (wood gas) would be introduced, an alternative fuel that was used during the World War II. To prepare for gengas, Anders and Alex went to the woods and cut down birch trees, the best wood for producing gengas. The logs had to be cut with a saw and chopped into small pieces. The bus traffic could resume if the busses were equipped with gengas. Trucks could also be powered by gengas.

Almost all the stores were out of imported staples like coffee, tea, chocolate, and sugar. If a store happened to have coffee and sugar, it sold only one package at a time to prevent hoarding. The food stores were open only during daylight hours. The hospitals received acute cases but couldn't do much for them with only generators for power. Many men abandoned their homes in the cities and began to walk from farm to farm, begging for food and sleeping in haylofts.

One late afternoon, a woman came to the farm on a bike. She said she had sewing notions that she wanted to trade for milk for her children. One child sat on the back of the bike and one in the front. Both were bundled up against the cold and had dripping noses. The youngest was asleep. Lena's heart ached for them and asked their mother where they came from and where they were headed.

"We started in Gothenburg and we're going to my parents' farm outside Trollhättan. I try to cover 20 kilometers a day, but it takes a long time."

"Where do you sleep?"

"In a pup tent," she said, pointing to her heavily loaded bike. She looked at the darkening sky and seemed anxious to continue.

"Ma'am, do you need any needles? I have darning needles in case your socks are getting worn?"

"They sure are. The men's socks are getting thin. I haven't mended socks for years, but now that we can't buy new ones, darning needles would be good to have. What else do you have?" Lena bought most of her supplies before filling up the children's sippy cups with milk. "It's free," she said. When it started to rain, she said, "You shouldn't have to be on the road a night like this. Our sauna is warm and you're welcome to go there and bathe yourself and the children."

"That's the nicest thing anyone has done for us."

When Anders came up to them, Lena explained the woman's situation and told him she had offered her the sauna.

"Go ahead. It's already nice and warm, and I have carried in water," Anders said.

"I'm so thankful. My name is Astrid. I worry about the girls. They both have colds. My hubby rode his motorbike to Norway. I hope he made it. He knows where the girls and I will be, and he'll come for us whenever he can."

"If you'd like to stay in the sauna and sleep there tonight, you're welcome to it. We can use it tomorrow," Anders said. "Just don't tell anyone about it because then the sauna will be occupied all the time." He was as moved about the woman's story as Lena.

"I promise I won't tell anyone, and I appreciate your kindness more than you'll ever know," Astrid said.

"There are clean towels in the sauna. It will be warm all night so I don't think you need any blankets."

"I have blankets." Astrid turned her bike toward the sauna.

"I'll bring you supper," Lena said.

In the morning, Anders found a thank-you note in the sauna from Astrid.

The story about the runny-nosed girls made Mia think about how much she wanted to be a mother, and she had an inkling that it might come true.

One evening when Alex and Mia had gone to bed, she whispered, "I'm almost positive that I'm pregnant."

"I can hardly believe it."

"I haven't had my period and I feel nauseated in the morning."

"It would be wonderful if we could finally have a child, but the circumstances are not the best right now."

"I'm so worried, Alex. We need to move to Norway."

"I agree."

Hugging and kissing his wife, Alex promised her he would do everything in his power to get them to Norway.

"We have no gasoline for our car and we can't take the diesel car from Pappa. I'll think about it. But there's something else I want to do first. I need to get the milking machine to work."

When Alex told his parents that Mia was pregnant and they needed to move to Norway, Anders said he would be glad to drive them to the border. From there, they could call Toby and ask him to pick them up. "Your child must come before everything else. You've been here and helped us long enough. We have light and heat and can manage ourselves. I just have to be sure to be home before the evening milking."

"But you need the diesel yourself, Pappa."

"Don't you worry about that? When that's gone, I can drive on gengas.

"It's too hard for Mamma to milk by hand and you can't milk all the cows yourself twice a day. If I can find a generator, I can get the milking machine to work, and then I'll find a way for Mia and me to get to Norway."

"I heard there will be an auction next week at Hans Olsson's. He's going to quit farming. All his children are in Norway, and he and his wife want to move there. I'm almost certain he has an old generator. Most farmers used them for threshing before they had electricity."

The hacker: *Alex is more resourceful than I expected and Anders displays a lot of wisdom. I cannot wait to see what the two of them will do to make life easier on the farm. It will still be hard, and one never knows what unexpected event can occur. Watching this Swedish family at work is like watching a movie.*

Chapter 7

Toby met his son and daughter outside the school after their first day of classes. "How did it go?" he asked.

"It will be too hard. You should see the books. Why do we have to learn to read and write Norwegian when we're going back to Sweden?" Emil asked.

"At least you have to try," Emil. "It's not that hard."

"My teacher said we can write in Swedish to begin with," Lynn said. "If I need help with the Norwegian language, there're Swedish-speaking assistants who can translate for me. Students from other countries get help and so can we."

"I can call the principal and see if we can arrange temporary help for you," Toby said. "Some words in Norwegian are different from the Swedish, but most are similar when you see them written. It's easy to change from one language to the other on the computer. I experimented today. You can also get words and sentences translated quickly online. I know you study English and other languages, but it's good to know another Scandinavian language. Norwegian is important because it's the only Scandinavian language that appears on the instructions for dishwashers and washing machines. I'll work in English at my office, so I depend on you to teach me Norwegian," he said with a chuckle.

Emil snorted. "Don't hold your breath, Pappa."

"Come on Emil. We really can't complain about anything. We have a comfortable apartment. Think about your friends in Sweden. They have no heat, no light, nothing electronic, and no warm food. They can't take showers or use the toilets in the bathroom."

"Why can't they use the toilets?" Lynn asked.

"Because when the electricity is gone, the pumping stations can't operate and new water can't get into the house. I bet the kids don't get any allowances either because the parents have very little cash and the charge cards don't work."

The children were quiet for the rest of the way home. A few hours later, Ella came home carrying food bags.

"I bought bread, milk, potatoes, a salad, and a cake until I can bake myself. The rest is in the fridge."

"Then I'll start the potatoes if you fix the rest," Toby said.

The children came to the kitchen and said they were hungry.

"You had lunch in school, didn't you?" The children nodded.

"Good, then you can set the table and learn where everything is."

When they were finished with their meal and had cleaned up in the kitchen, the doorbell rang. A family with two teenagers stood outside the door. The woman held a bouquet in her hand. "We heard you're from Sweden, so we wanted to welcome you. We're from Gothenburg," she said.

"So are we!" Toby exclaimed. "Please come in. How nice of you to come." They said their names, and Daniel and Toby shook hands while Karoline gave the flowers to Ella.

"Thank you. They're beautiful."

"These are our children, Melker and Mathilda," said Karoline.

"Hi, how old are you?"

"I'm 14," said Melker. "And I'm 15," said Mathilda.

Ella called on her children. "We've company from Sweden."

Emil and Lynn came at once and said hej before they asked Melker and Mathilda to come with them to the basement. Ella and Karoline went to the kitchen, where Ella put the flowers in a vase.

"We just arrived in Oslo," she said. "How long have you been here?"

"We came a year ago. Daniel works for S-oil and I work at a hospital."

"What a coincidence. I work at the hospital in Ullevål and Toby at the S-oil office. We can learn so much from you and your children. Emil and Lynn will have many questions because they started school today. We came to Norway so the children could attend school. I have a sister here in Oslo, and she's also a nurse. We stayed with her at first."

"We live in a furnished apartment in this building, but we'll be moving soon. We had planned to bring our furniture from Sweden, but now we'll have to buy everything."

"Do you want a cup of coffee? I bought a cake today," Ella said.

"We'd love to, if it's not too much trouble. I can go home and get sodas for the kids."

"Good, because I haven't bought anything like that yet," Ella said while filling the coffeemaker with water. She opened the coffee can and put a filter in, measured the coffee, and hoped it would be strong enough.

The coffee was ready, and they joined the guys.

"This is fantastic. What a coincidence," Toby said. "We have the same occupations. We are from the same city, and have children at about the same age."

Ella called the kids.

"We can take the chairs from the dining set so all of us can sit around the coffee table," Toby said and started to move chairs. "I'd like to hear what Melker and Mathilda have to say about the school." The kids heard what Toby said.

"Emil complained about school, but I told him he has nothing to worry about," said Mathilda. "We've been here almost a year and we speak Norwegian and have no problem reading and writing. We're doing almost as well as the Norwegian students."

"Did you get help in the beginning?" Toby asked.

"We did."

"I'm guessing you're going to the same school as Emil and Lynn."

"Yes, but not in the same classes. The discipline is stricter here."

"I like that," Toby said with a wry smile.

"Isn't it strange? Toby and I both graduated from the University of Gothenburg. We have so much in common," Daniel said. "I asked Toby many questions about Sweden. We're glad to be here, but both Karoline and I have parents and siblings in Sweden, and we worry about them, especially since we can't communicate with them. We wish they could come here."

"It's the same for us," Ella said. "I have nightmares about it."

While the women talked with each other, Toby began a discussion with Daniel.

"My Norwegian brother-in-law says that NATO is guarding Sweden from the air."

"But the burning question is if the power grid can be restored without concessions."

"I've wondered about that, too," Toby said.

"If ransom had been paid, the power would have been back by now."

Their previously good mood had disappeared.

"I don't understand how the city people can stand it," Karoline said. "They have no wood-burning stoves and no outhouses. Older farms might have those things even though they haven't been used for years."

"Yes, my parents are farmers and they have kept things like that in case they lose power," Toby said. "My brother and his wife went home to help them, but also so they wouldn't starve, but now they aren't making any money."

"We rented out our house before we came here, and we can't collect the rent. We shouldn't be selfish though. It's worse for those who live there," Daniel said.

The children chatted happily about television programs, data, video games, etc. They agreed to accompany each other to school the next day.

"Perhaps we can ride together to work, Daniel?" Toby suggested.

"Going by car would be cheaper for two. You can ride with me until you're familiar with the route. Do you know that S-oil in Fornebu has the most modern-style office complex in the world?"

"Yes, I saw it yesterday. It's unique."

"And Ella and I both work at the largest hospital," said Karoline. It has more than 24,000 employees in various locations. I take the trolley there. It's the easiest."

"I drove the electric car today because I needed to shop on the way home," Ella said.

"Do you have an electric car? Then you can charge it for free at S-oil while you work, Toby. You can also drive in the fast lane," Daniel said.

"Great! Then I'll take that car to work and you can ride with me."

When the guests had left, the family gathered in the kitchen. Everyone was happy to have met a Swedish family.

Toby called Kurt, but his number was no longer available, probably because he had a new cell phone. Having looked up the website for TalTek, Toby found Kurt's name on the faculty, his new number, and email address. "That's great," Toby said to himself and fired off an email to congratulate Kurt on his new position.

The hacker: *I think Toby feels guilty about having left his parents without saying goodbye to them. More than anything else, he wishes he could contact them. He and his new friend, Daniel, might be correct in their speculation about a worst-case scenario, but we will just have to wait to see. Now I want to see what happens on the farm.*

Chapter 8

Alex and Anders looked at everything that was to be sold at the auction. The generator was broken, but Alex thought he could fix it. Anders thought about bidding on the horse, but it would probably be too expensive. He felt sorry for Hans Olsson. He would lose a lot by selling almost everything he owned.

The auction began with the livestock. Anders bid on the horse and was glad to get it for 300 crowns. The cows sold for 200 each. Their milk was more valuable, but Anders had enough cows. Alex bought the generator and other miscellaneous items. If the generator had been in good condition the price would have been much higher. Mia bought soft yarn she planned to use for knitting baby clothes and cotton bedsheets that she would make into diapers in case they couldn't move to Oslo. Everything was cheap.

As soon as Alex had the chance, he began to clean and fix the generator, so it could power the milking machine with the help of diesel. He tested it the same evening and it worked. Next, he wanted to make a mechanical butter churn and asked his mother if he could use an old spinning wheel.

"You may, because I don't use it."

Alex mounted a whisk upside down so the mechanism could be used to make butter instead of spinning yarn. Lena tried it and it worked so much faster than churning by hand.

People had started to attend church more often, and Anders and Lena joined them. Dressed in their heavy winter clothes, they still shivered in the unheated church until all the people in the pews made it feel warmer. Many elderly people had trouble reading the fine print in the hymnal in the dim light from just candles. After the service, they stopped outside and greeted one another. They asked how their relatives in town were doing and how others managed under the primitive circumstances. They found out who had gone to Norway and how they had traveled. They hadn't seen a newspaper for a long time.

The army had exercised in the area for a week. While Alex inspected the damage done to the fields, he discovered a barrel of gasoline in a ditch and felt a jolt of hope. The gasoline could be the ticket for him and Mia to drive to Norway. He went home and got the tractor, a trailer, ropes, and planks. Anders came with him. He said he had a hand pump that could be mounted on the barrel to pump up the gas. The two men rolled the barrel onto the planks until it was on the trailer and then raised it for safer transport.

"Now that you have gasoline, you and Mia can leave," Anders said. "You have helped us so much. The milking machine and the butter churn are great. We have lights and heat in the house. I think you should leave before the snow comes."

"I thought we could wait until after Christmas, but you're right, Pappa. For Mia's sake, we should leave sooner. Just think how happy she will be when I tell her."

Alex entered the kitchen with a broad smile on his face. He took Mia in his arms and danced around with her.

"Why are you so happy?"

"We can leave for Norway tomorrow. I've found a barrel full of gasoline. The army left it in a ditch."

"Is it true?"

"As true as I'm standing here. We can go to Ella's sister and ask where Toby and Ella live. When I think of it, I have Malena's number and we can call her as soon as we're in Norway. In Oslo, you can see a doctor, and you can give birth in a hospital. I can start to work and make money. Pappa and Mamma can manage on their own."

"You're making me so happy, Alex. I'll go and pack right now. Lena is taking a nap, but when she wakes up, she will be super happy for our sake. But it will be difficult not to be in contact with her and Anders."

"The mail has started to work on a small scale, so don't give up on that. I saw a letter carrier on a bike the last time I was in town. We'll write to my parents as soon as we are in Oslo."

It was hard to say goodbye. Lena wiped away a few tears.

"Alex, do you have the phone number to Malena and Svenung?" she asked.

"Yes, I do, and our laptops and important papers. I don't think we'll have any problems getting into Norway. If so, we'll be back."

The weather was still mild in the daytime. The rain drizzled on the windshield as Alex drove north. At night it could freeze and it would mean slippery roads. If everything went well, they would be in Norway before dark although darkness fell early in November. Alex had a can of extra gasoline in the trunk.

"We have only two suitcases," Mia said. "It will be like starting over with two empty hands. I'm thinking about everything we have in our apartment, all the furniture, rugs, bedding, decorations, and our summer clothes."

"Hopefully, we'll be back. It will be a large expense to buy everything, but we'll start with as little as possible. Most importantly, we'll buy what we need for the baby."

"Hope our Swedish health insurance is valid in Norway."

"I'm sure it is until we can get Norwegian insurance. Norway has universal healthcare the same as Sweden."

There were no other cars on the road until they came closer to Norway when they saw cars with Norwegian license plates. Before they crossed the border, they stopped to eat the food that Lena had packed for them and drank coffee from a thermos. Alex topped the tank with the gas he had brought. They couldn't wait to get into Norway for their toilet needs, so they went into the woods.

"I hope it's the last time we have to do this," Mia said.

"I'm sure it is."

There was no line at the border. The guard sat inside but came out to meet them. He said that the Swedes didn't come as often anymore.

"We want to stay in Norway. I have relatives in Oslo," Alex said. "I am an electrical engineer and my wife is a teacher. Here are our passports. If you need anything else, I have references."

"Just fill out this form. Make sure the writing shows on the copy. Write down your license plate number."

Passports had not been needed between Sweden and Norway for years, but now they were stamped. Alex began to fill out the form. When he was done, he gave it back to the guard, who pulled out the copy and gave it to Alex.

"Welcome to Norway," he said. "Sweden took in 50,000 Norwegians during the war, so we're happy to return the favor."

Now that they were in Norway, the cell phones they had charged in the car worked just fine. Alex clicked Malena's number and she answered.

"This is Alex, Toby's brother. Mia and I have just arrived in Norway and we need the address to Toby and Ella."

"Hi, Alex. You surprised me. They live in a large furnished apartment and they will be happy to welcome you. Do you have a pen?"

"Mia is writing for me." She was ready with a paper and pen, and a wide smile on her face. Alex had his phone on the speaker.

"Thank you so much, Malena."

"Looking forward to seeing you both. Just so you know, Toby said that Swedish debit cards no longer work here."

"Thanks for telling us. I'll avoid the toll road."

"Now we have Toby's address, and we're in a country with electricity." Alex entered the address to the GPS.

"Never in my life had I imagined that we would leave Sweden like this, almost like refugees," Mia said.

"No, we Swedes have always been proud and stubborn. We thought we were the best in the world and had it better than everyone else. Norway was a poor country after the war, but now it's rich thanks to the oil, richer than Sweden."

Mia sat up straight and looked at the lights, the traffic, and the store signs, all lit up in bright colors. "It's so beautiful," she said. "I can drive if you want to take a break."

"No, I think you should rest. I feel great and I don't mind driving. I'm so glad you will get good maternity care in Oslo."

The hacker: *Alex will have reasons to worry about his parents. With so many beggars coming to their door, their safety is at risk. I am glad Alex found a way for him and Mia to get to Norway. Cannot wait to follow them in their new country.*

Chapter 9

Alex and Mia received a warm welcome from Toby and Ella.

"We knew you were coming because Malena called," Toby said. "How're Mamma and Pappa?"

"They're fine. We have big news for you. Mia is pregnant, so we just had to come here."

"That is wonderful news. Congratulations," Ella said. "Are you alright, Mia?"

"I feel great now, but for a while, I was nauseated in the morning. I think I'm in the third month, but now I can finally see a doctor."

"Malena can recommend one for you. Don't you have any suitcases?"

"They're outside the door." Alex brought them in before they took off their leather jackets and hung them on the coat rack by the door.

"You can stay with us. We have plenty of room," Toby said. "Ella has everything ready."

"It feels good to be here," Mia said.

"Do you want something to eat?"

"Thanks, but we already ate. Mamma made sandwiches. She's baking bread in the big oven, and Mia has helped her," Alex said.

"It's the best bread I know," Toby said. "You must tell us everything about life on the farm. We don't know anything. Come to the living room. I can't wait any longer."

"Mamma and Pappa sent their love, of course. They hate not to be in touch," Alex said, as he sat down.

Emil and Lynn came and greeted their uncle and aunt. They were as curious as their parents and wanted to know first-hand about life in Sweden.

"It's worse in the cities than in the countryside," Alex said. "You're lucky to live here."

Mia described everything Alex had done on the farm. "He built a windmill that gave us lights and installed heating stoves in the bedrooms." Mia continued to relate in detail about everything Alex had accomplished. The children's eyes were open wide.

"Pappa worked just as hard," Alex said. "He went with me to the woods to cut down trees. We used a lot of wood for the cooking stove and to heat the house. We prepared for gengas by cutting down birch trees. We expected a big demand for birchwood when the buses began to run on gengas, but it hasn't happened yet."

"What is gengas?" Emil asked.

Alex explained the process that had been used during World War II when Sweden could not import gasoline. "The gasoline in storage is reserved for the military and the police."

"How were you able to drive here when you didn't have any fuel?" Toby asked, and Alex told him about the barrel of gasoline the military had left behind.

"What a stroke of luck. Have people resorted to stealing yet?"

"Maybe in the cities. Many hungry people came to the farm and asked for food. It's pretty quiet so far, but there could be problems if the crisis continues. I don't want to think about anyone hurting our parents. Pappa has nothing to defend himself with."

"No, the only ones who can have guns are the hunters and the police. We owe you both for going to the farm instead of leaving for Norway right away. I left without saying goodbye and I feel guilty, but we left for the sake of the children. Kurt had just arrived in Tallinn when he found out what had happened. We're in touch. He thinks he'll be able to finish his dissertation in Tallinn. So now, all three of us live outside Sweden."

"I'm glad he is safe. Living on the farm was alright. We had plenty to eat. But I haven't had any income for a long time," Alex said. "I need a job. Do you have any suggestions, Toby?"

"You can look at the ads in the newspaper tomorrow, and I'll ask at the office if anyone needs an electrical engineer. You must be tired from all the driving. There's a bedroom and a bathroom in the basement for guests. Hope it will do?"

"We're thankful just to have a roof over our heads," Mia said.

Ella came with a bowl of fruit. "Take this in case you get hungry."

"Bananas and oranges! We'll love it. On the farm, we had apples and pears from our trees, but no other fruit," said Alex. He carried the fruit bowl downstairs.

"Take it easy tomorrow morning and sleep in. We'll leave coffee for you. There's bread in the breadbox, and you can find eggs, cheese, and butter in the fridge." Ella followed them downstairs. "Here's the bathroom," she said.

Mia looked at the tub and said she would take a long bath. It was just what she had longed for.

Alex woke early and went outside to fetch the newspaper. He leafed through it until he found the ads for available jobs. One consulting firm wanted an electric engineer who was willing to travel to Asia, but Alex didn't want to travel now that he was going to be a dad. His eyes eagerly looked for something else until he found a position at a hydroelectric powerplant that sounded promising. He tore out the ad and saved it. Mia was still asleep. She had been so happy last night. This morning, he had stood and looked at her beautiful face.

Her long hair, the color of ripe wheat, spilled out on the pillow. While he shaved with his electric razor for the first time in many weeks, he thought about how lucky he was to have Mia by his side and smiled at his image in the mirror. Having dabbed aftershave on his chin, he whistled Bobby McFerrin's eighties hit song "Don't worry, be happy."

Mia woke up when she heard Alex whistling. She stretched her arms and legs. All the wonderful reality felt like a dream. She let her hand glide over her tummy. There were no movements yet from the baby. Today, she could be lazy. She didn't have to wake up in a cold room and work in a primitive kitchen. But she thought about Lena who now had to do all the indoor chores alone.

"Good morning, sweetheart," Alex stepped out from the bathroom with a towel wrapped around his hips and went directly up to Mia and kissed her. "I love you. You and our baby fill me with happiness."

"Good morning, honey. I love you, too, and I love to be here. You smell good. I've enjoyed staying in bed, but now I'll get up. She stretched her arms above her head and sighed with pleasure. She found her robe in one of the suitcases and wrapped it around her still slim figure.

"Your shirts need to be ironed," she said.

"Yes, but I'll put on a sweatshirt for the time being. I saw an ad in the paper for a job that looks interesting."

"That's good."

"Aren't you curious about it?"

"Whatever it is, I'm sure it will be fine." She smiled at him as she walked into the bathroom, leaving the door ajar. Alex heard her flush the toilet. It was a good sound to hear. He smiled ruefully as he hung his suits in the closet and smoothed out the wrinkles. Before the blackout, he had taken everything for granted—running water, flushing toilets, gasoline, a good job, and easy access to money. Now he had to start from the beginning to earn a living.

They had breakfast together while it was still dark outside. "I'll call the power plant at 9 o'clock," he said, thumbing the ad.

"So, it's a power plant. Sounds good. Perhaps I should look for a job."

"You can do what you want, honey, but you deserve to take it easy. It's best for the baby. If I get a job, you don't have to stress."

"I can knit baby clothes for the time being."

"Pappa must have milked the cows by now. Hope the milking machine works. It's hard not to think about the farm."

"Yes, I know."

Mia put the cups and plates in the dishwasher. "What a luxury," she said. "On the farm, I would have been glad to have running water."

Alex picked up his cell phone and called the number for the power plant. A man by the name of Ole Olafssen offered him an interview the same day. Like all power plants, this one had safety rules at the entrance, and Olafssen explained how they worked.

Alex liked the mature, jovial man as soon as they met. Olafssen probably liked Alex as well, because he hired him the same day and introduced him to the other personnel. As a plant operator, Alex would start up, shut down, and control the generator output.

Alex and Mia were both in a good mood when Toby came home from work. Hearing about Alex's new job, he asked many questions about Sweden's electric grid.

"The latest figures I can recall are from 2015," Alex said. "That year, Sweden got 47 percent of its electricity from hydro, 34 percent from atomic energy, and the rest from wind and solar. Most of the power lines are in the ground. Sweden's main grid is federally owned, and it normally exports power to Denmark, Finland, Germany, the Netherlands, and the United Kingdom. Then there are regional and local grids that work in concert with the federal grid. With our smart grid and the internet, we're vulnerable to cyber attacks.

In 2016, Ukraine experienced 6,500 cyber attacks in two months."

"I must visit Mamma and Pappa before something worse happens," Toby said.

"How about we write a letter to them? We might get an answer. I saw a letter carrier in town the last time I was there."

"Oh, that's promising. What's the military doing?"

"Not much. I heard the soldiers are transporting civilian supplies. If I had stayed, I might have been called up, but I want to do more with my life than deliver supplies."

The hacker: *Alex is a smart fellow and he might surprise me by being able to do more for Sweden now that he lives in Norway. The fact that Toby and Alex are together in one place will be of importance in their lives.*

Chapter 10

On the first Sunday in Advent, Anders and Lena went to the cemetery to decorate their family graves with wreaths they had made from greens and spruce cones. They lit a thick candle and put it inside a small lantern as was the custom at Advent. Carefully, Anders placed it on their little daughter's grave and lit it. The girl was born between Toby and Alex but had a heart defect and died when she was only two years old.

"I don't see any other lanterns. Usually, there are so many," Anders said.

"Other people need the lanterns at home. It would have been the same for us if Alex hadn't built the windmill. I hope he and Mia are with Toby and his family."

The church bells pealed and they walked toward the church entrance, greeting people they knew along the way. Walking into church, Anders took off his hat. He and Lena chose a pew in the back and bowed their heads. The church was faintly lit with live candles.

Before the minister began the sermon, he said, "It's heartening to see so many parishioners in our church today."

After his sermon, he read congregational messages. Anders and Lena were shocked to hear about a recent death.

"Farmer Nils Johansson in Krokhult has died at an age of 55 years, 11 months, and 4 days." The small church bell rang for Nils.

Anders and Lena were still shaken by the sad news as they left church. They stopped in the vestibule to read the announcements about what was for sale and where auctions would be held. Many others did the same. It was a way of getting messages when there were no newspapers.

Outside, Anders and Lena greeted friends they hadn't seen for a long time. Anders asked his neighbor, Lennart, what had happened to Nils Johansson.

"He hanged himself in the barn. I suppose he couldn't take it any longer. Now there might be an auction at his farm too."

"How awful. I feel bad for his widow."

"I heard that Alex has left for Norway."

"His wife is expecting a baby, so they had to leave."

"You're pretty comfortable with everything Alex managed to fix for you."

"Yes, we are lucky. Have you had any news from the cities?"

"From what I've heard, they fight over food and clean water. They dig latrines in their yards. I heard that retirees are demonstrating outside the government offices demanding their pensions and other benefits. The buildings are empty. People are desperate for cash. I won't be surprised if they start burning down government buildings."

"It would only delay the benefits," Anders commented.

Some of the men began to talk about the much anticipated gengas. "I can't understand where we're supposed to mount the equipment to the tractor. We can't hang it behind because that's where we'll have the manure spreader, the sowing machine, and the reaper if we can't use the big machinery," Lennart said.

"I don't understand it either," Anders said. The women talked among themselves.

"Somebody has stolen hens and eggs from me," Lisa Andersson

told Lena.

"It doesn't surprise me. You live close to the highway. When people are hungry, they don't hesitate to steal. I hope it doesn't happen to me."

Anders and Lena said goodbye to their friends and went to get their bicycles. They rode side by side on the narrow road because no cars were coming. Once they were home, they changed clothes before going outside to do their chores.

"Alex said that the falls in Trollhättan are 32 meters high. Just think if we could use all that power locally," Anders said. "It would save lives. If we hadn't combined all the power in the land, we would still have electricity."

"You can't be sure of that," Lena said. She was on her way to the henhouse to gather the eggs when she saw chicken feathers outside. She picked up a white feather with specks of black from the ground and wondered what had happened. Inside the henhouse, she looked for the speckled hen, but it was gone. She gathered the eggs while fuming over the lost hen.

"Anders, somebody has stolen my best laying hen. I hope they don't kill her for food." Anders was on his way to the house with a pile of chopped wood in the crook of his left arm.

"I wonder how the thief knew it was your best laying hen," he said. "It could have been worse. He could have taken more hens. I'll put a padlock on the henhouse."

"We don't have any locks on any of the outbuildings. Somebody could come and lead out a cow," Lena said.

"You're right. Guess I'll have to put a padlock on the barn door, too."

It made Lena feel better, but she still missed her best laying hen.

"What happened to Nils Johansson was worse," Anders said. "I'm afraid he won't be the last farmer to give up."

"You mustn't give up, Anders."

"Of course not. I would rather take my wife with me and drive to Norway."

"Then we would be forced to sell all our farm animals, and we would hardly get anything for them."

"But Norway has food, and no superpower dares to attack Norway because they are members of NATO. But it would be hard to give up our farm that's been in my family for generations."

Monday morning, a young man came to the farm on a bicycle and went up to Lena with a letter in his hand.

"I have a letter for you from Norway," he said. "It's the first that has come to this area. It will be 10 crowns."

"Ten crowns!" Lena said. "But it has stamps." Lena could see the stamps, and she was eager to read the letter.

"Stamps are no good anymore. The postal offices aren't open and I don't get paid. But if you would rather give me some bread, it's fine."

"Come with me to the door then."

Lena handed him the bread. Her hands shook as she grabbed the letter.

"It's from my son," she said. "Thanks a lot. Are we able to send letters to Norway?"

"I think so. I haven't received any yet, but if you see me come by, you can stop me. I come only when I have letters to deliver. Perhaps we'll meet in town. Thanks for the bread." He put it in his bag that looked empty.

Anders had seen the mailman and walked toward Lena. "Did we get mail?"

"Yes, it's from Alex. Let's go inside and read it." Lena told Anders what it had cost her.

"But it was worth it," he said.

Lena lit the kerosene lamp and moved it closer to her.

"Do you want to read it, Anders?"

"No, you have better eyes than I."

The letter was dated a few weeks earlier.

Dear Mamma and Pappa,

We think about you all the time and hope you are well. We had no problems getting into Norway. We found the building where Toby and Ella live, and everything has gone better than expected. I was hired by a power plant right away. We still live with Toby and Ella, but we'll get an apartment after Christmas. We are registered in Oslo, pay taxes, and have healthcare. Mia has seen a doctor. We can welcome our child sometimes in May. Has anyone begun to use gengas yet?"

Tears filled Lena's eyes, and she couldn't continue to read. Anders took the letter, smoothed it out, and read the rest holding it close to the lamp.

Kurt is in Tallinn, Estonia. He took the ferry there just before the power went out, and now he teaches at a university in Tallinn. Mia, Ella, and the children send warm greetings. They are fine. If my letter reaches you and we get an answer, Toby will write next.

PS. Here is Kurt's address ....

"This letter is what I've been praying for," Lena said and wiped her eyes with a corner of her apron. Just think, Kurt is in Estonia and they must have electricity there. We can write to him."

"We can write, but we don't know if there's any ferry traffic between Stockholm and Tallinn at this time. Do we have any paper to write on? I have a pen."

"I can fetch the paper," Lena said. She had a bounce in her step when she hurried away.

The hacker: *I knew there would be suicides and much worse. Lena feels better now that she can get mail from her family in Oslo and she has news from Kurt, but there will be other reasons for her to worry.*

Chapter 11

Since Ella worked at the hospital and was often tired when she came home, Mia took over the cooking and baking for the two families. Ella praised Mia's cooking, saying, "You're a good cook, Mia, and I'm happy to be able to sit down at the table and enjoy it when I come home."

"I would like to learn to cook," Lynn said, surprising them all.

"Then you can watch me make dinner when you get home from school, and you'll learn." Mia didn't think Lynn was serious, but she was. "I want to learn everything, which ingredients are needed and how you prepare," she said. "I also want to learn how to bake the good bread you make, Mia."

"Then you should come with me to the store tomorrow. We can take the car and buy more than usual."

"It would be great if you could teach Lynn to cook," Ella said. "Then she can help with the cooking when you've moved. Emil should learn, too."

"No thanks," Emil said. "But if you make some good cookies, I might be interested."

Lynn asked Mia if she missed her job teaching domestic life skills.

"I haven't had time to miss it yet. On the farm, I cooked on a wood-fired stove and we had no running water because of the cyber attack. It was chilly and dark all the time, and we didn't have much variety in our meals. It was mostly meat and potatoes. We had lots of meat because the freezer was almost full, and Lena had to preserve it by canning. Sometimes we ate herring or other fish for dinner. We always had good bread, milk, butter, and eggs. Whenever the stores were open, the shelves were almost empty. I'm happy to work in a modern kitchen again and have access to a large variety of products."

"Mamma always bakes gingersnaps and Lucia buns for Santa Lucia Day. Could you show me how to do it, Mia?" Lynn asked.

"Of course. Let's make a list of what we need."

"In Norway, people don't celebrate Santa Lucia as much as we do in Sweden," Ella said, "but we do it in our family. Malena has a Lucia crown. You can be Lucia this year, Lynn."

Early in the morning on December 13, Ella helped Lynn into a long white nightgown, put the Lucia crown on her head and turned on the battery lights, to symbolize the saint who had brought food to hungry people during a famine hundreds of years ago.

"It should be live candles, but this is safer," she said as she gave Lynn a tray with Lucia buns flavored with saffron and ginger snaps to carry. "Now, we'll sing the Santa Lucia song and surprise the others." Ella began to hum the tune. The family acted surprised and enjoyed the coffee, juice, and home-baked treats.

One day, a letter arrived from Sweden. Mia put it on the table in the hallway so Toby and Alex could see it as soon they came in the door. She looked at the handwriting on the envelope and thought it must be Lena's. The letter was addressed to Tobias and Alex Almåker, with families.

"Oh, a letter from home," Alex exclaimed as soon as he saw it. "But we have to wait to read it until Toby gets home."

"It's almost as special as when the letters arrived from America years ago," he said. "Pappa told me about it. Perhaps they came only once a year, usually before Christmas. Someone read the letter aloud as everyone gathered around. After that, the letter circulated among all the relatives and friends until it almost fell apart."

"I know," Mia said. "I've read Vilhelm Moberg's books about the Swedes who settled in Minnesota."

"Me too, but now we're spoiled with email and cell phones. I never thought I would have to wait for regular mail," Alex said.

After dinner, they all gathered in the living room. Alex got the honor of reading the letter. He opened it carefully with his penknife and took out two sheets. Anders had filled his sheet with large lettering, while Lena's script was small. They had been to church on the First Sunday of Advent and heard about a suicide.

"I was afraid something like that would happen," Alex said. They sympathized with the loss of Lena's hen but couldn't help smiling about the way she told it.

In a P.S. Lena wrote: "I had stamps so I used them. Your letter carrier might still want money. Ours is not paid by the Postal Services. When I got the letter from you, I traded it for bread."

Everyone was surprised but glad the Swedish mail carrier worked voluntarily. When the women and children had left the living room, Toby began a serious conversation.

"Do you think it's possible to start up the local power plants in Sweden, Alex?"

"If we could limit the power to the local grid, it would be possible. Restoring power to the entire country should be left to computer experts. Kurt is better educated for that than I am. Since the power has been gone for so long the hacker must have destroyed the backup systems."

"Couldn't be any worse, could it?"

"No, it's a big problem."

"I read in the paper that Norwegian reporters have crossed the border to record interviews," Toby said. "Aftenposten had a long article today. Norway ferries food to Gothenburg and takes sick Swedes on the return trip. Denmark delivers food to the city of Malmö, but food distribution inside the country is difficult."

Toby continued: "At the office, I heard about Swedes who have sailed here. It's cold to sail this time of the year and the weather could be stormy. Svenung told me that most city people avoid the shelters. They might go there to sleep and eat, but that's all. He also told me that the Swedish Navy has begun to evacuate civilians from Stockholm to Finland, Estonia, and the other Baltic countries."

"It means that more and more people are willing to leave Sweden. I wonder how many immigrants have gone back to their homelands," Alex said.

"Svenung told me many of them fled as soon as they could. It seems that people who have changed country once can do it more easily a second time. Busses provided by the state are leaving Stockholm every day with immigrants. Many believe the Swedish government is happy to see them leave. When they come to Denmark, the Danes put them on busses to Germany with the intent of returning them to their home countries. The Ruskey is probably waiting for Stockholm to empty so they can move in. The large corporations have moved to other countries, and entire office complexes are empty. Svenung hopes that NATO will defend Sweden if needed, but I doubt it. The Swedish prime minister and the other ministers are confined to bomb-proofed bunkers."

"It's a deplorable situation, and meanwhile Pappa and Mamma could be robbed and hurt," Alex said. "I worry about them. If we could convince them to lease out the farm, we could pick them up. But we run the risk of being robbed, and we must think of our own families. I can't leave Mia now that she is pregnant."

"I know, and it's up to me to go and get them. You've done so much already, Alex. But first we should answer their letter. I'll point out how good they could have it in Norway. Mamma and Pappa are still healthy and not ready to retire. They could support themselves here."

"I agree, but it will be tough for them to leave the farm."

"I know. By the way, how do you like working at the power plant?"

"I like the work, but it's important to save as much money as possible. After what happened in Sweden, I'm afraid of depositing money in a bank. I'll probably buy a fire-proof safety box for my cash and important papers."

The next time they talked, the subject of Alex's salary came up. Toby said his company needed electrical engineers. "If you want me to put in a word for you, I will."

Alex said he would think about it but didn't think it would look good to jump from job to job. He said he might ask for a raise.

"I'm glad you're staying with us over Christmas."

"But I should pay you for room and board."

"No, Mia takes care of our household and that's worth a lot. We appreciate her work. Ella is exhausted when she comes home from work, and I'm glad I don't have to cook and clean. Mia is teaching our daughter to cook and bake, and it's also valuable. Daniel and Karoline have moved and we don't have any friends to socialize with yet, so we appreciate your company."

Toby gave Alex a paper to write on. "Our parents will wonder if we have received their letter, so start writing, bro."

Ella came into the living room. "You are good sons," she said when she saw that both had written a few lines. Greet them from me. Don't forget to email Kurt about the letter from your parents."

"It's done," Toby said.

When Alex came downstairs, Mia was in bed.

"I can feel small movements from the baby," she said. "It's unreal and wonderful at the same time."

"May I feel it?"

"It's not enough for you to feel, honey. I feel it only from the inside."

The hacker: *This is a touching scene. Toby and Alex apparently feel that they have to get their parents out of Sweden because something awful could happen to them if they stay. It will be interesting to find out if they can talk their parents into leaving the farm. Now I want to check in on Anders and Lena.*

Chapter 12

The meat packing plant was closed like everything else. A former butcher had promised to slaughter a hog for Anders before it grew too big. It wasn't easy to corner the fattest hog in the pigpen, but after many tries Anders had him inside the cage on the horse-pulled wagon.

To the butcher, he said, "I want a back part and the head if it's alright? Lena wants to make headcheese. I'll wait for the blood, so she can make blood pudding today. The rest I'll pick up tomorrow."

Anders watched as the butcher killed the hog and blood poured into a pail. He whisked it so it wouldn't coagulate and continued to watch while the butcher poured hot water on the hog to remove the bristles. Anders knew the process well. His grandfather had butchered hogs on the farm. The next step was to winch up the hog so the butcher could open it completely and remove the organs and everything else. Anders wanted to check the thickness of the bacon. The butcher then weighed the hog and told Anders how much the pork was worth.

On the way home, Anders held the pail with the blood between his legs so it wouldn't spill out. He thought about how it had become necessary to return to the old ways after the cyber attack. When he came home, Lena took the blood and mixed it with flour and salt, and baked the mixture in the oven. It would be enough for several iron-rich meals. Anders liked it best when she sliced the blood pudding, fried it in lard, and served it with lingonberry preserves.

Anders boiled the hog's head in a large three-legged kettle placed over an outside firepit. He chopped more wood and fed the fire. It didn't take long before the aroma spread to the highway. A wanderer smelled it and came by, but when he saw what was cooking, he left. Then a dog came and sniffed it. He had no collar and Anders guessed it had belonged to townspeople who could no longer afford to feed him. He judged it to be a labrador. Anders patted him and wondered if he might want to stay. He could use a watchdog. The dog lay down beside him while waiting for food.

After a while, more dogs approached but the lab kept them at a distance with loud barks. Anders picked up a stick and chased them away. Steam rose from the kettle, and the lab stayed at a safe distance. Anders went to the kitchen to get a pot to put the head in when it finished cooking.

"We have a dog now. It's a beautiful dog," he told Lena.

"A dog! Do you think he'll stay?"

"If we give him food, he might stay. Come and see."

Anders left, carrying a large kitchen pot, and Lena grabbed a jacket and followed him. The dog came up to Lena and wagged his tail.

"You're a nice dog," she said, patting him. "Do you want to stay with us? You can stay if you are house-trained."

"It looks like he's fully grown, so he's probably house-trained. He could watch the outbuildings."

"Not when it gets colder," Lena protested. "Then, I'll take him inside at night."

"He could be in the barn, or I could make him a doghouse."

"We'll see." Lena liked the dog already. "What should we name him?"

"I'm sure you can think of a suitable name for him." Lena tried common dog names like Fido and Karo to see if he listened to them, but he just looked at her with his big brown eyes.

"I can make a temporary collar and a lead for him," Anders said. If you watch the kettle, I'll go and get a rope."

"Can't we give him some food?"

"I'll give him some after it has cooled."

Lena bent down and rubbed the dog behind his ears. "How about we call you Bruno since you are light brown? Yes, Bruno is a name that fits you." Anders came with a rope and tied it around the dog's neck, leaving enough for a lead.

"Now you can walk him and see if he's obedient. I can make a better collar later. Perhaps you have an old belt I can use."

"I'm sure I do." Lena walked around with Bruno in the farmyard and had no trouble handling him. Anders stood and watched. "I can see he's trained to walk on a lead," he said.

When the fire had died down, Anders moved the hog head to the kitchen pot and carried it inside. He was afraid a long line of hungry dogs would show up and maybe people, too. Bruno followed him and lay down outside the door. An airplane passed overhead, and Bruno barked at it. "It's okay," Anders said. "It's one of ours."

Bruno was still on the steps when Lena came outside with a piece of cooked pork for him. Bruno devoured it and sent an appreciative look at Lena. She went back to the kitchen and started to assemble the headcheese. First, she lined a dish with a big piece of pork rind. Then she began to cut meat from the cheeks. She packed it down piece by piece until the form was full. Then she poured the salty brine she had prepared over the meat and weighed it down before placing it in the cold cellar. It would be ready to eat for Christmas. Her mouth watered as she thought about it. She put the ham in a big crock and covered it with brine. It was heavy so she would ask Anders to carry it to the basement. Tomorrow, she planned to make sausage.

Anders helped Lena make the sausage. They used an old meat grinder and a funnel-like attachment. He turned the handle and Lena guided the sausages through the funnel until they fell into a large pan one after the other.

"I wish the children could come home for Christmas as usual, but it's impossible," Lena said with a resigned look on her face.

"They're better off where they are. Hope we'll get a letter from them soon."

After a long wait, the mail carrier finally came. Lena was ready to pay for it with bread. Anders and Lena read the letter several times. Alex and Toby had penned it and posed questions at the end. As expected, Alex and Mia had moved in with Toby and Ella. All the grown-ups except Mia had jobs, but she kept the house clean and cooked their meals, which was just as important. All was well. But Toby had written something that worried them. He had recommended that they lease out the farm and move to Norway. He promised to come and pick them up.

"I don't want to move to Norway," Anders said. "I think we're doing fine. We have everything we need to survive. A tenant farmer would need a loan, and I don't think the banks issue loans. It would be hard to leave our family farm in the hands of strangers, especially if we live in Norway and can't check on it."

"But we would be more comfortable in Norway. What I hate the most is to have to go to the outhouse and not being able to take baths."

"We are lucky to have the sauna, but of course it would be nicer to use the tub and shower."

"I'm thinking about what Toby wrote," Lena said. "Malena's husband flies for NATO. Perhaps he knows something we don't." Lena looked at Anders with worry in her eyes.

"If only we could call them instead of waiting for letters." Anders thought about what Toby had written and admitted that he might be right.

"I'll miss the family so much at Christmas time," Lena said, looking sad.

"We have enough meat for a lot of people."

"But I'm worried about running out of bread flour. It will soon be gone. We need more."

"Alex was hoping the gristmill in the park could be started up, but now that he isn't here, I wonder if anyone will attempt it. Perhaps the old miller could do it if he gets permission," Anders said.

"I hope so. I'll start a letter to the children tonight and ask them for pictures of everyone. They all have cameras, and they can take pictures with their cell phones. All I want for Christmas is pictures of them all."

The dog stayed put outside the door and it looked like he felt at home. But in the evening, Lena let him inside so he wouldn't run away during the night.

"You stay here, Bruno. You'll be good company for us in our loneliness," she said and patted him on the back.

The hacker: *Anders and Lena are resourceful and have a lot of survival skills. I was born in Moscow and had no idea about how hogs were butchered, and all the work it takes to preserve meat the old-fashioned way. Anders and Lena might change their minds about staying in Sweden. Now, I am beginning to wonder what's happening with Kurt, but for now, I am interested in Alex.*

Chapter 13

As soon as Alex mentioned to his boss that he had a chance to get a job at S-oil, Olafssen asked if his salary was too low.

"I need to make more money. We couldn't take anything with us from Sweden, and we're hoping to get our apartment in the new year. We'll have to buy everything from kitchen utensils to furniture. My wife is expecting our first child and needs to take it easy."

"I understand, and I'll do what I can."

Toby said he was sure Alex would get a raise, but if not, there were alternatives. "I talked to my boss, and he said you could pick and choose jobs. We have departments for wind and solar energy. S-oil is concentrating more and more on renewable energy, and we are changing the company name to deemphasize oil exploration."

"Perhaps I should mention that I built a windmill in Sweden," Alex said with a laugh. "It had merits considering the material limitations."

The two brothers always had a lot to talk about in the evenings. Ella and Mia were good friends, but Ella's work hours made her mealtimes different from those of the rest of the family, and it resulted in more work for Mia. The children didn't always listen when she asked them to do something. It happened that they told Mia she was not their mother, so she couldn't tell them what to do. It hurt Mia's feelings and she went downstairs, crying.

"I don't understand why I cry so easily," she said to Alex, "but the kids are testing my patience."

"I'm sure your pregnancy has something to do with it, honey. Emil and Lynn are at a difficult age. It will get better when we have our own apartment."

"Yes, I'm sure. I've been thinking a lot about that. We could buy used furniture to save money and buy our kitchen stuff at IKEA."

"Yes, but we should buy new beds. We can pay for them in installments."

"And we'll need a car seat for the baby and lots of other things. It will be fun to go shopping for things like that."

When Alex was called into Olafssen's office he felt anxious. Would he get a raise or not?

"Please sit down, Alex." Olafssen paused before continuing. "Our policy is to offer new employees a modest salary until we know what we can expect of them. You're an asset to us, Alex. Your salary will be considerably higher than we offered you at first. Here it is," he said and wrote it down on a piece of paper that he slid across the desk to Alex.

"Thank you," Alex said with a wide smile. "It's much better."

"It's well deserved." They pumped hands, and Alex felt a big sense of relief.

It made Mia very happy. "Now I can plan for our new apartment. Perhaps I can buy a few Christmas gifts, too."

"Yes, but please wait until I get my first paycheck. I know it will be before Christmas."

"I have a piece of news for you. I got called in for a sonogram next week."

"I have heard about those, but how do they work?"

"It's a scan. Pictures of the baby will show up on a monitor. We'll get an image to take home. Just think, Alex, we can see our child before it's born. Other mothers have talked about it, but now when it's about me, it's amazing."

"I want to see it, too."

"Of course."

"It's not because they're worried about something is it?"

"No, not at all."

"Good. I must say I'm a little curious about what the baby looks like at this stage. Do we find out if it's a boy or a girl?"

"If we want to."

"Do you?"

"I haven't decided yet."

The second letter from Anders and Lena arrived sooner than expected. Anders asked if Svenung had said something to them that could be interpreted as a warning about what might happen to Sweden. "If so, we'll listen to you," he wrote. He told them about the butchering and added, "We have more hogs ready for the market, and I would like to sell them or trade them for something else." Both parents wrote about the dog that had come to them and stayed. But Toby and Alex read between the lines. "They don't write about the starving people who come begging for food," Alex said. "I can imagine that Mamma feels sorry for them and gives them as much as she can."

"If a lot of people come and beg, Mamma might give away too much," Toby said. "I'm surprised about Pappa's reaction to my advice. He seems more uncertain than before. How should we answer him?"

"We can write that we get worrisome news from Sweden. We can point out that they have a better chance to lease out the farm because it has heat and lighting, but that it's up to them to decide."

"We must take pictures and send to them. That's what Mamma

wants."

"Yes, we can do it on Saturday when everyone is home."

When the pictures were taken of all the family members, individually, and in groups, Toby ordered prints online. "I expect everyone to write something in our letter tomorrow. It has to arrive before Christmas."

"Our Christmas break lasts until after New Year's. I want to go and see a movie," Emil said.

His father said, "You're watching movies on TV. Isn't that enough?"

"But I want to go to a theater and see a movie with a friend. I want to go out like everybody else. If we had lived in Sweden, I would have gone to the movies. We want to see the new Star Wars."

"Yes, you can, Emil, but first, invite your friends here. I don't know any of your friends, or their parents, like we did in Sweden. Lynn has had girls over here."

"Okay, Pappa, but do we get chips and pop then?"

"Yes, of course."

Alex and Mia were all smiles when they came home from the sonogram and told Ella about their experience.

"Look! Here's the first picture of our baby," Alex said. "It's 16 weeks and we can see how it's formed. We heard the heartbeat. Look here!"

Ella examined the image. "I can't see the sex," she said.

"No, we can't either but we don't want to know," Mia said. "It doesn't matter as long as it's healthy."

After Alex and Mia had gone to bed, Alex put his hand on Mia's tummy and caressed it. After a while, he thought he felt something.

"But it could just be air," Mia said with a laugh.

The hacker: *So far, it is going well for our Swedes in Norway, but the idea of getting the parents out of Sweden could have consequences.*

Chapter 14

"Anders, this can't continue," Lena said. "Five beggars have been here already this morning and they all want bread. I can't give away any more. Men and women come, carrying backpacks. They smell bad. I don't think they have bathed since the power went out, and how could they? They say they have hungry children. They put the bread in their backpacks and walk on. I can't help but feel sorry for them. Some bring empty bottles and ask for milk. Milk I can spare, but not bread. Bruno barks at them, but they pay no attention to him."

"I can put up a sign by the road. Then I'll talk to the old miller. We must start up the gristmill so we can grind flour. He said he had received permission from the museum board. We can't wait for the power to come back."

Anders took his knife and carved the words, "Inget bröd" (No bread) on it. Then he nailed it to the fence post by the road while he was on his way to Lasse Persson. Lasse had demonstrated the windmill now and then.

"Are you ready to test the mill, Lasse? My wife says she is out of rye flour."

"Javisst, the wind is strong enough today." Lasse put on a cap and a warm jacket. He was tall and thin and leaned to one side while walking.

After Lasse had started the mill, a thick layer of dust covered every surface. He and Anders had dust in their eyelashes, noses, and beards. They took off their caps and slapped them against their legs. Then they went outside to inspect the wings.

"They're still turning," Lasse said. "We can mill oats. It's best to start with something for the animals. Tomorrow, you can bring a sack of oats and we'll do a test run. Why don't you tell your neighbors about it?"

"Sure, I can do that. See you tomorrow morning at eight o'clock."

Anders shoveled oats in a sack that Lena held up for him. When it was full, he tied it at the top with a string. He could just as well bring a sack of rye at the same time. He wrote his name on it, so it wouldn't be mixed up with anyone else's grain. He hitched the horse to a cart and was ready to leave.

Bearded farmers came from all directions. They pushed the sacks on wheelbarrows or bikes. Big Jon carried his sack on his back. When they had gathered, it took a while before they had shaken hands and talked about the long power outage, the weather, and the wind.

"We have to do a test first," Lasse said. "Do you volunteer to be the first to try it, Anders?"

"I suppose so."

"I'm starting the mill now. Stand to the side," Lasse said.

When the millstones began to grind, the men covered their ears to screen out the worst noise. Lasse shut off the mill and looked at the coarse meal and said it was mixed with dirt. "There might be some mice droppings in it too, but it's good enough for the pigs."

Anders tied up his bag and moved it aside.

"Next," Lasse said. "Stand aside. Here we go again."

The oat flour looked better and better with each milling. When all the men had had their oats ground, Anders wanted to grind some of his rye as a test.

"Of course, but first I have to change the setting."

"How fine can it be?"

"These old gristmills can't grind fine meal. It will be coarse even at the best setting."

"Better coarse meal than no meal."

Anders mounted a clean white sack to catch the flour when it came out.

"You can pour in the rest," he told Lasse.

Anders was satisfied when he had loaded both the oat flour and the rye flour on the horse cart.

Lena met him in the farmyard. "Did it work?" Bruno followed close behind her.

"Yeah, but if we are going to grind wheat, it will be too coarse for coffee bread."

"I have saved some white flour for special occasions. No beggars came today. I feel guilty about not being able to give them bread."

When Anders and Lena were in town to sell their milk and butter, they also brought some of the bread Lena had baked from the coarse flour. She called it hårt bröd (hardtack), and it was hard but not crisp like it was supposed to be. Lena said it was the best she could do using the coarse meal. She wouldn't waste precious yeast on it. She could make yeast, but for that she would need lots of sugar.

All the sellers at the farmers' market were dressed in warm, padded jackets, and wore knitted caps on their heads, and cut-off mittens that freed their fingers. Their customers surprised them by bringing white flour, oatmeal, and sugar in trade for bread, butter, and milk.

Lena couldn't believe her eyes. "Where did you get this from?" she asked.

"Swedish planes dropped it from the air, but we can't use it."

"I gladly take it in trade," Lena said. It was her lucky day. No cash was needed.

"I hope the planes will drop food that you can use the next time," she said.

"Typical bureaucrats," Anders snorted.

While he walked around looking at what was for sale, Anders met the mail carrier who recognized him and pulled a letter from his mailbag to show to him.

"Come with me. My wife can give you something in return. But I've got a question for you. How do the letters get to and from Norway?"

"I give them to a mail carrier from the next town. He gives them to the next mail carrier who goes south. It works like a relay until it comes to Gothenburg where it's loaded on Norwegian ferries. The letters that come here move in the opposite direction."

"No wonder the mail is so slow. So, there's ferry traffic between Norway and Gothenburg?"

"Yes, Norway has started a new ferry route to Gothenburg. Many people have fled to Norway on those ferries. They take cars, too. Another mail carrier told me about it. Norway donates a lot of food to Sweden like crispbread, butter, cheese, and milk powder. The ferry to and from Denmark is still running. I imagine it's used for the same purpose."

"It sounds like the ferries carry good food for city folk who can't cook anything," Anders said. He stroked his beard and thought about what the mail carrier had told him.

"We have a letter from Norway," he told Lena.

"Oh, great!" Lena smiled when she saw the mailman. "Is it okay if I give you carrots in trade?"

"Yes, please. We can eat them raw."

"It's a thick envelope so I think they sent pictures," Anders said. "Do you want to wait until Christmas to open it?"

"No, I want to read the letter today."

When Anders had milked the cows, and they had eaten their supper, he and Lena sat down at the kitchen table, and Anders opened the letter.

"Here are the pictures in a separate envelope. Do you want to place them under the Christmas tree?"

"No, I want to look at them now. We don't have a tree yet. Give them to me, please."

Lena looked at everyone in all the pictures before she handed them to Anders.

"They all look happy and healthy. We should frame the family photos."

"Yes, of course, I have frames, but I'll miss them all so much at Christmas. Look here, how cute the kids are."

"Yes, I know, but now I want to read the letter," Anders said. "Toby has written most of it," he said as he unfolded the letter.

Mia wrote about her sonogram and that everything was well with her pregnancy.

"So, the baby is due in May. That's what I thought," Lena said. "I hope everything goes well."

The hacker: *I never thought about the consequences of not having power. It is nice that Norway is willing to help Sweden with food, but in the long run this cyber attack was not supposed to be about food but control and having the upper hand. I wonder if Toby will visit his parents or if it's just talk on his part.*

Chapter 15

Toby really wanted to visit his parents between Christmas and New Year's and explained to Ella how he would do it. "Norway sends food and other supplies to Gothenburg on ferries that bring Swedish refugees back to Norway. I can board the ferry as a paying passenger."

"The weather can be bad at that time of the year."

"I know, but it's the only week I have time off from work. If you don't mind?"

"No, I don't mind, but is it safe?"

"I'll be careful."

Toby was surprised to be called to see his boss. The boss had papers in front of him, but that was nothing unusual.

"Tobias, I understand you're going to Sweden to visit your parents," he said. "Do they live in the vicinity of Gothenburg?"

"Yes, they live out in the country about an hour's drive from Gothenburg. I plan to take the ferry over."

"Perhaps you could do an errand for us in Gothenburg. It's like this. We bought an empty office building and have a contract on it. But we need to make a down payment and pick up the signed contract. You'll get a substantial bonus if you can do this for us. We could have a man meeting you at the ferry." The boss saw Toby's hesitation.

"Everything is of course legal," he said. "You can count on our integrity, but we don't want you to tell anyone about it, not your wife, or brother, or your parents. No one. It's sensitive these days."

"I understand and I'll take care of it if the contact person meets me at the ferry. But it's a big responsibility to carry a lot of cash."

"We'll give you a briefcase that you can lock. We trust you, Tobias."

"Alright, but I need the name of the man meeting me. I will ask him for identification. And he has to know when the ferry docks."

"We'll arrange all that in advance."

Toby was glad for the opportunity to be a courier for the company and looked forward to the bonus. It would be welcome when they had to furnish the new apartment. But he wondered why he couldn't tell anyone about it, not even Ella.

When the two families had celebrated Christmas together and Toby had bought gifts for his parents—candy, chocolates, coffee, tea, sugar, white flour, yeast, rice, and batteries for their flashlights, he asked Alex if there was anything else he could think of to buy for their parents.

"Maybe lutfisk. I don't think they can get any this year, and it's not Christmas without it. A camping light might be a good idea. It's dark to walk to the barn and the outhouse this time of the year."

"Perfect," Toby said. "It will be better than the soft gifts we never wanted when we were small."

Alex laughed. "I don't think they need clothes. I want to send something though. Aspirin and cough medicine are hard to find in Sweden. Wish I knew what they need."

Ella wanted to send candles. Mia wanted to bake something for Toby to bring.

Emil and Lynn wrote cards, wishing their grandparents a happy new year.

"I'm ready to leave," Toby said and hugged them all. "I can't use my cell phone in Sweden, but I'll call from the ferry on the way home as soon as I get a connection."

It rained on the drive to the ferry. During the crossing, it was stormy, but Toby sat below deck, bought food, drank coffee, and read Norwegian newspapers. Reporters had been over in Sweden and taken pictures. Large black headings, ANARCHY IN SWEDEN, caught Toby's attention. The pictures showed people breaking into stores and fighting over food. It was horrible, and it strengthened his belief that his parents must move to Oslo before they got hurt. Toby put the paper in his case.

Gothenburg was completely in the dark. No street lights, no illuminated store signs, only the headlights from a few cars with Norwegian license plates. The contact person met Toby, and having checked his ID, he gave him the envelope with the cash, got a receipt, and the contract.

As Toby resumed driving, he wondered what it looked like at Påskgatan where they had lived. To see it would mean a detour, so instead he drove north from the city and passed the little town where he had attended school. It was eerily dark everywhere. He took for granted that his parents would be home. A barking dog met him as he drove into the farmyard. He had heard about the dog. There were no lights in the house.

They can't be in bed already. I hope nothing has happened to them. Toby got worried. No smoke came from the chimney. He knew where the key was and decided to use it, but the dog stood in his way barking. Toby looked at his watch. It was 8:30 in the evening. Walking back to his car, he saw the faint light from a flashlight down the road. He was sure it was his parents and went to meet them.

"It's Toby," his father exclaimed shining his light on him. "Toby, is it you?" Lena could hardly speak. "It's like a dream come true." Toby hugged them both.

"It's Santa arriving a little late," he said.

"Are you alone? How did you get here?"

"I'm alone. I came on the ferry. If you'd help me carry in what I brought, we can talk more later."

"Lennart and Lisa invited us for supper. We didn't know you were coming. Did you write?"

"No, I didn't write. I wanted to surprise you."

Anders led the way with his flashlight. Toby carried the cartons. "I brought a camping light and extra batteries. It's much brighter than a flashlight," he said.

"This will be better than Christmas," Lena said and hung up her coat. "I just have to light the kerosene lamp.

"Alex told me about it," Toby said as he placed the cartons on the counter.

"I'm going upstairs to start the fires in the stoves, so it's warm when we go to bed," Anders said. The fire had died out in the kitchen stove, but Lena lit it again. Then she began to open packages.

"Oh, you brought rice. Then I can make the Christmas porridge. Pappa and I felt so lonely at Christmas but we had good food, everything except lutfisk and rice."

"Here's the lutfisk," Toby said, handing Lena a well-wrapped package with a smile. "Everyone sent something. Wait until Pappa comes down and I can show him at the same time." Toby looked at the framed pictures that stood on the kitchen table.

"Thank you for the pictures and the cards from the children. We enjoy them every day."

"It's good that the mail is making it through even if it's slow."

"We wrote a letter to Kurt, but we don't know if he got it."

"He called us on Christmas Eve. He's fine, and he got your letter. He still teaches at a university in Tallinn."

"Glad to hear it. Aren't you hungry? You've come a long way."

"I ate on the ferry, so I'm not hungry, only thirsty."

"Please make yourself at home. I'll put on the tea kettle."

"I've been thinking about how nice Christmas used to be when we were all together, but we shouldn't complain because we have our health. Many people are ill."

It was midnight before they had gone through everything that Toby had brought, and he had answered all his parents' questions. Lena was so excited she couldn't fall asleep. In the morning she overslept and didn't wake up until she smelled coffee. Had Toby made coffee? It was her job. The first thing she did every morning was to start the fire in the stove and make coffee. She had put the old coffee pot to good use.

Instead of dressing, she wrapped her robe around her, stepped into her slippers, and went to the bathroom. For once she used the toilet and flushed it with water from the pail. It was a luxury, but she did it because Toby was home, and she didn't want to go to the outhouse. To wash, she took a scoop of water from the pail and poured it into the basin. She brushed her hair and put it up in a bun before going downstairs.

"Good morning, Mamma. Did you sleep well?"

"When I finally fell asleep. I'm just so happy to see you and get news from the rest of the family. Sorry, I overslept."

"You deserve to sleep in for once, Mamma. Please, sit down and I'll serve you coffee."

"What time is it? If Pappa is done with the milking, I have to make oatmeal."

"No, you don't have to make oatmeal today, Mamma. I brought something you'll like, an ostkaka (cheesecake, but more like a custard like pudding made with rennet). It's warming in the oven. Mia made it. I could bring it thanks to the cold weather."

"How nice of Mia. I've got lingonberry preserve in the pantry." Lena rose to get it.

"Did you have time to pick lingonberries this year, Mamma?"

"Yes, I did, before that awful thing happened. But oh, how wonderful it will be to have ostkaka for breakfast. It's party food."

When Anders came in from the barn, he said, "It smells so good in here. What is it?"

"It's ostkaka that Mia baked," Lena said.

Anders took a scoop of water from the pail and poured it into the sink, picked up the soap bar, and began to wash his large hands. When he was done, he dried them on a towel that hung on a hook. "Oh, by the way, that camping light Alex gave us is great. I used it when I walked to the barn this morning and also inside the barn."

"Do you have enough chopped wood, Pappa? If not, I can chop some."

"That would be good because we never know how long the winter will be. As you can see, Toby, we have gone back to living like in the old days. We miss our modern conveniences, but many are worse off. The city people have no light and no heat. They have no food either and have to go begging for it. I don't understand why the government isn't doing anything."

"It can't go on like this all winter long. Sweden has been so proud of its technology, and now it can't even restore the power."

"I don't know the reason, but we had to do something while we waited. We started up the old windmill in the park and milled some flour. It's very coarse, but we must have bread." Anders sat down at the table, and at once, Lena stood up. But Toby told her to sit down. He would serve the ostkaka.

"This is so wonderful I want to cry," Lena said. She tasted it and said, "It melts in my mouth, and it's delicious. Thank you, Toby, and please thank Mia."

Anders asked how long Toby could stay. "The ferry leaves Gothenburg the day after New Year's Day. Do you have any diesel left, Pappa?"

"Yes, I don't use it much now that I have the horse."

"It would be good if you and Mamma could move to Oslo. We worry about you getting sick, especially now when healthcare is hard to come by. Alex sent some over-the-counter medications, but it's not for anything serious."

"I heard of a woman who died because she couldn't get her blood pressure medicine, but Mamma and I don't have any problems like that."

Toby got no further with his plea, at least not until he showed his parents the newspaper he had bought on the ferry. Anders put on his glasses and looked at the pictures first.

"Is it really that bad? Can this be true? Can this be Sweden? It's horrible. I'll save this article. Right now, I can't even comprehend it. We're lucky compared to these people." He promised to think about leasing out the farm. Toby had another suggestion, but one thing at a time.

The next day, Toby chopped wood, and then he made up a fire in the ceramic fireplace in the living room where the Christmas tree stood decorated without the usual electric light strings. Lena had found the old clip-on candle holders, and just before they ate their lutfisk dinner, she lit the small candles that Ella had sent. "It's beautiful, Mamma," Toby said. It was windy outside and the light from the windmill dimmed at times, but the candles in the tree and on the table gave a festive glow.

Toby took the opportunity to tell his parents that he had been contacted by a Norwegian man who was interested in buying their farm. He had wrestled with the idea because selling was more serious than leasing out, but now it seemed appropriate to at least tell his parents about it.

"But we don't want to sell," Anders said, and Lena agreed. Toby left it at that. He had a few more days to convince them. It was important because both he and Alex worried about what could happen to their parents if they stayed.

All too soon, it was time for Toby to leave. He couldn't wait to tell his family about the result of his proposal. On the way to the ferry, he took a detour to his former home in Gothenburg. The destruction was worse than he expected.

He sat in his car and was almost scared to look. Their furniture was spread out on the lawn, and he could smell the burned wood and upholstery. Toilet paper littered one corner of the yard, and as Toby let the car roll forward, he smelled crap through his rolled-down window. His anger rose. His heart beat so fast he could feel the pulse in his ears. He hit the empty seat beside him until his knuckles turned white. He swore aloud but found no relief. Like a madman, he drove to the apartment house where Alex and Mia had lived. The chilly wind from the open car window cooled his anger. The destruction there was even worse. The upper floors were burned down and showed only a skeleton of steel beams. The third floor where Alex and Mia had lived was gone, along with all their belongings. An entire housing complex lay in ruin. He remembered the last time he was in the same parking lot, just after all the lights had gone out.

The computer specialist was right when he said it was a cyber attack that had destroyed our power grid. He's probably safe, but I wonder what happened to the woman who said she had nowhere to go. Where have all the people gone? No bombs or enemy soldiers were responsible for all this destruction, but who could have done such an awful thing?

Toby knew he couldn't tell his family about what he had seen. He had to keep all those awful pictures hidden in his mind. He shook his head, stepped on the gas pedal, and left the area, thinking of people living in high-rises. How would they be able to walk up all the stairs when they were fatigued by hunger and the elevators didn't work. He had read about suicides by jumping from the windows.

Without planning it, he found himself outside the university where most of the windows were broken. His student years passed before his eyes.

I ought to drive past the office building I bought for my compa-

ny. The contract is in my case, but it won't be worth anything if the building is destroyed.

He was relieved to see it still standing. Plywood covered the entrance and the windows. Debris filled the sidewalks. Toby felt sick, and he couldn't reach the ferry fast enough to get to Norway. The site of his home and the apartment complex where Alex and Mia had lived were etched on his brain.

The hacker: *Toby's home used to be one of the nicest in the neighborhood, and now he feels terrible about having left it unguarded. I wonder what his company will do with the building it purchased in Gothenburg and if Toby gets the bonus when he gets back to work.*

Chapter 16

As soon as Toby was back at work, he handed the envelope with the contract to his boss, who opened it and checked the signature.

"Thanks for taking care of this, Tobias."

"I took a look at the office building. Plywood has saved it from being vandalized."

"Thanks for checking. Here's your bonus," his boss said, handing over a thick envelope. Toby peaked into it and saw a lot of cash. He felt his face heating up.

"Put the money in your briefcase, lock it, and store it in a safe place. We trust you won't say anything about this bonus to your colleagues. It would be difficult to explain. We'll let you know later what the building will be used for."

"I understand." Toby did what he was told and set the combination. He said, Tack så mycket (Thank you very much), and left the room with only one question in his mind. Why does it have to be a secret? He was glad to have the money to buy furniture for the new apartment when it would be available to them, but he had to use it gradually so Ella wouldn't get suspicious.

As soon as Toby got home, Ella, Alex, and Mia wanted to know if he had convinced his parents to sell the farm.

"Pappa said right away that he wasn't interested in selling, and that buyers could not get loans.

"I told him that the man would pay with a check drawn on a Norwegian bank and that it could be cashed in Norway. Pappa asked how much the man would be willing to pay and if he planned to work the farm himself. I said I didn't know all the details, but most likely he would rent it out. All the livestock and machinery would be included in the sale."

Alex asked how Toby knew the investor.

"He contacted me."

"So, had you convinced Mamma and Pappa to sell before you left?" Alex asked.

"I think Mamma came up with the best reason for selling. She thought it sounded much better than the Ruskey taking the farm and not paying anything. She said she wouldn't mind moving to Norway since she had two sons and grandchildren there. 'It would be a new chapter in our lives,' she said. 'I'm tired of baking bread that is hard as a rock, going to the outhouse, and not being able to take a bath in our own home. It's cold and uncomfortable. I haven't complained before, but now that we have a choice…' Her voice broke and she looked helplessly at Pappa."

"What did Pappa say to that?"

"He said, 'You're right. It's not easy.' But he was still hoping that the power would be restored. Finally, he said it wouldn't hurt to find out how much the investor would pay for their farm."

"I told him he shouldn't be surprised if the investor came to their door and asked to see the place. So, now I must call the investor. If he's still interested, he could take over in the spring."

"I hope it will work out," Mia said.

"Mamma can hardly wait for spring. We can only hope that nothing serious happens before then."

"One of us will have to pick them up," Alex said.

"Pappa said he will drive to the ferry himself if he has enough diesel left. I'm surprised no one has stolen diesel from his tank. I don't think he has a lock on it, but there aren't that many who drive on diesel and I don't think the farmers want to steal from each other," Toby said. He thought about all the destruction he had seen in Gothenburg and felt like telling Alex but decided against it. He didn't want to upset Mia.

Instead, he said, "Pappa talked about the gengas that had been installed on busses. He said he hoped he could sell birch wood to the bus companies. He sells firewood to people in town. Mamma sells butter and milk. But the prices are low and people don't have cash. She uses the eggs for trade in the grocery store. I went there with her, and the shelves were almost empty. If everyone could withdraw money from their savings account the economy would get a boost."

Mia asked if many beggars still came to the farm.

"Yes, I saw some of them. They looked thin and Mamma can't say no. She gave them milk in the bottles they brought. You'd think the power would be back by now. It's been gone for almost three months. I don't know what the problem is."

Ella and Mia went to the kitchen to finish dinner. Toby and Alex continued to speculate about what would happen if Norwegian and Danish companies bought up farms in western and southern Sweden, and, heaven forbid, if enemies occupied all the empty buildings in Stockholm.

"They could occupy Gotland and Öland, too. And who would defend northern Sweden with its many gold, silver, copper, and iron ore mines? The Russians, Germans, and the British could help themselves. The Swedish government couldn't do anything to stop them. Would Sweden be divided like Germany after World War II? Perhaps Stockholm would be divided into zones like Berlin. Would there be anything left called Sweden?" Alex raised and lowered his arms to show how helpless he felt.

"Norway must step in," Toby said.

"Yes, it would be best if Norway took over all of Sweden. We could have a new union to save Sweden. It could be dissolved later."

"Since Norway is a member of NATO, Sweden could get in without paying!"

In the kitchen, the women continued to talk about the current problems. Mia asked Ella if she was afraid of hackers stealing her identity online.

"Yes, there's a risk. I remember 2017 when 74 countries were attacked in cyberspace. The hospitals in the UK could not receive patients. Doctors could not access their journals online. Businesses were forced to pay off the hackers, who were sitting somewhere in eastern Europe doing their dirty work. The children are in danger when they surf the internet. I've warned Emil and Lynn not to answer texts from strangers and not to use sites other than those allowed by their schools." Ella talked as she set the table.

"The temptation to use the internet is always there," Mia said while stirring a pot. "We don't use dictionaries or encyclopedias anymore, and the internet seems to have the answers to everything. Facebook has given out information about their customers' accounts. Nothing is private anymore. We can't trust our own banks. Our bank accounts in Sweden may have been confiscated by hackers sitting in another country."

"It makes us afraid of losing control, but we can't put the cash under the mattress either. The house can burn and cash is not insured," Ella said. "I feel sorry for the elderly who can't handle charge cards and don't know how to pay bills online even if they have a computer. Now, they need more help than ever, and they will probably end up in eldercare much sooner than necessary. In Sweden, it's not even possible to pay bills online without electricity."

"But the state wants the elderly to live in their homes as long as possible." Mia carried the food to the table and rinsed out the pots.

"But if they can't keep up their homes, they will deteriorate. So, there's so much to consider," Ella said before calling the men and children to the dinner table.

During dinner, Alex thought about something he needed to tell the family. His boss, Ole Olafssen, wanted him to visit the power plant in Trollhättan on behalf of the company. Alex assumed he would go there in February.

Having thought about it for a while, he said, "I'd like to visit Mamma and Pappa. Now that Mia and I won't get the apartment until March, I have time for a trip to Sweden." He looked at Mia, but she didn't seem to have any objections.

"Bring white flour," Toby said. "Mamma misses that more than anything else."

"It's almost unbelievable how things have changed. Now we're talking about white flour for our parents, something we always took for granted," Alex said. But more importantly, he wondered why his boss was sending him on an errand to the power plant in Trollhättan.

The hacker: *Toby and Alex are asking the right questions, but they are not getting any answers, not yet. Ella and Mia are well informed about Sweden's so-called safety nets that no longer work, and they question all the technology that was in place before the cyber attack. Cashless societies are a paradise for us hackers. Guess we have to wait to see why Alex is going to the power plant in Trollhättan and if Anders and Lena will sell the farm.*

Chapter 17

January came with snow and cold winds. Anders and Lena hoped the winter would be short. Having the cows inside meant more work in the barn. Anders was glad for the horse, though. If they got enough snow, he could use the sled to get around, perhaps even to church like in the old days.

A car that Anders didn't recognize stopped outside and a well-dressed man stepped out and looked around. "It must be the investor," he said, observing the man dressed in a black overcoat through the kitchen window.

"Let him knock on the door," Lena said. Hastily, she took off her apron and pulled a comb through her hair. "He's going to want to look at everything. Hope I have cleaned well enough."

The man took off his hat, overcoat, and galoshes inside the door.

"My name is Johanssen. I'm interested in your farm," he said and shook hands with Anders and Lena. He wore a dark suit, white shirt, and tie. His head was almost bald.

"Please come in," Anders said. "It's cold outside, but the kitchen is warm. Was it hard to drive in the snow?"

"No, not yet, but there can be more snow, so I want to get back to Gothenburg as soon as I can."

"That would be wise because the roads won't be plowed."

"You're heating the house with wood, I suppose, but normally you have electric heat?"

"Yes, that's correct."

"Do you have enough timber?"

"You bet. There's lots of spruce and pine in the woods."

"How about a cup of coffee," Lena asked. She saw that their guest carried something and wondered what it could be.

"Yes, please, if it's not too much trouble. I see that you have both a wood burning stove and an electric one." His eyes scanned the kitchen. "I brought some coffee bread. Hope you don't mind. Perhaps you bake yourself."

"Yes, but I can't bake coffee bread because I'm out of white flour and can't get anymore. Thank you very much," she said, as she took the bread to the counter. "Please sit down at the kitchen table. We can't heat the living room for everyday use."

"Of course not. I'm sure you miss your central heating and other conveniences."

"Yes, very much so," Anders said. "I had two old heating stoves stored away that we installed on the second floor. When the power is restored, we can remove them."

Johanssen helped himself to cream and sugar and stirred it into the coffee, but he didn't take any bread. Lena said it tasted good.

"We separate the cream from the milk," Anders said. "The separator hadn't been used for ages, but it works well. We got the cube sugar from our son in Norway."

"The coffee beans, too," Lena said. "We probably won't get any more."

Johanssen thanked Lena for the coffee and rose from the table.

"Now, I'd like to take a look at the rest of the house and the outbuildings."

Anders said he would show him around the house before going outside.

Johanssen followed Anders to the second floor. Lena stood at the bottom of the stairs and tried to hear what they said. When they came downstairs again, they put on their coats. Anders pulled on his boots and Johanssen stepped into his galoshes.

They are very practical, Lena thought. She hadn't seen galoshes in years.

"We'll be back in a little while," Johanssen said. Lena watched as Anders led the way through the snow. Perhaps she should have invited Johanssen to stay for dinner. She had planned a simple meal of pork sausage with mashed potatoes and could add some carrots. Best to start peeling the potatoes.

The potatoes, carrots, and sausage lay in separate pots ready to be cooked when the two men came back inside and sat down at the kitchen table. Johanssen took out a large envelope from the briefcase he had brought in from the car.

"I had a contract drawn up, and if you agree, all we have to do is to add the figures," he said. "Your son, Tobias has read it. We can pay 300,000 Swedish crowns for the farm, inventory included," he said while looking first at Anders and then at Lena.

Anders gasped. "But that can't include the livestock?" he protested. "I haven't seen prices like that since the '80s."

"It includes everything. We can't compare the situation today with the prices before the cyber attack. You couldn't sell the farm to any Swede at any price."

"But we have a windmill that gives us light and a generator to power the milking machine. We have a flour mill nearby where we can grind our grain. You can't find another farm like it. We can't accept that price."

"Of course not," Lena said.

"I can go as high as 350,000."

"This farm has been owned by the same family for several generations and it has been well cared for. Your offer is disrespectful."

"It's not enough. We'll not sell the farm for that price," Lena said.

"Then perhaps I'll look elsewhere."

"You do that, but I'm sure you won't find a farm like this one. I know all the farmers around here, and no one would sell at rock-bottom prices."

"Would you consider 500,000?"

"No, we won't. The price will have to be in the millions."

Johanssen looked surprised but scribbled some more numbers on a pad.

"Here's is my highest offer," he said and showed Anders the number.

"My wife and I have to talk about it. We'll be back soon." He and Lena went into the cold living room and closed the door.

"He has already increased his offer quite a bit, it's a good sign," Anders said.

"I wonder where he got all that money from. Perhaps he made it in the oil industry. We know that oil has made Norway rich."

"That's true. He can probably afford to pay two million. The Norwegian crown is worth more than the Swedish. Should we go for it?"

"We don't want to do anything we will regret later. I heard that an apartment in our little town sold for nearly one million before the cyber attack."

"In that case, our farm should be worth at least three million."

Mr. Johanssen was still busy jotting down figures on a separate piece of paper when Anders and Lena stepped into the kitchen.

Anders cleared his throat. "We don't see any reason to sell below three million," he said.

Johanssen drew in his breath and looked shocked. "Oh. Why is that?"

"Because we don't have to sell. We have no debts. We're healthy and can work this farm until the power is restored, and then we can get at least four million for it. We're not far from Gothenburg and it won't be long before the real estate developers come this way."

Johanssen looked thoughtful and scribbled some more figures on the paper.

"If you're not interested, you can return to Norway without a deal," Anders said.

Johanssen looked out the window and saw the snow blowing into drifts. The windows of his car were white.

"We need a 20 percent down payment right now," Anders said.

"You're driving a hard bargain."

"You're getting a bargain, and you know it," Anders said.

Anders looked on as the man took out a big checkbook. "This is the only way, we can pay the down payment," he said. "You can cash the check in Norway." Anders wondered who "we" were but assumed Johanssen was married. He didn't sign the check right away. First, he wrote in the sum of three million crowns on the duplicate contracts and dated them.

"We can close on April 1. The papers are the same. I will take one and you can keep the other. "You can't cash the big check until you have left the farm. Put the contract in a safe place."

When all three had signed the two copies, and Johanssen had signed the checks, Lena asked if he had time to stay for dinner.

"No, I'm sorry, but I must leave before the weather gets worse. It's still snowing," he said, looking out the window." They said goodbye and Johanssen walked with long strides to his car. He had taken care of his errand and looked satisfied.

Anders hugged Lena. "We did it! What's for dinner?"

"Mashed potatoes and our homemade sausage." Lena took up the stove rings and put the pots directly over the fire.

"It will taste good, now that the contract is signed. We can write to Toby and tell him that Johannsen paid a lot more than he had planned."

Lena sounded happy and hummed a tune.

The hacker: *I would not be surprised if Anders and Lena will regret the sale of their farm. It also looks like they forgot something very important when they signed the papers.*

Chapter 18

The two Almåker families gathered around the TV in their home in Oslo to watch the evening newscast. Everyone was anxious to hear if there was any news from Sweden. Today the news was bad.

A few miles outside Stockholm, a man has killed another man to get food for his children. The murdered man's wife heard someone call out, "I have three children and no food." Her husband called her name, but before she could come to his rescue, the murderer had pushed her into a closet and barricaded the door. She could hear him enter the pantry, and it sounded like he swept cans from the shelves. When she finally was able to get out, she found her husband lying on the steps in a puddle of blood. The woman ran to a neighbor and yelled, "Come quick and help me. I think Albert is dead. A thief has killed him."

The neighbor went with the woman and found Albert dead. When he turned the body over, he saw that the back of his head was crushed. A bloody club lay beside him. It was too late to catch the murderer. More neighbors came to help the woman who had just become a widow. They cleaned the body, made a casket, and dug the grave. It was the only way Albert could be buried. A pastor came and read the rites. The death was announced in the parish church.

"It's not the first time a desperate man has killed another human being to get food for his children, but in Sweden! It would have been unthinkable before the cyber attack," Alex said. "Mamma and Pappa have more food in their pantry than most people and I worry about them. I'm glad they sold the farm, but they aren't moving until spring."

Ella hugged her children to calm their fears. Mia put a hand on her swelling tummy and was glad she didn't live in Sweden anymore.

As the shortage of food became more acute it led to peaceful demonstrations in Stockholm against the government. Starving people took the matter into their own hands and broke into empty homes and raided them of everything edible and any cash they could find. They lounged in their living rooms and slept in their beds until they got hungry again when they went to the next house to continue their relentless search for something to eat. The owners, who had fled to other countries in a hurry had left their cookie jars, candy stacks, crackers, chips, dry groceries, and canned food behind. There was usually something left for the hungry to eat, and if they were lucky, there was wine in the cellar. Sometimes they found money in the strangest places.

The British press, always available in Norway, carried an editorial about Sweden.

The Swedes aren't as likely to demonstrate as, for instance, the Americans. But there have been demonstrations in the past against immigration and the government's immigration policy when buildings and cars were burned. The political party," Anders (The Sweden Democrats), has carried out a campaign against the large immigration to Sweden. Some of its hardliners demand that Sweden should be a country for Swedes only. The party has gained popularity and is now represented in the Riksdag. At this time, however, people in general probably believe their government is working on a solution to the crisis from the shelter. If hunger becomes more widespread, there may be uprisings. With all communications down, it takes a long time before word gets out about how bad the conditions are. We probably know more than the average Swede.

Malena called and asked if they had heard the news about the murdered man. "I don't understand why the Swedish military can't transport enough food to the starving people," she said. "The military has trucks and gasoline, and Sweden has large warehouses filled with food. I hope Norway can help. And why hasn't the United Nations done anything to help? Are they afraid of the Ruskey too?"

"Toby had answered the call and related to the family what Malena had said. "She has a point," he said, "but Russia has veto rights in the UN."

Alex was getting ready to leave for Sweden. He told Mia he was going on a business trip so it wouldn't cost them anything. Mia never questioned his decisions, but after she heard the news from Sweden, she worried about his safety. Alex took the same route as Toby, but from Gothenburg, he drove directly to Trollhättan. He passed a bus pulling a gengas generator. Outside the city, he saw a few trucks powered by gengas. He didn't see any other vehicles, only a few bikers.

The weather was cold and a thin layer of frost covered the trees and grass. The power plant in Trollhättan, located at a beautiful place by the river, looked the same to Alex. The director lived in a large, brightly lit villa with a view. Alex continued up a hill, parked his car, and listened to the noise from the roller dam. He walked up several steps and knocked on the door. A man with an accent opened it and let him in as soon as he heard his name.

"Let me take your coat. You're expected." Alex followed him.

"Hello, Alex. I hope you had a good trip." The gray-haired director came toward him and they shook hands. Alex didn't have a chance to speak before he was addressed.

"I understand that you worked here at one time, Alex." He pointed to a chair, while he went behind the desk to sit down.

"Yes, I did. I've come to deliver a letter from my company," Alex said, putting the letter on the desk. The director picked it up, opened it, and read it. Then he took a piece of stationery from a shelf and wrote something in longhand, put it in an envelope, and wrote Olaf Olafssen's name on it.

"Please, take this letter to your boss," the director said, handing it to Alex.

He was on his way to his parents. His trunk was loaded with white flour, fresh coffee bread, rusks, and cookies that Mia had baked. He had sent a letter to his parents, so he hoped they were expecting him.

The daylight was gone when he drove up the road to the farm. His father came out to meet him. Alex let the car run to give them light.

"How nice of you to come and visit us, son. Mamma is so happy." Alex hugged his father.

"It's fun for me too."

"Hope the family is well."

"Yes, everybody is fine. I brought 25 kilos of white flour."

"That much. It will be welcome, and there's room for it in the pantry. I'll take the sack."

"Then I can take the cartons."

"Here, I come with a sack of flour on my back," Anders said when Lena opened the door.

"Is it white?"

"Yes, Mamma, I heard that you don't like the coarse flour from the gristmill," Alex said with a big grin.

"Welcome Alex, with or without flour." She stretched her arms toward him, and he hugged her with one arm while holding the carton with the other.

"I brought some things that Mia baked. Here, can you take this carton? Then, I'll go and get my suitcase." Lena put the carton on the counter.

Alex decided to go to the outhouse while his car still lit up the yard. He washed his hands in the rain barrel before getting his suitcase from the trunk, shut off the engine, and went back inside. He pulled off his leather boots and hung up his winter jacket.

"Here, you can borrow a pair of slippers," Lena said. "The floor is cold in the living room but the fireplace is lit."

Anders brushed flour from his jacket before hanging it up.

"We're so happy you could come and visit us," he said. "You don't have to milk cows this time. The milking machine is great, and I can do it myself, thanks to you, Alex."

Lena was busy unpacking what Mia had baked. Alex's visit had helped her realize how much she had missed him and how wonderful it would be to move to Norway.

"Mia shouldn't have gone to all this trouble," she said, but it will be good to have it until I can bake myself. Supper is almost ready."

Anders was anxious to talk to Alex about the sale of the farm.

"Do you think we should have held out for more money?"

"I don't know much about farm prices, but I'm glad you sold."

"I hope nothing happens to the animals before the new owner takes over," he said. "It doesn't say anything about that in the contract."

"It's a risk he has to take. You might get some new calves, too."

"Yes, but now that we can't get any more insemination there won't be any more calves, and the milk will dry up."

"It will be the new owner's problem. Perhaps someone has raised a bull calf. They grow up fast."

"Please stop talking about cows and calves. I'm more interested in hearing about my family in Norway," Lena said.

So that was the subject during supper that they ate in the kitchen. But when they were seated in the living room after dinner, Anders wanted to know if there were any suitable jobs for him in Oslo.

"Farming is all, I know," he said.

"There are nurseries that might be hiring in the spring."

"I don't know much about flowers and such."

"But I can teach you," Lena said. "I know quite a bit about flowers and scrubs. After all, I'm the daughter of a master gardener."

"Well, then you can work at the nursery, and I'll find something else to do."

Anders said goodnight first.

"Goodnight, Pappa." Alex heard his father go out the back door and come in again.

Lena turned to Alex. "I'll be glad to work with flowers. Pappa worries too much."

"It will be a big change for him to work for others. He's used to being his own boss, so I'm not surprised if he feels bad about leaving the livestock to other people."

Alex's visit made Lena even more eager to move.

Alex could only stay a couple days, but he was happy with his trip. It was still dark at 9 a.m. as he drove toward the ferry. All of a sudden, the road was blocked by boulders and he wondered why. He couldn't pass and stepped out of the car to see what could be done.

The hacker: *Unfortunately, Alex did not see the rock that was aimed at his head. A lot of violent acts are committed in order to get out of the country and to obtain food. But there were crimes in Sweden before the cyber attack, especially in the immigrant communities. I haven't heard anything about what has happened to Malena's and Ella's parents.*

Chapter 19

Malena called her sister Ella, saying that a letter had arrived from their father. "They're in Denmark," she said.

"Oh, that's good news. I want to read the letter. Can you come over? Take the kids with you. Is Svenung home?"

"No, he isn't home yet, but perhaps he can join us later. I'll bring the kids. Is 7 o'clock alright?"

"Yes, of course. I can hardly wait. How is our family doing in Denmark?"

"Everybody is fine."

"I'm glad. See you later."

"We are having company this evening," Ella told her children. "Malena has received a letter from our father. Everyone in our family is safe in Copenhagen."

"Are Hedda and Thorsten coming? It would be so cool," Lynn said.

"Yes, they're coming with Malena."

"I can serve the cookies I baked," Lynn said.

Mia set the table in the living room and placed a flowering plant in the center. Ella made coffee and tea. Toby and the kids helped to get everything ready.

"Remove the newspapers, and the shoes by the door," Ella said.

"Turn off the TV, Emil."

They were prepared when the doorbell rang. Everyone talked at the same time until they had sat down in the living room. Malena took out the letter from her purse and read it aloud:

Dear Malena and family,

Hope you are all well. We have been in Copenhagen a few weeks now and like it here. The Danes are generous and kind. They picked up my grandmother and took her to a home for the elderly. Critically ill Swedes who need surgeries have been taken to a hospital here in Copenhagen. In addition to the Swedes who drive over on the bridge from Malmö, large numbers are coming across on the ferries every day. A national organization is shipping food and medicine to Malmö and Helsingborg.

We live in temporary housing and have jobs. Our grandchildren have started school. Copenhagen can receive many Swedes. Now we're longing to know if you have heard anything from Ella and her family? Write as soon as you can. We don't have phones yet.

Your father

At the end of the letter, everyone had signed their names and written a few words. Malena and Ella hugged each other and cried with relief. The children had listened to the letter and asked questions.

"We haven't seen our Swedish cousins in a long time," Hedda said. "Is there any way we can visit them now that they are in Copenhagen?"

"We would have to fly," said Ella. "Ferries take too long."

"It sounds like Denmark is doing a lot for the Swedes," Toby said. "People in Skåne are lucky to have Copenhagen just across the strait. Norway has no large cities at the border to Sweden. Halden and Fredrikstad are the closest. I don't know how they cross up north, but I'm guessing the Swedes just drive or walk across the border like the Norwegian refugees did when they fled to Sweden in the 1940s."

"I read in our school books that the Danes ravaged Sweden in the 17th and 18th centuries when the two countries were enemies. Skåne was Danish and Norway belonged to Denmark," Emil said.

"That's correct. But if we go back in time, Denmark, Sweden, and Norway were united. That's why we have the three-crown symbol."

"Do you mean like the hockey team, Tre Kronor, Pappa?"

"Yes, but they didn't come up with the name. The symbol has existed since 1398 when a union was formed between the three countries."

Ella interrupted the conversation. "It's time for coffee. The kids will have tea in the kitchen. Bring the tray with the cookies."

"I already put a plate with cookies in the kitchen," Lynn said.

As the adults enjoyed the coffee, Svenung came and surprised them all.

"The children let me in," he said. "I was late coming home, but if you have any coffee left, I'll have a cup." He spoke Norwegian, but everyone understood him. Svenung was tall, and his light hair was cut short.

"Here's a chair. Sit down and I'll get you some coffee," Toby said.

"Have you read the letter yet?" Svenung asked.

"Malena read it to us. Our relatives are lucky to be in Copenhagen." Toby had an idea. "Perhaps Norway and Denmark should get together and take care of western Sweden."

"It could be done. I wonder how many Swedish refugees have come to Norway and Denmark?"

"We have heard of thousands," Toby said, "but it's probably closer to one hundred thousand by now. Sweden took in about two million immigrants and refugees during a 20-year period."

"Ironically, Sweden used to have a shortage of housing," Mia cut in.

"Yes, and now thousands of apartments are empty because most people can't stand living in the cities anymore. The garbage is not collected and bags of waste are tossed out the windows," Svenung said. "In Stockholm, the situation is critical."

Toby thought about what he had seen in Gothenburg but kept it to himself. "But what's NATO doing?" Do you know anything about that,

Svenung?"

"We're observing the situation. As you know, Finland has restored most of its power. The Finns are clever and they have a good defense. They haven't closed their military bases as Sweden has. Finland put up a fierce defense during World War II, and still, it had to give up the Karelia region to the Soviet Union."

"But we can't expect NATO to defend Sweden, or what do you think?" Toby still wanted to know, one way or another.

"I'm not privileged to the information." Svenung didn't sound as certain anymore.

"Do you know how Germany and Great Britain are reacting?"

"We fly over Kalmar and Öland, and I've seen German ships in the area. I also know that Germany delivers food to Trelleborg and picks up Swedish refugees on the ferries that sail from and to Travemünde. The UK also ships food on ferries to Malmö and takes refugees on the return trip."

"Sweden planned to make military service mandatory for girls and boys, but I don't think the law had been passed before the cyber attack," Toby said.

"Here in Norway, healthy boys and girls can serve for one year, but it's still voluntary because we have enough volunteers. Our defense has been strengthened even though we belong to NATO."

"SAAB has joined Boeing in a T-X project to educate pilots. The pilots are just as important as the planes," Toby said.

"I hope there won't be another war," Mia said, shuddering at the thought.

"I want to fly to Copenhagen and visit our family there," Ella declared. "Malena, you'll come too, of course. The children are excited about going. Best to travel while we can."

"The Swedes who used to travel so much for recreation are now limited to fleeing their country. Just think how everything can change,"

Svenung said. "One can never depend on prosperity to last."

"Is Alex still in Sweden?" Ella asked Mia.

"Yes, but he'll be home tomorrow. I can't relax until he calls from the ferry and is on his way home."

"I'm sure he'll call as soon as he can." Ella placed a hand over Mia's.

"What were your impressions of Sweden when you were there, Toby?" Svenung asked.

"It was dark everywhere and very quiet without the usual traffic. In the countryside it's calm, and the farmers seem to have adjusted to the primitive conditions, but people in the cities are struggling to survive. Most businesses are closed. Windows and doors are covered with plywood to keep looters out. Both men and women beg for food from the farmers. In the cities, they sleep in cold rooms. In some places, I saw they had burned furniture outside for heat and cooking." Toby didn't mention what he had seen at his house and Alex's. It was just too painful.

I'm guessing that some city folks are staying at their summer houses," Svenung said, "but they'll freeze there too if they don't have wood burning stoves."

"Have you heard that Pappa and Mamma have sold the farm to a Norwegian and they're moving here?"

"Yes, it was a surprise. If more Norwegians are planning to buy farms in Sweden, Norway could ship over fuel to the farms they buy."

The hacker: *Sweden and Norway are alike in many ways, but when it comes to defense, they are very different. Norway was occupied by the Nazis during the last war, so, after the war when NATO was formed, it did not hesitate to join. Sweden stayed out of the war by declaring itself neutral, and neutrality meant it could not join one side or the other. I'm sure it will be regretted. Now, I want to see if Alex is hurt.*

Chapter 20

Alex felt something wet on his aching head and touched it. As he withdrew it, he saw blood. He couldn't think clearly. What had happened to him? He lay on the ground without his warm jacket, and when he looked for his car, it was gone. He saw the boulders. Trying to stand up, he swayed. He shivered and realized he must try to walk, but where to? When he saw the sign to the ferry he began to stumble forward. Slowly, it occurred to him that the person who had hit him on the head was on the way to the ferry in his car, with his jacket, ticket, wallet, and cell phone.

Feeling shaky, he feared he wouldn't make it to the ferry in time. When he saw a car approaching, he managed to raise a hand. A Norwegian man rolled down the window and talked to him.

"What happened? I can see blood on your face, and you don't have a jacket."

"I was hit on the head."

"Did you have a car?"

"Yes, I should have been on the ferry now. I'm Alex Almåker ... and I live in Oslo. The attacker has my wallet...." He couldn't continue. The man stepped out of his car and helped him into the passenger seat of his car before removing the rocks that were in his way.

"I'm heading for the ferry myself. I'm Oystein. You're bleeding and it has to be taken care of. The attacker is probably on the way to the ferry with your identity. We must report your car stolen, so the thief can be arrested."

"Thanks for stopping, Oystein. I've got a terrible headache and I'm dizzy." Alex touched his forehead and moaned.

"You don't have to talk. I understand."

When Oystein drove onto the ferry, he told the man who checked his ticket what had happened. "Alex Almåker here was attacked and robbed. Could you check if someone with his identity and car is on board the ferry?"

"Almåker, yes, he's onboard."

"No, it's not Almåker but someone who stole his ticket and car. Almåker is here with me and injured. He needs help, and the police in Oslo have to be alerted."

"We will tell them and ask them to stop Almåker's car. Now, you must drive onboard."

Alex saw his car on the ferry as soon as they had parked.

"There's my car, the blue one!"

"I'll give the license number and description to the crew. Are you able to walk up to the passenger deck with me?" Alex nodded, and Oystein helped him up the stairs. When they came to the dining area, the other passengers stared at Alex. A crewmember came and asked what had happened and Oystein explained. The man assured Alex he would get his car back, and said they had a nurse on board who could clean his wound.

On wobbly legs, Alex went to the restroom. Looking in the mirror, he didn't recognize himself. His hair was sticky, and he had blood on his face and neck. He tore off paper towels, wet them, and cleaned himself as well as he could. He couldn't do anything to the cut on his head, but it looked like it had stopped bleeding.

Oystein stood outside the door and waited for him. "Is there anyone I can call for you?" he asked.

"My wife."

"What's her number?"

Alex felt terrible about not remembering his wife's phone number. "It's in my cell phone," he said. He felt for it in his pockets until he remembered it was gone.

"My brother, Tobias Almåker in Oslo," he said, but he couldn't remember his number either. "I must have a concussion."

"Don't worry about it. When we get closer to Oslo, I can look up your brother's number. Are you hungry?"

"I'm thirsty, but I don't have any money."

"I'll pay, of course."

"Thanks. I'll reimburse you."

"Don't worry about it. You need to see a doctor. You can't drive."

"Maybe Tobias can pick me up."

Alex felt better after the nurse had tended to him, and he had consumed two cups of coffee with a sandwich. He sat in a chair and soon fell asleep. Oystein kept an eye on him and wasn't sure it was good for someone with a concussion to sleep that long. After several hours, he got a signal on his phone and began to search for the number to Tobias Almåker. When it came up, he clicked on it.

"Tobias Almåker here."

"Hi, Tobias. My name is Oystein Larsen. I'm on the ferry from Gothenburg with your brother, Alex. He was attacked on the way to the ferry. I think he has a concussion. Could you meet him at the ferry in Oslo?"

"Yes, of course. That's bad news. I'll tell his wife. Where's his car?"

"It's on the ferry. The attacker used Alex's identity. But if we're lucky, the thief will be arrested before he can take the car. He also has Alex's jacket, wallet, and cell phone. Your brother needs a doctor. He's sleeping and has been sleeping a long time."

"I'll leave right away, and I'll bring someone to take Alex's car home. Tell him I'm coming. Thank you, Oystein, for helping my brother. Hope I'll see you at the ferry." Mia began to cry, and the happy gathering in his home broke up.

Toby had never driven so fast in his life. Mia and Svenung were with him. They arrived in the harbor just as the ferry approached. A police car tailed Toby. Svenung explained to the police why the speeding was necessary. When Oystein drove off the ferry, he had Alex with him.

"There is my brother. He made it," Alex exclaimed and pointed to Toby's car. Toby at once ran up to them and helped Alex out of Oystein's car.

"Thanks for helping my brother, here's is a little something for your trouble."

"Glad I could help. Good that you made it in time. Hope Alex feels better soon."

Mia and Svenung came up to Alex and Toby, and Mia put her arms around her husband.

"So, sorry this happened to you, honey."

"Take them to a safe place," Toby told Svenung. "I have to find Alex's car."

Thanks to Toby's speeding, the police were already there and arrested the attacking thief, a man with light, straight hair that fell over his eyes and had no likeness to the dark-haired Alex. The police searched the thief and found Alex's wallet and car keys in his pocket.

"Where's Alex Almåker now? I need to return his belongings to him and verify that they are his," the policeman said.

"He's here, but injured." Toby pointed to Alex. "I'm his brother, Tobias Almåker, and I'll take him home."

"Take his car then." Toby got the car keys and drove the car off the ferry.

Alex and Mia stood side by side and waited for Toby. The policeman came up to them and asked Alex to identify his wallet and phone.

"Yes, they are mine. I don't remember how much I had."

"But your charge cards could have been used, so call your bank. I'll write a report and you need to sign it. Do you want to sit down?"

"Yes, I'm dizzy and I have a terrible headache." Alex sank down in the passenger seat of Toby's car, and Mia slid into the backseat.

"We can send for an ambulance if you like."

"No thanks, I'll wait until I get home to see a doctor." The police wrote the report, and Alex signed it.

"Toby, I'll drive Alex's car," Svenung said. "See you at home. Drive slower this time. It's best that Mia calls home and tells the family that you have Alex with you."

It was not until they sat in the car that Mia noticed that Alex didn't have his jacket. The thief must have put it in his bag. Sweden had become a dangerous country. Mia put her hand to her forehead and sighed. She was glad Anders and Lena were moving to Oslo.

The hacker: *A member of the Almåker family has been injured. They think that Anders and Lena's move to Oslo will solve all their problems, but I do not think so.*

Chapter 21

Toby and Mia took Alex to the ER the same evening, where he got his wound stitched and was diagnosed with a concussion. He had to stay home from work for three weeks and take it easy. Mia waited on him hand and foot. He could hardly do anything but take walks. His headache was not as bad as before, and sometimes it disappeared. He was anxious to get back to work.

When Alex returned to the office, he found out that his company had purchased shares in the Trollhättan hydroelectric power plant, and that Olafssen would be moving there with his wife. It explained why Alex had met with the director of the plant in Trollhättan. He would miss Ole at work and wondered who his new boss would be. He was happily surprised when he learned that he would take over Olafssen's position. As the operations manager, he would supervise all electrical, mechanical, and maintenance workers.

"Alex, I understand you're waiting for an apartment," Olafssen said. "If you're interested, I could rent my house to you, all the furnishings included?"

"Of course, I'm interested. It would be a good solution for us because we still don't know when we can get the apartment."

"You and your wife can come and take a look at the place. I'll give you the address."

"Great. I hope you can start up the hydro plant in Trollhättan."

The news about the house thrilled Mia. "Wow, it sounds too good to be true. A whole house? Then your parents can live with us."

"You wouldn't mind?"

"No, not at all. We lived with them, and they were so sweet and kind to me."

"Pappa was worried about finding a job here, so it would be perfect for him. He could take care of the yard. Olafssen said that there is a large orchard on the property."

"And Lena can help me with the baby. I'm so inexperienced."

"We have to look at the house first and find out if we can afford it. But I forgot to tell you I've been promoted; my salary will be higher."

"Congratulations, sweetheart. You make me so proud," Mia said, kissing him.

"You taste delicious, honey. Here's the telephone number and the address to the house," Alex said as he fished out a paper from his inside pocket. "I trust you completely if you want to go there by yourself."

"But I want you to come along. You know better than I how much we can afford to pay."

"Then it has to be on Saturday."

"It's Thursday today, so it should be fine. I'll call and ask when we can come."

Mia sat down in a comfortable chair and put her hands on her tummy. The baby moved. Mia thought about her mother who had died at such a young age. She felt as though she was telling the story of her childhood to her unborn child.

When I was little, I couldn't say Marie, so I said, Mia. Then everyone called me Mia. I have only a vague memory of my mother and have only a faded picture of her holding me. I can't remember my father at all. He went his own way and I don't know if he is alive. I grew up with my moster, my mother's sister. But now I have a new family. Your dad and his parents, Anders and Lena. They are my closest family. I hope you'll have siblings. I'm sure you'll have good genes from your father. I don't know much about my genes.

Mia loved Olafssen's house. "This will be the baby's room," she said to Alex. "We'll buy a crib and put it here. The sun shines in the window, and here I want to sit and nurse."

They strolled through the yard and looked at the fruit trees. The house was located on the outskirts of Oslo, and Alex and Mia liked both the house and the location.

"We have many different kinds of fruit trees," Olafssen said. "I'm afraid I've neglected the orchard."

"I know the right man for the job. My father is a farmer in Sweden," said Alex. "Hope you don't mind if my parents live with us? They are coming in April."

"No, we don't mind. Farmers are dependable people. They have cared for their farm, and they could take care of my property the same way."

"How much is the rent?"

"I wouldn't rent it out to just anybody, but I know that you and your wife will take good care of it, so the rent will be low—just to reimburse me for the expenses of keeping the house. I'll pay for repairs should there be any. "

"I would like to see how much the bills amount to every month," Mia said.

"It's a good idea. You have a smart wife, Alex."

The three agreed on the rent and how it would be paid and shook hands on the deal.

Alex photographed their new home while asking Mia if she was pleased.

"How could I not be pleased? I've never lived in such a beautiful house. Well, your parents' house was nice, but this is newer and larger. I can't wait to move in. It's great that they'll leave everything as it is. We don't need to buy anything. I'll be happy here."

"I'll write to Mamma and Pappa and tell them they can live with us for the time being, but I want to order prints first. I'm sure they'll be pleasantly surprised."

Toby and Ella were happy for Alex and Mia but said they would miss them.

"We can still visit each other," Alex said. "By the way, I have more good news. I'm taking over Olafssen's job."

"Congratulations, bro."

"I'm glad I stayed at the power plant."

Olafssen and his wife left for Trollhättan, and Alex and Mia moved into the house the next day. Mia couldn't have been happier as she walked from room to room. Then she went to the store to buy food. When she had put away the groceries, she looked out the window and was surprised to see large snowflakes coming down. She still admired the snow when Alex came walking toward the house. She watched as he shoveled the snow from the walk. It wasn't much, but it might freeze later.

"Tomorrow, I'll wear my boots to work," Alex said as he took off his wet shoes inside the door. Do I get a kiss?"

"You can have two." She offered her lips, and Alex took full advantage.

"I'm glad you came home early."

"I saw the snow and thought you might need something from the store."

"I have already been to the store. How was the bus ride?"

"It was longer than usual, and I had to walk part of the way."

"Tomorrow you can take the car if you want. Are you hungry? I haven't started dinner yet."

"Dinner can wait. We're alone now. We can do what we want whenever we want." He drew her into his arms.

"I love you, Mia. You're the softest and most beautiful woman I know."

"I love you just as much, Alex, but I can't say you're the softest man I know."

Alex led her to their bedroom and closed the blinds.

The hacker: *Mia is a kind soul, almost meek. It must have something to do with her background. She comes from a humble beginning. She is not likely to have any enemies, but if Alex follows his ambitions, he might cause her pain and anxiety. Now I am anxious to learn how Anders and Lena are managing.*

Chapter 22

When a letter from his parents arrived, Toby gladly paid for the postage.

He read it right away.

We are happy for Alex and Mia. They live in a nice home and we are looking forward to living with them. It won't be long now. The days pass quickly. Please, thank Alex for the pictures.

Our neighbors, Lennart and Lisa, came to visit us yesterday. They had heard that we sold our farm to a Norwegian investor and asked if he would be interested in buying their farm as well. Both would like to move to Norway. They have no generator for their milking machine and must hand milk. As you know, their farm is about the same size as ours, but they don't have as many cows. I wouldn't be surprised if more farmers around here want to sell to Norwegians. I have gasoline left and promised Lennart he could have some so he can drive to Halden.

The rest of the letter described their daily chores. Toby put the letter back in the envelope, called Alex, and asked him if Olafssen had made any progress at the power plant in Trollhättan.

"He has, but it will take time because many of the employees have left the company. That's all I know."

"Pappa wrote that more neighbors want to sell their farms. He asked me to contact Johanssen. He could make good deals, especially if the power is restored to the area."

When Toby called Johanssen saying that more farmers might be interested in selling to Norwegian buyers, he said he would think about it. Toby assumed there was a company behind Johanssen's business dealings.

In March, another letter arrived from Pappa Anders:

Johanssen has bought Lennart and Lisa's farm and two more nearby. We are afraid of the beggars who come every day now, so we keep the door to the house locked. I've told mamma not to open it when she is alone. Bruno scares away some of them but not all. At the cemetery, they can't dig graves fast enough for all the people who die of hunger and disease. They don't have any fuel for the bulldozer and have to dig by hand. I don't know how long this can go on. We hope Norway sends over more food and that the power stations can be restarted. Mamma says she will make cheese and butter instead of trying to sell the milk because no one has money to pay for it. She has no time to write. We hope to leave in a few weeks. The man who will lease the farm from the Norwegian was here and looked at everything. He seems to be a capable man, and he can take over on the first of April.

On April 1, Toby took the night ferry and slept on board to be in Gothenburg early in the morning to escort his parents to Oslo. They were busy loading as much as they could into their car.

"I'm glad you are here, Toby, because we don't have more room in our car."

"Then we'll put it in mine." Toby began to carry boxes.

"I milked the cows for the last time this morning and gave the milk to the calves," Anders said.

Lena looked exhausted. "Go and sit down in my car. Mamma. You don't have to carry anything else."

"I have to get my purse and see so I haven't forgotten anything. I don't think I will ever see our home again." Tears ran down her cheeks. When she came back outside, she wiped them away with a tissue. Toby led her to his car. "Think about the nice house you'll move into and the new grandchild soon to be born, Mamma."

"We're ready to leave," Anders said, closing the trunk. "I'll follow you, Toby. You know the way."

Bruno lay on the ground watching it all, but now he began to bark. He came up to Anders and Lena and whimpered.

"Oh, my goodness," Lena said. "I forgot to say goodbye to Bruno." She got out of the car and began scratching him behind his ears and talking to him. "I'm so sorry we must leave you, but you can stay on the farm and you'll be well taken care of." Bruno wagged his tail.

Lena looked for Martin Gustafsson, the man who would be in charge of the farm, and saw him coming toward them. "Here is your new master, Bruno."

Martin grabbed Bruno's collar and held on to it. "I'll take care of Bruno," he said. As the cars started up, Lena listened to Bruno's bark for the last time. "Wish we could have taken him with us," she said.

"Pappa, we are driving through Dalsland. It's the safest route. If Mamma wants to rest, I will stop at a suitable place."

"Okay, don't drive too fast for me."

They drove E-45 past the familiar towns built along the railroad track and some farm country before they came to Trollhättan. Lena wondered if they could see the power plant from the road.

"No, not from here. The locks are closed and the ships that were stranded in Vänern when the cyber attack hit have to stay there."

"And now they can't get to Gothenburg?"

"No, not until the power is restored. The bridges can't open either."

"So much depends on electricity, much more than I realized."

They drove across the high Stallbacka bridge north of Trollhättan and passed Vänersborg at a distance before reaching the plains of Dalsland. Having passed Mellerud, they drove northwest toward higher elevations and wooded areas. Lena was asleep as Toby drove through Dals Ed with the beautiful lakes in full view, but she woke up when they reached the border. Their two cars were quickly cleared to pass. In Moss, they stopped for a break. Lena looked with amazement at the bustling activities in the brightly lit city. "Wait till you see Oslo," Toby said.

"I'm so stiff," Lena said when she stepped out of the car in front of Alex and Mia's home. It was evening and every room was lit up. Mia was heavy with child but said she felt fine.

"You have too much light here, it's blinding me," Lena said, and Anders agreed. "We aren't used to strong lights anymore."

Alex and Mia invited them inside, while Toby began to carry boxes and suitcases from his car.

"We can empty my car tomorrow morning," Anders said. "You don't have any thieves around here, do you?"

"I don't think so, Pappa, but I can put your car in the garage if you give me your keys. I'll be back tomorrow with Ella."

"Thanks for your help, Toby. See you tomorrow."

"What a beautiful house," Lena said as soon as she entered.

"We like it." Mia showed Anders and Lena the first floor before they went upstairs.

"Here's your room, and here's the bathroom. Alex uses the shower in the basement."

"Then I can do the same," Anders said.

"Hope you will be comfortable here. You can put your clothes in this closet."

"I want to go to the bathroom first and wash up. I wonder if Toby brought in my case," Lena said.

"I think so. When you're ready, we'll have supper in the kitchen." Anders walked downstairs to get their suitcases.

When Toby and Ella arrived the next day, Alex went outside to meet them.

"How's it going?" Toby asked.

"Great. I showed Pappa the orchard, and he's eager to get to work. Spring is here."

Toby offered to unpack his father's car, but it had already been done.

"Our parents were up early. How was it to cross the border?"

"No problem at all. The guard laughed when he saw how packed our cars were.

"You're welcome to Sunday dinner at our house. The children can't wait to see their Farmor and Farfar," (grandparents on the father's side) Ella said.

"Pappa and Mamma are sitting in the living room. They took baths in the tub and now they don't know what to do. They're not used to being idle."

Toby touched Alex's shoulder. "We have accomplished our goal to bring our parents here, but you know what that means, don't you, bro?"

"Yes, it means that one of us has to stay in Oslo," Alex said. "We can't abandon them here."

"It makes our move more permanent, but I still feel like I have unfinished business in Gothenburg, and Sweden will always be my homeland."

The hacker: *I think it will be hard for Toby and Alex to keep their commitment to their parents.*

Chapter 23

Anders and Lena watched TV mostly to learn the Norwegian language that sounded strange to their ears, but they were also interested in news from Sweden.

The regular program was interrupted by a special report.

"What has happened now?" Anders asked aloud.

"The following bulletin has come in from Stockholm via shortwave radio:

Last night, Russian soldiers invaded the castle in central Stockholm. A staff member, who managed to escape, related the event to a Swedish reporter. The castle was lit up by generators. No royals were present. The king and queen live at another castle, but they are evacuated to an unknown location.

"Svenung was right," Anders said and moved closer to the TV to hear better. The broadcast reported:

As soon as the Russians had entered the Royal Castle, their captain ordered us to serve them vodka. I went down to the wine cellar and got wine instead. The captain looked at the bottles and spit at them. "Vodka," he yelled. Another member of the staff and I then picked up as much vodka we could carry and took it to the captain. We thought they might drink a lot and get drunk, and we were right. The captain and his soldiers drank from the bottles, made toasts, and howled. After a few hours, they were asleep. We took their weapons and escaped. I knew where a reporter lived and ran as fast as I could and told him what had happened.

Large crowds have gathered outside the castle protesting the unthinkable invasion. One man stood in front of the protesters, yelling: "We have a castle guard with soldiers on horseback that are supposed to protect the castle night and day. The guard is changed at regular hours. Why didn't the guards protect the castle?" After a while, the crowd chanted, "Where's our military?" and "Why isn't the government doing something? Ni är fegisar!"(You're cowards!)

"I'm glad they are protesting because the power has been out for almost six months," Anders said.

"As Svenung pointed out, the Big Bear can do what he wants," Mia said. "But why can't the Swedish military defend our capital from such a small invasion?"

"It's hard to believe," Lena said. "And if we had lived in Sweden, we wouldn't have known about it."

"That's what the Russians are counting on. I think it's part of a larger plot that began with the cyber attack," Anders said. "I fear what will come next."

When the station went back to regular programming, Mia called Alex at work.

"Did you hear?"

"Hear what?"

"We heard on TV that Russian soldiers have invaded the castle in Stockholm."

"Really? Svenung was right. I don't have a TV here, but I can check the internet."

"It's so awful, Alex. We were there not long ago. It's very upsetting to our parents."

"I can imagine."

"I'm glad we aren't in Stockholm anymore."

Reporters analyzed what had happened, and Anders listened until Toby called and said he could hardly believe the Russians had entered central Stockholm without being discovered. "Nybroviken is not deep enough for subs to hide. They would have to surface."

Young Swedes were out protesting on Stockholm streets just as the situation changed. The next morning, the Oslo station had news from Stockholm:

We can now report that Swedish troops entered the castle this morning. The hungover Russians were defenseless and unable to resist arrest. The demonstrators that have gathered outside the castle are jubilant.

"Bravo," Anders exclaimed. Mia and Lena clapped their hands.

"The danger is over for now, but the Russians will probably get more aggressive. This is humiliating for them, and they'll take revenge," Alex said. "The Swedish military has to strengthen its defense."

Svenung called and said he had seen more Swedish troops marching to Stockholm.

"That's good," said Anders. "They will be needed."

Another special report interrupted regular programming:

Several Russian submarines are on the way to Stockholm. Sweden's most capable warship, Viby, is advancing toward Stockholm at a speed of 35 knots. It's armed with torpedoes and anti-sub shells. Swedish fighter planes have been seen in the area. NATO is observing from the air.

"I hope Viby wins," Anders said.

"This is unbearable." Lena could hardly stand it. "When we lived on the farm, we weren't as worried as we are now."

"There will be a race between the Russian submarines and the Viby," Alex said, looking at Anders. "If it sinks a Russian sub, it might start a war."

"But if Viby sinks an enemy sub in Swedish waters, it has the right to do it."

"The next time Russian soldiers come to Stockholm, they won't dare to get drunk," Lena declared.

"Let's change the subject," Mia suggested. "We're invited to Toby and Ella's for dinner, so let's try to relax and not think about what's happening in Sweden."

"I'll bring cheese and butter," Lena said. "They're the only presents I have."

"Tomorrow I want to go to a bank with the big check we got for the farm," Anders said to Alex.

"But first you need a Norwegian ID. Mia can take you to the right office. Mamma has to come also. You both need an ID to open a bank account and get health care. Then you can go from there to the bank and deposit your check. It would be wise to invest some of the money in bonds that will give you a good return."

"But I want access to the money if I need it. After what happened in Sweden, it's difficult to trust banks."

"The banker can give you advice about the safest investments. Tell him you want regular dividend payments. It will be like a paycheck every month."

"Can you come with us so we don't do anything wrong?"

"If you're uncertain, you can put the money in CDs and a regular savings account for now and decide later how to invest it."

"Well, then we'll head for Toby's place. It will be fun to see them again and where they live," Anders said.

Anders and Lena noticed that Emil and Lynn mixed in some Norwegian when they spoke Swedish. Both had turned a year older, and Lena promised to buy them birthday presents as soon as she had Norwegian money.

Toby took Alex aside and asked, "Did you hear the latest news?"

"Do you mean about Viby? We heard it was on its way to Stockholm."

"Yes, but the very latest is that it sank a Russian sub in Swedish waters. It hasn't been confirmed though."

"So, does this mean war?"

"We hope that Russia takes it as a warning," Toby said.

"It's good to know that NATO is on our side. It could also mean assistance from German and British forces."

"But we cannot be sure about NATO. It wouldn't surprise me if the American president goes against it."

"It's possible considering what he said earlier about the financing of NATO. He says European countries don't contribute enough, and Sweden hasn't paid anything," Alex said.

"More Swedish troops will be needed to defend Stockholm."

"Hope the enforcements arrive in time. But for now, we won't say anything about this to our families."

Lena sliced the homemade cheese and served up the butter she had made.

"This will be so good, Mamma." Toby picked up a bit of cheese. "I'm testing it. Yum, I think it's just right."

"Pappa will say it needs to be stored longer."

"Food is expensive here in Norway. It's about 30 percent higher than in Sweden, but salaries are also higher here."

"It feels almost sinful to eat such good food when we know most Swedes are starving," Lena said.

The hacker: *How can the Swedes think they will win any fight with my country? Anders and Lena are shocked by all the bad news from Sweden available to them on Norwegian television. The news never got to them in Sweden. I wonder how they will adjust to their new environment. Will Lena be able to take more bad news?*

Chapter 24

Anders worked in the orchard, cutting away dead branches, and had no idea what was going on in Sweden. Lena stood and watched him.

"This will take time," Anders said. "There's a vegetable garden in one corner of the yard if you're interested."

"Oh yes, of course, but it's still too early. Perhaps in a couple of weeks. The flowerbeds could use some flowers. Pansies can be planted now." Lena got excited and said she would buy pansies and seeds right away for both vegetables and flowers. "We have money now."

"Yes, it feels good to have money in the wallet again."

They took a coffee break and checked the TV for news from Sweden.

Norwegian television reported from Stockholm:

As we reported earlier, the Swedish Viby is chasing Russian submarines outside Stockholm. One of the subs had gotten ahead and surfaced in Nybroviken without being discovered. After dark, Russian soldiers advanced to the parliament building. Muffled shots felled the guards posted outside the empty building. An eyewitness related the event.

In the moonlight, we could see the guards fall to the ground and be replaced by Russians. We think the robbers had strong flashlights because we could see beams of light through the windows. After a while, the first Russians came out carrying what looked like electronic equipment with cords dangling behind. The last Russians carried heavy statues and paintings. Everything was loaded on the sub that lay above water close to the castle. Central Stockholm is almost deserted. Only a few of us civilians saw the entire coup. We could hardly believe our eyes. Our guards didn't have a chance to fire. The Russians left their guards outside the building.

The TV showed pictures of the parliament building and reported that the structure was erected in about 1900 and enlarged in the early 1980s.

Apparently, Stockholmers were afraid of protesting outside the building where the Russians had posted guards, so they took to the streets instead. Haggard looking starved men and women carried signs saying "Get the Ruskey out of here. Get our government back." The storefronts were covered with plywood. There were no police officers in sight.

"It's hard to believe our government is still in hiding while all this is happening. The ministers might be dead," Anders said. Lena was shocked and scared. Although she felt safe in Norway, she would always love Sweden more. When Alex came home in the evening, Anders asked him if he thought a war was imminent.

"It's possible, but what can little Sweden do against such a goliath. The parliament building is on Helgeandsholmen opposite the castle. City Hall could be next."

"It feels like someone has thrown a wet blanket over us," Lena said. "I was so happy making plans for a garden and planting flowers and then comes all this bad news from Sweden. But for Mia's sake, we mustn't talk about it. In her condition, she needs to stay calm."

Svenung came home and surprised Malena and the children one evening.

"How come you got time off?" Malena asked.

"It's very strange. We were ready to help Sweden when the mission was canceled."

"Do you know why?"

"The American president is against it. Since the U.S. is the largest financial contributor by far to NATO, his words carry weight."

"What will happen now?"

"I'm afraid Sweden will be lost."

Malena's legs buckled and she went down on her knees moaning. Svenung led her to the sofa, where she buried her face in a pillow.

"NATO was our only hope," she said.

"There might be another way.

"Like what?"

"I can't talk about it."

"But can Sweden defend itself?"

"I doubt it. The soldiers don't even have uniforms. The fatigues and boots that have been stored for years are too small for today's recruits. Angela Merkel has offered Sweden uniforms."

"But wouldn't it be better if Norway sent uniforms to Sweden?"

"Yes, I agree."

Toby and Ella had heard the bad news and came over.

"It's only getting worse. Where will it end?" Ella asked.

"Probably with our dear homeland becoming Russian," Toby said.

"I don't want our children to go to war," Ella said with conviction. "We have to move again."

"But where? If there will be a war, most countries will be involved. That's what happened during World War II."

Ella and Malena could not sleep. Still, they had to get up early and go to work. At the hospital, their work required all their focus. Patients in need of surgeries came from Sweden every day via Norwegian ferries and then in ambulances to the hospital. The nurses heard them talk about the awful situation in Sweden. "There's no medicine, and the terminally sick people are screaming for help. Some have committed suicide."

Both Malena and Ella were close to collapsing when their workday was over.

"I can't take it anymore," Ella said. "If I don't get transferred to another ward, I can't continue," she said. "Today, I changed the dressing on a friend from Gothenburg. She held on to me and said that her seriously ill parents would die if she couldn't get to them. Another patient told me that a young man had died of a burst appendix. It's so unnecessary. I told Toby that if Sweden becomes Russian, I don't want to live in Norway any longer. I want to live far away from Scandinavia."

"But I'm married to Svenung, and he flies for NATO, so we have to stay here," Malena said. "I don't think you should act in haste. NATO defends Norway, so we're safe here, and our parents are just as safe in Denmark. If we only could get a few days off, we could fly to Copenhagen and visit them."

"Yes, we could use some time off." Ella straightened her back and felt a little better.

The bad news from Sweden also affected their children.

"I wonder how our friends in Gothenburg are doing," Emil said to Lynn as they walked home from school.

"Me too," said Lynn. "Jelena's parents are divorced and I don't think her mom can afford to leave Sweden. I wonder if they have enough food and a warm place to sleep. The mother is from Croatia, and she and Jelena would be better off there. It has a warmer climate, too."

"My best buddy, Sebastian, has an older brother who is probably in the military now," Emil said. "He could be on his way to Stockholm, and there he could be shot by a Ruskey. I wrote a letter to Sebbe, but he hasn't answered yet."

"I haven't heard anything from Jelena either."

"I feel privileged. Here, I've just seen Star Wars, and in Sweden, they can't even watch television. If I lived in Sweden, I think I'd be out protesting against the government."

"I'd probably do the same, but now we're home and I'm hungry. An apple, chips, and a Fanta will taste good."

"A sandwich for me," Emil said.

The hacker: *So, the Swedes sank one of our subs, but I am sure they will pay dearly for that mistake. This is going on much longer than I had anticipated, but now Sweden can definitely give up on help from NATO. Ella is getting restless, and Mia is close to giving birth.*

Chapter 25

Children and teenagers played ball wherever they could, but more often they went to the soccer fields. Emil was selected to play on a team, and his parents and Lynn were there to cheer him on. Lynn had played on a girls' team in Gothenburg and wanted to play again. It didn't take long before she was in uniform with football shoes on her feet, ready to train and play against other teams. The sport was an amazing unifier. Emil and Lynn played with kids of many different nationalities. Norway had received immigrants and refugees who had adjusted to Norwegian society. Brown and black faces could be seen among all the white ones.

Mia had been told she would give birth sooner than expected. She had packed a small case with baby clothes and another with essentials for herself. She was ready for the big event. The weather warmed up. The birches sprouted little green leaves. The birds built their nests and insects buzzed.

One evening when Alex and Mia had gone to bed, Mia felt the first contractions. They were light to begin with, and she didn't say anything to Alex because she knew the pains would get stronger and continue a long time with the first child. She let Alex sleep.

Hours later, Lena heard that Alex and Mia were up early and guessed why. She cracked her door open and asked, "Is it time?"

"Yes, Mamma, but you can go to bed again. I'll call from the hospital when the baby is born," Alex said.

Lena stood by the window and watched as the car pulled out of the driveway. It was 4 a.m. and the sun shone brightly. She yawned and went back to bed. Anders was awake.

"What's going on?"

"Alex and Mia are on the way to the hospital."

"Already?"

"Yes, it's a little earlier than expected. Hope everything goes well. Mia doesn't know what is ahead of her."

"You didn't know either the first time."

"No, that's true."

Alex called at 8 a.m. when he knew his parents would be awake. Anders answered.

"Has anything happened yet?"

"No, Pappa, they say we can't expect the baby to be born until later today. The contractions are stronger now. I'm coaching Mia. I'm supposed to be with her the whole time."

"Mamma is asking if everything is normal."

"Yes, tell her everything is normal. The baby has a strong heartbeat."

"Call again when something has happened."

"Of course, I will." Anders hung up and told Lena what Alex had said.

"Just think that Alex will be a father. They had almost given up hope of having any children."

"That's when it happens," Anders said.

The baby boy was born at 4 p.m. weighing seven pounds. Mia was tired but happy. Alex cradled his son in his arms and walked around with a big grin on his face. He photographed Mia and the baby at all angles.

"I have a son! We have a son. You did a fantastic job, Mia. I never thought it would be so painful for the mother. It feels like a miracle that we have been blessed with a child after waiting for so many years."

"I know. Are we going to name him Andreas as we agreed on if it was a boy? We can call him Andy."

"Yes, I like that. It will be almost like my father's name, yet different. But he should have a second name."

"We talked about Nathanael. Don't you think Andreas Nathanael sounds nice? Or Andreas Alex Nathanael?"

"Two names are enough. Andreas Nathanael, now you have to go back to your mamma for a while because I'm going to call your grandparents and tell them they have a new grandchild."

"And that we're the parents of a little Norwegian," said Mia. "Tell them to come and visit us."

After the call, Alex went to the hospital's flower shop and bought red roses for Mia. The next day, Anders and Lena came with flowers and the bag with the baby clothes. Toby and Ella came with flowers and a knitted blue hat for the baby. Mia sat in a chair by the window and enjoyed all the attention.

"You deserve it, honey," said Alex. "I don't think you can stay here very long, so enjoy it while you can. By the way, I forgot I have a job to go to. My boss doesn't know why I'm absent."

Toby laughed. "At least you should show up and tell the good news. Then you can take paternity leave."

"All I can think about is my son and Mia. We're a family now, it's a wonderful feeling, and I'm so thankful it happened here and not in Sweden."

One trip to his office was all that Alex managed before it was time to pick up Mia and the baby at the hospital.

"Don't forget the car seat," Mia said.

Little Andreas looked so tiny that Mia felt bad about fastening him in the car seat. She sat beside him in the backseat while Alex drove. Anders and Lena waited for them with coffee and a cake that said, "Welcome Andreas."

The house soon smelled good of everything that comes with a newborn. Little Andy slept at one end of the crib with a teddy bear at the other end. Mia picked him up and sat down in the chair by the window and nursed him. Alex snapped several pictures of the idyllic scene.

"I wish I had a mother to write to about my happiness," Mia said.

"I can understand that, but you have my mother."

"I know, I'm glad she and Anders are here. I love them as if they were my parents. We worked well together on the farm."

Andy woke up, and Mia changed his diaper while Alex went downstairs to open the door for Toby and Ella.

"Where is Mia?" Ella asked.

"She's with the baby." Ella headed upstairs.

Anders watched TV and didn't hear Toby and Alex coming into the living room.

"Hi Pappa," Toby said. "Any news from Sweden?"

"No, I was just watching a soccer match. You probably know more."

"Norway is delivering food to Gothenburg and it helps. Everyone is waiting for the power to come back on. Trollhättan is lit up though." Toby said.

"Trollhättan has electricity?"

"That's what I heard at work. Eventually, the power will be restored along the west coast. Norwegian electricians are working on the transformers in Strömstad and Gothenburg. Sweden is getting a lot of help."

"And what does Svenung have to say?"

"Svenung says that Finland ships food to Stockholm. The problem is the distribution. Trucks marked UN drive off the ferries and continue to the nearest hospitals with medical supplies. For many of the patients the help comes too late."

"It's about time that UN is doing something," Alex said.

"Where's Mamma?" Toby asked.

"She's in the kitchen cooking up something for us," Alex said. "There have been many changes in our lives, but Mamma still cooks for us whenever she has the chance. That part has not changed."

The hacker: *I am glad for Mia's sake. She will be a good mother. The Big Bear will now turn its attention to northern Sweden.*

Chapter 26

While Toby and Ella visited Alex and Mia, more terrible news came on the airways. Something unexpected had happened in the north while the Swedes had their eyes on Stockholm. Russian parachute troops had landed in Kiruna and Malmberget. And that's not all. Russian naval troops had gone ashore in Luleå, a port to the Bothnian Sea, and easily occupied the city as they handed out food to the locals, as well as kerosene, gasoline, and coal, all of which were gratefully accepted. The Russians could easily infiltrate the city because the citizens of Luleå had not received any assistance and felt neglected. In Piteå, members of the Leftist Party welcomed the Russians and the much-needed supplies.

"What we feared has already happened up north," Toby said.

"Damn it! That's what I was afraid of." Alex listened intently. "They mustn't get to our power plants," he said, gesturing broadly.

"Norway and Finland have to take action against this," Toby said in a stern voice. "The Swedish military is too weak to make a difference."

The women voiced their concerns. To have their arch enemy on Swedish territory in the north resulted in fear and angst among everyone in the family.

"We definitely need Finland to assist us in driving out the Russians before they do much damage," Ella said.

"I agree," Alex said. "Swedish volunteers helped Finland during the war, and Finland is just on the other side of the river, Torne Älv, so it's in Finland's interest as well."

"And Norway has to protect its port at Narvik," Toby said. "If the Russians try to stop the export of Swedish iron ore through Narvik, NATO has to act because Narvik is Norwegian territory."

Soon after the Norwegian parliament had met, young Norwegian men on active military rolls were called to duty. If Norway mobilized, Toby and Alex might have to serve. Both had done their military service in Sweden, and when they registered in Norway, they had agreed to serve if needed. They never told their wives because they didn't think it would happen. Toby was 36, but he could still be called up in case of war.

Ella and Mia watched as young Norwegian men and women in military uniforms marched to the train station for transport up north.

"I can't believe what I'm seeing," Mia said. "It's like a movie."

"If Emil had been a few years older, he could have been among them," Ella said, looking at the marchers with fear in her eyes.

While Toby and Ella visited Svenung and Malena, they talked about Norway's preparations for war.

"We haven't heard what the parliament decided. Best not to tell the Ruskey," Svenung said, "but I can guess what's going on." He still waited for orders to fly to northern Sweden. He felt powerless as he followed the news from Stockholm on TV, and showed it by slumping in his chair.

"The immigration from northern Europe to America has decreased quite a bit since the presidential election," Toby said, looking at Ella. He was afraid she toyed with the idea of emigrating once again.

"And the United States needs educated people to join their corporations," said Svenung with conviction.

"But Canada is okay, don't you think?" Ella said. Quietly, she wondered if Toby would agree to immigrate to Canada.

"In some ways, Canada is more like Europe," Svenung said, just as his cell phone rang. "I have to take this call," he said and went into the next room. The others could hear him say "Understood, sir. I'm on my way. Roger and out."

"It was the order I've been waiting for," he said as he ran toward the closet where he had his uniform and the pistol on the highest shelf. He got dressed quickly and hugged and kissed Malena and the children. With the NATO cap on his head, he gave a salute and was out the door. The family left behind heard his NATO car start and drive away.

"I'm used to these sudden goodbyes, but they're still upsetting," Malena said. "I never know when he'll be back and if he will be back. Planes can crash."

"We understand," said Ella. She felt the tension. "We should leave now," she said to Toby.

"Yes, of course. Hope that Svenung will have good news from the border." They hugged Malena and her children a little tighter than usual before leaving.

On the way home, Toby and Ella talked about what had happened in northern Sweden and what else could happen. The situation could be a threat to Norway.

"Of course, we have to show solidarity with Norway," Toby said. "Norway has been good to us and given us new opportunities."

"I agree, but I still worry about our children having to fight in wars."

"We don't know what the situation will be when they are old enough, so let's not worry about it, and for heaven's sake, do not talk to the kids about the seriousness of the current situation. They might know what has happened up north, but they don't understand what consequences it could have. So far, the Russians are only on a gift-giving expedition to gain trust. It's too bad that we have neglected to send supplies to that area." Toby turned into their parking spot and shut off the engine.

"I don't want to see injured soldiers coming to our hospital. We have enough of bad civilian cases from Sweden," Ella said as she unfastened her seatbelt.

They didn't have to say anything to their children before Emil and Lynn let them know they were well informed and wanted to know more. Emil had a question for his father as soon as he came inside the door.

"Pappa, what do you think will happen in Norrland?" (Northern Sweden).

"I don't know. We have to wait and see."

"Here's what I think. Norwegian and Finnish soldiers will chase the Russians out, but I wish the Swedish military would take part in the defense."

"So, do I, Emil."

"Would you have been called up if we had lived in Sweden, Pappa?"

"Not to start with. I belong to the Reserve."

"How old do you have to be to enter the Swedish military?"

"The training begins when they are about 19."

"How can the Swedish recruits be trained when they don't have electricity?"

"It's difficult, but it was possible in the old days when there was no electricity."

"But Trollhättan has power, and it has to be defended because of its waterfalls and locks."

"That's true. It was heavily guarded during World War II. Why are you so interested, Emil?"

"I think it's exciting. It's happening in real life and not in a movie."

"Wars are awful, Emil. It's a lot worse in reality than on film. Go to the library and borrow some books about the big wars. The Vietnam War was awful and it lasted longer than World War II."

"I've never liked to read about wars, but now I wish I had paid more attention. Our teachers say we can learn from history."

"It would be good if we could learn to avoid wars."

"Where did you train when you were in the military, Pappa?"

"At K3 in Karlsborg."

"And what did you train for?"

"For quick response in mobile units."

Lynn asked how old the girls had to be to serve in the Norwegian military.

"It's voluntary. Don't worry. I think you should go to bed now. You have school tomorrow," Toby said.

He said goodnight and "sleep tight" to the children, but it took him a long time to go to sleep. There was too much to process. He had not been totally honest in answering Lynn's question.

The hacker: *As a nurse, Ella has a different perspective than Toby. They do not always agree and this could be a source of conflict between them. Toby skirted the truth when he talked to his children. Girls can be called into service if needed, but Lynn is too young and so is Emil. In recent months, everyone in the Swedish family has learned they cannot take their future for granted.*

Chapter 27

On Sunday, Anders and Lena went to church for the first time since they had arrived in Norway. The bells pealed as they walked toward the white church that looked so much like their church in Sweden. They carried their Swedish hymnals. Seated in a pew, they noticed a man and woman beside them who also had Swedish hymnals. Anders showed them his psalmbok, and they smiled and nodded to one another. When the service was over, they walked out together with Ove and Kerstin Nilsson.

"Are you new here?" Ove asked. "We haven't seen you before."

"We came from Västergötland in April," Anders said. "Where are you from?"

"From Dalsland. When we needed medical care and couldn't get it in Sweden, we moved here," Ove said, adding, "our children were already here."

"Two of our sons live here," Lena said.

"There are many Swedes in this area. We have started a Swedish Club, and we are serving coffee in the parish house today," Kerstin said. "Please come with us, and we can talk some more."

Kerstin welcomed Anders and Lena to the coffee hour and introduced them to the others. The Nilssons were former farmers, and Anders and Lena had much in common with them. At the coffee table that was spread with all kinds of Swedish baked delicacies, they talked about Sweden's difficult situation. Ove and Kerstin had been back to visit their son, who was now taking care of their farm in Dalsland.

"As soon as the power is restored, he'll sell it," Ove said.

Anders wondered if Ove and Kerstin would understand how he had felt when he left his family farm to strangers.

"Our son got robbed when he went over there," Lena said.

"Our son has been robbed a couple of times," Kerstin said. With all the bad news on TV, Lena had felt sad, but having met Kerstin and Ove and shared their experiences, she was in a much better mood.

"The Swedish Club will meet here in the parish house on Wednesday afternoon at 3:00," Kerstin continued. "You are both welcome to join us."

"We wouldn't miss it for anything."

"You can bring something if you like, Lena."

"I'll be glad to do that."

Anders and Lena were happy to have met other Swedes. So far, they had stayed at home and not gone anywhere but to the store. Now they had new friends. They told Alex and Mia about it during dinner.

"That's great," said Alex. "You need friends to feel at home here."

On Wednesday, Lena put the cookies she had baked especially for the Swedish Club in a tin.

"Anders," she called from the back door. "Hurry up, did you forget we're going to the Swedish Club?"

"No, I didn't forget. I just wanted to finish my work."

Lena wore a summer dress and her best shoes. Anders showered and shaved.

"You should wear a suit jacket," Lena said.

"Guess I have to since you're so dressed up."

Carrying the cookie tin in a bag, Lena tried to keep up with Anders in her high heels.

"Please walk a little slower," she said.

"Oh, I'm sorry. I forgot you're wearing heels. We could have taken the car."

"The weather is too nice for that."

They heard Swedish spoken as soon as they came close to the Parish House. Kerstin stood by the door and welcomed them.

She had a list in her hand and asked Anders and Lena to write down their names, addresses, and phone numbers. Many different Swedish dialects were spoken, but most of the people were from Dalsland, Värmland, and Västergötland, provinces close enough to Norway. There were at least 25 people in the room. Anders and Lena sat down at the same table as Ove and Kerstin. Another couple, Tore and Gunnel from Västergötland, joined them, and they were soon engaged in a lively conversation. Lena related their background, how they had lived primitive lives on the farm, and how their son had made a small wind turbine and fixed a generator to power the milking machine.

"You were lucky," Tore said, and Gunnel thought so, too. "We had to hand milk all winter long," she said. "We ran out of bread flour and lived mostly on potatoes."

"I baked bread, hard as a rock, because the grain came from the gristmill," Lena said. "But we were lucky to get white flour from Norway when one of our sons came to visit."

"We've heard of other Swedes who got supplies from Norway," said Tore. "Have you been back to Sweden?"

"I went back once, but we sold our farm and have nothing to go back to," Anders said.

Kerstin invited them to come to the coffee table to get a cup of coffee, pastries, and cookies to bring back to their tables. "Then we'll have a short meeting," she said.

While Anders and Lena waited their turn at the table, they talked to other Swedes, who had lost their jobs in Sweden. In Oslo, they had found similar jobs. When the meeting began, Kerstin asked everyone to introduce themselves and tell why they had come to Norway. Many had relatives in Oslo, and they were used to visit each other. It was impossible to avoid talking about Sweden's situation although it dampened the good mood. Someone suggested that they take up a collection to the Swedish Red Cross.

"I suggest that we give the money to Salvation Army instead," Tore said. "Their people feed the hungry and pick up the dead, and do a lot of other good work."

"I don't think Salvation Army here in Oslo can accept funds to be used in Sweden," Kerstin said. The discussion ended with taking up a collection to the Swedish Relief Fund handled by the Red Cross. Anders gladly contributed to the collection.

"If you know of any other Swedes in this area, please welcome them to our club and let them know when we meet," Kerstin said. "Please help yourself to more coffee."

As Anders and Lena walked home, they were happier than they had been in a long time.

"I didn't know it would be so much fun to meet other Swedes," Lena said. "The Norwegians are always so friendly, but we feel more connected to our own nationality."

"Yes, I'm sure that's how our emigrants felt when they came to America. Grandpa said he belonged to Swedish organizations."

"Isn't it strange how history repeats itself? I haven't had so roligt (so much fun) since I came to Norway," Lena said.

"But you have to stop saying 'roligt' because it means quiet here."

"We've been away for hours, and Alex must be home by now. I should be making dinner."

But she didn't have to. Mia had dinner ready. Lena apologized. "I'm so sorry I'm late. You shouldn't have to cook, Mia."

"Nonsense. You had prepared it, so it was no trouble at all. Andy is asleep."

Alex came home and wondered why his parents were so dressed up.

"We went to the Swedish Club meeting. It was interesting to hear other Swedish people telling their stories," Anders said.

When Kurt called, he was glad to hear that Pappa and Mamma were adjusting to Norway. He said he would come and visit them in June.

"I'm so glad," Lena said. "It will be good to see him again. If we had lived in Sweden, Kurt could not have visited us.

The hacker: *Lena is happy when she can socialize with other Swedes and have her sons close. But that might change.*

Chapter 28

While waiting for Mia to finish nursing the baby, Anders and Lena sat in the living room and watched the news. The dinner was kept warm in the oven. When the newscast changed to Danish, Lena became frustrated.

"Do you understand what they're saying, Anders?"

"No, only a few words, but the pictures look scary. We can ask Alex when he gets home."

Although Anders and Lena couldn't understand everything that was said, they could tell from the pictures that the news was bad. When Alex came home, he went directly to the living room.

"What are you watching?" he asked.

"It's in Danish so we don't get it," Anders said.

Alex watched and listened with a look of fear on his face.

"This is bad," he said. "A Russian unit has gone ashore in Malmö."

"That's what I thought," Anders said. "The Ruskey is getting bolder now that NATO is staying away."

"I can't stand this," Lena said. "Sweden is being attacked from all directions."

"There's nothing we can do about it," Anders said. "What do you think, Alex?"

"The Danish forces are our only hope."

"The Ruskey is playing with us like a cat plays with a mouse before he kills it," Anders said.

"Unfortunately." Alex lowered his voice. "I don't want Mia to hear about it."

Lena went to the kitchen to get dinner on the table. If it hadn't been for Mia's talk about how the baby had gained weight and always was hungry, the mood would have been subdued. After the meal, Alex went outside with cell phone in hand to call Toby.

"Did you hear the latest about Malmö?"

"Yes, the Russians are playing with us. I fear that Gotland and Öland will be next, and then it will be serious."

"I hope not. Have you heard from Svenung?"

"No, not yet. But the pressure on NATO is increasing."

"You would think there would be negotiations by now. Sweden is a member of the European Union, for heaven's sake!"

"But it's only an economic union. I can't understand how the government can still be in seclusion," Toby said. "And how can the different parties get along when they are used to disagreeing all the time?"

"Denmark won't like to have the Ruskey across the strait," Alex said. "The Danes will step in. Let me know if you hear anything from Svenung."

The outcome of the conflict in Malmö surprised many. Alex and Mia and Anders listened to the report:

Malmö police have put up a strong defense, and Securitas has disarmed bombs or moved them. Several Russians were killed when the bombs exploded. Danish soldiers fired on the invaders. Four policemen were injured but no Swedes were killed.

The defense of Malmö has become the turning point the Swedes needed to save their reputation, but it was thanks to the police force, Securitas, and the Danish soldiers. The Swedish military had nothing to do with it. Civilians came out of their homes and cheered for the brave defenders.

"That's much better," Anders said. "The Swedish police force is small and nonaggressive, but here it took a stand. I'm surprised the police still have gasoline. Perhaps they have an emergency supply."

"I hope the Russians have learned a valuable lesson," Mia said.

Ella and Malena hoped they would soon be able to fly to Copenhagen, but Toby advised against it. He said he wouldn't be surprised if the Russians came back on all fronts.

"The risk is there," Alex said.

Alex went for a walk to shake off his worries. When it didn't work, he returned to the house. Mia changed Andy's diaper.

"Do you want to try?" she asked.

"Sure, it can't be that difficult. But wash him first, please. Mamma can do it much better than I."

"Sure, she's an expert, but if you practice you can be an expert, too." She watched while Alex put the diaper under Andy, stretched the fasteners, and applied them.

"Make it tighter so the diaper stays put."

"With these disposable diapers it's easy," Alex said and tightened the diaper. He held his son's head while placing him against his shoulder. At once he felt happy and relaxed.

Anders summed up the situation for Lena when they were alone in their room.

"Sweden is now occupied on three sides, to the east, north, and south. The Swedes are trying to defend Stockholm, but they are badly prepared. Norway and Finland defend the north. Now we're expecting the Danes to defend the south. I don't think that any other country will defend Gotland and Öland for us. Russia will probably occupy those islands next."

"I thought the worst that could happen was the cyber attack, but it was only the beginning," Lena said with a deep sigh.

"The Russians knew what they were doing when they attacked our power grid. It was a way to get Sweden on its knees."

"I'm worried that Alex will be called up to serve in the Norwegian Army. He has skills that could be used."

"Let's not worry about it. One day at a time. Tomorrow, I'll mow the lawn."

"And I'll bake bread."

They went to sleep holding each other's hands. All the bad news tied the families together, especially those who had come from Sweden. It was more important than ever to unite. Children kept close to their parents and listened to them, trying to understand why all the awful things had happened. People who seldom or never attended church began to seek solace there.

Back in Sweden, stress tore family members apart. Spouses could not agree on what to do. Mothers of young children had to stay home and take care of them no matter how poor they were. The fathers could go out and beg for food but didn't always bring it home to their families.

When the mothers were unable to find food, they starved until their legs no longer carried them. The babies died first. Anders and Lena had heard a heartbreaking story at the Swedish Club about a woman named Anna.

Even if Anna had been strong enough to dig a grave, she didn't have a spade. She took a sheet and rolled it tightly around her dead child. The older children asked why the baby didn't move. She collected rainwater and gave it to the children who were still alive while being dehydrated herself. She no longer felt the hunger. One day, a Salvation Army officer opened her door, holding a hanky in front of his nose.

"Has anyone died in here?" He had to repeat the question before he heard a faint, 'yeah.' Then he left. Anna didn't think he would return. He would go somewhere else. But he did return with an assistant, disinfection spray, gloves, facemasks, a sack, and a paper carton. No one wanted to carry the smelly box, so they pushed it in a wheelbarrow.

"We'll bury the dead child," the man said as he left. "Someone will bring water and food to you." Anna's prayers had been answered.

After Anders and Lena had gone to bed, Lena said, "I feel so sorry for Anna. There could be many more women like her in Sweden."

"It's hard to believe that something like that could happen in Sweden. Its welfare system has fallen apart," Anders said.

The hacker: *The story about Anna is sad, but it could have been avoided if the Swedish government had accepted our conditions. Like Anders said, Gotland and Öland could be next.*

Chapter 29

Norwegian television reported that Russian troops had killed two young Finnish soldiers in Norrland. They were mourned not only in Finland, but also in Sweden, Norway, and Denmark. The Swedes felt guilty. The young victims were honored as heroes, and the Swedes were downgraded to weaklings.

Lena and Mia cried. "It isn't right that our neighbor countries should do our fighting," Mia said.

"They do it for their own sake as well," Alex said. "The Norwegian troops are placed at Norway's border to Sweden, and the Finnish soldiers defend the border between Finland and Sweden. They have to defend their borders."

"I hope they're successful, but more of their soldiers could be killed or wounded in action."

"The Russians can't count on going unscathed either."

"There have to be peace negotiations," Mia said.

"Sweden has nothing to negotiate with. We need the UN for that."

The United Nations met in Geneva and discussed the problem. The meeting ended in a declaration that admonished Russia for invading Sweden and a warning against further border transgressions. More UN soldiers would be sent to Stockholm with food and water to the needy.

"We Swedes have always believed in the United Nations, but now it appears to be rather tame," Alex said. "Russia, of course, has veto power, as does the United States, so there's not much that can be done."

Malena and Ella worked hard at the hospital to care for all the refugees from Sweden. Their work burden had increased enormously. Toby had taken over all the shopping and cooking at home with the help of the children, but Malena's husband didn't even come home in the evening. She had to do all the shopping but trusted her daughter, Hedda, to do the housekeeping and cooking as well as she could. Hedda was a mature 16-year-old young woman, who had learned to cook by necessity.

When Malena and Ella happened to run into each other at work, they only had time to exchange a few words.

"My back hurts," Malena complained. "I'll start to work nights tomorrow. How're you doing, Ella?"

"My feet hurt worse than my back, and I'm always tired. At night, I crash. Now they want me to work nights. Perhaps I'll accept because then I can see Toby and the children more."

"I'm waiting for Svenung to come home. But I must hurry and hand out medicines."

"Hope we can see each other soon in private."

When Hedda came home from school, it was up to her to make dinner. Her 14-year-old brother, Thorsten, was always hungry and could not wait for dinner. He took out a bowl from the cupboard and poured cold cereal to the top before gradually adding milk.

"Thorsten, I want you to do your share of work here," Hedda said. "You can pick up your dirty clothes from the floor in your room and take them to the basement. You should vacuum your room. You have dust under your bed. I can't do everything around here. Mamma doesn't have time to clean, and I'm not cleaning your room."

"When is Pappa coming home? He has been gone a long time."

"I don't know, Thorsten."

"What's for dinner?"

"If you helped me in the kitchen, you would know what's for dinner. Mamma works overtime almost every day, and we don't know when she'll be home."

Thorsten sucked up the last milk from the cereal bowl and put it in the dishwasher and then tossed the empty milk carton in the recycling bin.

"Hey, rinse out the milk carton and compress it before you recycle it." Thorsten reluctantly retrieved the carton and did what his sister said. He had grown so much that his jeans were too short.

When Hedda's cell phone rang she saw it was her best friend, Silva.

"If you need help with the cooking, I can come over," Silva said.

"Great. I can use both help and company."

"See you in a little while. I'll take the bike."

Hedda appreciated Silva's help and took out the potatoes that needed peeling and frozen meatballs from the freezer. The girls chatted happily while peeling the potatoes.

"I wish I had my driver's license," Hedda said. "I can't drive without a licensed adult in the car. And it takes longer to go anywhere by bus."

"I know. Do you need to go shopping?"

"Yes, Thorsten needs new jeans. He has outgrown all his pants."

"Can't he buy them himself? He can take the bus."

"Perhaps it's easier to buy them online. I'll ask Mamma. Despite everything, we have it better here than people in Sweden."

"I know. But I think about our Norwegian soldiers in Norrland. Did you hear about the two Finnish boys?"

"Yes, it's horrible. We don't have anything to complain about, really."

"And the Danes had to chase the Russians out of Malmö."

"It's getting worse all the time."

Dinner was ready when Malena came home. She smelled of medicines and said she was taking a shower.

"Hi Silva, so nice of you to be here to help Hedda.

"I'm leaving now. Mamma and Pappa are waiting for me."

Hedda called Thorsten. "Come and help me."

"I smell meatballs, my favorite," he said as soon as he came into the kitchen. He had ripped off his jeans above the knee and made them into shorts.

"You can set the table."

Malena came into the kitchen with wet hair and dressed in her bathrobe. She opened the refrigerator door and asked if there was any lettuce.

"No," Hedda said, "but there're tomatoes and cucumbers. Thorsten finished the last milk, so we have only water to drink."

"Do you want me to make gravy?"

"Silva made the gravy." Malena lifted the lid to the saucepan.

"How nice of her. We need to go shopping for groceries."

Malena cut up some tomatoes and sliced a cucumber. When they were seated at the table, she told the children she would start working the night shift. "Then I can shop during the day."

"I need new jeans," Thorsten said. "All my jeans are too short. Perhaps you could buy them online, Mamma?"

"I think you should try them on. I don't even know your size anymore."

"I want to come along, so I can practice driving," Hedda said.

"We'll try to do it tomorrow afternoon after you come home from school and before I start the night shift. We can eat at a restaurant for a change."

"Thanks, Mamma."

"When is Pappa coming home?"

"I wish I knew." Malena sighed.

"When are we going to fly to Copenhagen?" Thorsten asked.

"I can't get time off from work. We have so many new patients from Sweden. With the situation in Malmö, it's best to stay home. I ran into Ella today, and she's also starting to work nights." Malena tasted the food and said it was good.

The hacker: *Malena did not tell her children that she had treated starving Swedes who were sick from drinking polluted water. Life goes on, and for Thorsten it means that he needs new jeans. Now I am waiting for Sweden to show some action.*

Chapter 30

The church bells rang throughout Sweden to announce the mobilization, just like they had when the Germans had attacked Poland, which started World War II in Europe in 1938. With the power still out, no newspapers could be printed. Even the old typesetting machines needed electricity.

The youngest recruits were called up first. Men who had finished their training in the last two years had to report to the nearest police station for further orders. Women of the same age group could be called up if needed. Uniforms, tents, weapons, ammunition, fuel, and freeze-dried food packages had arrived from the United States.

Anders saw and heard the latest development on TV. The last part about the delivery from America surprised him. The tents would eliminate the need for barracks, at least during the summer months. Lena and Mia had not heard the news, but Anders told them.

"It's about time Sweden does something," Mia said.

When Alex came home, Anders asked him if he believed that the United States had softened its views of Sweden or if the pressure from other countries had something to do with it.

"The Americans may finally realize the importance of helping Sweden, but they want the Swedes to do fighting themselves. It's a good idea."

"I don't think Sweden has enough trucks and tanks. Normally

only about one thousand troops are recruited annually, and now it will be tens of thousands." Anders said.

There weren't enough vehicles to transport troops to Stockholm, so they had to march. Norwegian journalists were over in Strömstad and observed how the mobilization worked. The police chief reported on the confusion:

We don't have room for all the troops that have arrived here, and there aren't enough vehicles to transport them. We haven't received any orders about where to send them. A few old military trucks came, but they could only take some of the troops. We have private trucks with gengas and cars that run on gasoline waiting for orders.

We asked one truck owner what he thought about the request from the military. He said he expected to make more money driving recruits than supplies, but he carried so many bags of birchwood that he had very little room for soldiers.

While we waited for action, more private cars came and filled up their tanks from the military fuel truck. Eventually, busses arrived and they could take more troops than any other vehicle. A large number of civilians gathered to cheer on the recruits. We still don't know where they're going, but most of them are on the way. We expect that at least one unit will stay here in Strömstad.

Svenung had told Toby about what was happening in Norrland, and Toby relayed it to Alex as they took one of their usual walks together.

"The skirmishes continue up north. Norwegian and Finnish soldiers and Swedish volunteers are trying to chase out the Russians. Although we're at the beginning of June, the cold weather surprised them. At nightfall, our brave defenders raised their tents and stayed warm in their sleeping bags. The Russians had neither. They shivered and retreated to the harbor, where they thought their subs would be waiting for them. But the subs had been detonated. Swedish troops stood ready with their weapons trained at the enemy. Not one Russian could escape."

"So, we killed a few Russians, but in the long run, Sweden can't count on winning against mighty Russia," Alex said.

"Of course not. Russia has five million soldiers available. They can land thousands of troops on Gotland and Öland."

"But if they don't bring food, they'll starve."

"So, it would be best to take the sheep over to the mainland, using the Swedish Navy, and just leave some troops to defend the islands," Toby suggested. "Troops could be placed around the coastland to stop the enemy from landing."

"But Swedish troops also need food."

"Okay, leave enough sheep for our troops and ship in firewood from the mainland so the soldiers can roast lamb on a spit over an open fire."

"Sounds good, but you're not the general in charge," Alex said teasingly.

A piece of good news came from Gothenburg. Norwegian electricians had restored the regional power to the area, which might prevent the Russians from invading the important harbor city. A radio reporter described what he saw.

"Gothenburg is in ruins. Houses have been burned down. Furniture and rugs lie outside half burned. Broken glass is everywhere. The streets are full of garbage. Dead bodies are rotting in the gutters. The people who are still alive walk around like zombies."

"It's worse than I thought," Alex said. "Lots of sanitation work is needed. A large construction company like Skanska needs to come and rebuild the city."

"But where would the money come from? Skanska doesn't work for free. And who's going to pay the utility bills now that the power is back on?"

"I don't have the answer. The problem will be the same all over Sweden as electricity is restored."

"People will need medicine," Ella said. "I wonder what it looks like at Sahlgrenska Hospital."

"We're still waiting for the UN to do something," Anders noted while looking at Alex.

"I think it will be up to Norway," Alex said.

"You're probably right, but Norway has already done a lot."

Anders sat down to read the newspaper. He had learned to read Norwegian and didn't think of it as being difficult anymore. Lena didn't like to read the political news, but she recalled the families in Sweden she knew who had sons of military age and asked Anders if he remembered their names. The mobilization became more personal to them when they pictured the boys from their area in Sweden going to war. Lena also had relatives in Småland and feared for their sons.

To get away from the bad news on television, Lena liked to read the women's magazine that Mia subscribed to, especially about the flower gardens and how to decorate a home. She saw the pictures of men, women, and children modeling beautiful sweaters. Perhaps she should buy some yarn and knit something. Absentmindedly, she looked at the pictures of the royal family and movie stars. Most of the movies were produced in Hollywood. She put away the magazine and went to ask Mia if she could knit something for the baby. It would get her mind off the war.

"I have enough knitted clothes for him. They will last a long time. Why don't you knit a sweater for yourself? We could go to the store and look for patterns and yarn."

"I'd like that. Whenever you have time, Mia, and when Alex can watch Andy."

At the next meeting of the Swedish Club, all they talked about was the mobilization in Sweden. Everyone seemed to know someone who had been called up, or some family that had been affected by the mobilization.

"It could get serious, especially if Russia attacks Gotland," Ove Nilsson said. That comment started off a long conversation about what could happen. Lena helped herself to another cup of coffee, and asked Kerstin if she had any sweater patterns.

"Yes, I do, but perhaps we have to knit socks for the soldiers instead as they did in America during the world wars."

Lena doubted that, and said she would like to knit a Norwegian sweater for somebody in the family. "Those patterns are very complicated," Kerstin said. "Are you sure you can do it?"

"No, I'm not sure, but I would like to try."

"Start with something smaller then, like a hat, and get round needles."

"Okay, I will. Do you have a pattern?"

"Yes, I think so. I'll call you if I find one. It gives me an idea. We women could get together in our homes and knit. Would you like that, Lena?"

"Yes, I would like that very much. We could learn from each other."

"Knitting is very popular here in Norway, much more so than in Sweden. Now, of course, Swedish women don't have time to knit. They have more important things to do."

"Yeah, we are fortunate here in Norway. What about your son in Sweden? Does he have a family?"

"Yes, we have grandchildren who will soon be old enough to serve in the military, and we worry about that." Kerstin wiped away a tear. Lena gave her a hug and said she was sorry to have brought it up.

"I want them all to come over here, but it will be impossible to sell the farm if there is a war. You were lucky you sold when you did."

The hacker: *I am surprised Sweden has mobilized. It means the military has bypassed the inactive government. The soldiers do not know what they are in for. I wonder how Svenung reacts to that piece of news.*

Chapter 31

Svenung called from his plane and left a message that he was on his way home, but Malena was sound asleep after her night shift and didn't get it.

"My God, how you scared me," she said when Svenung came into their bedroom.

"I'm sorry, but I called."

"You don't know I'm working nights. I shut off my phone."

"Forgive me. I didn't know." Svenung undressed quickly—the tie first, then the coat, pants, shirt, and lastly his socks. He hung his uniform in the closet.

"Can I crawl in with you? I've also worked the night shift." Malena lifted the duvet and invited him in. He snuggled close. "The children won't be home for hours," he said with a grin.

"I know, and I missed you. Welcome home. How did it go?"

"I flew to Narvik to sleep and was in the air the rest of the time."

"How long can you stay home?"

"I don't know. Until the next order comes. I saw several fires from the air, but it has calmed down in Lapland and Norrbotten."

"You must have heard of the mobilization in Sweden."

"Yes, it was positive news. How're you doing at the hospital?"

"It's been very busy and strenuous. Some nights are calm while others are extremely busy. It's difficult to get used to the new hours."

"I'm so glad you were home. You don't know what a relief it is to come home to you. I love you, Malena."

"I love you, too and I miss you so much when you're away. The kids miss you, too."

Svenung did everything he could to show his appreciation. Afterward, they slept close together until they heard one of their children come home from school.

"Pappa, I saw your car. Where are you?" It was Thorsten who rapped on their door,

"I'm here." Svenung had jumped out of bed and hastily pulled on his pajama pants. "You can come in."

"I'm so glad you're home, Pappa." Thorsten threw his arms around his father.

"I'm just as glad to be home. I slept well."

"Hi, mamma. It's late afternoon, and you're still in bed."

"But I was awake earlier when Pappa came home." Thorsten left to get something to eat.

"Good afternoon, sweetheart," Svenung said as he kissed Malena on the forehead, smiled broadly, and looked happy.

"Good afternoon yourself. Hedda will be home soon. We can have dinner together. Then I must go to work."

"I'll miss you tonight," he said as he headed to the shower.

Hedda was just as happy as Thorsten to see her father's car outside the house.

"Here I am," Svenung said, embracing his daughter. "I heard you've been a good cook, but now I'll take over the job for a while."

"And you can shop. It will be great. I've got to do my homework."

"Where do you think you're flying next?" Malena asked her husband.

"I'm guessing the Baltic Sea. Our Norwegian troops will come home tomorrow."

"That's a relief."

Svenung opened the freezer door and asked, "What do you want for dinner?"

"There're pork chops in the freezer, but they take a long time to thaw," Hedda said.

"I made pea soup yesterday and there is enough left for today," said Malena.

"Then we'll take the soup today and the pork chops tomorrow. For breakfast, I can make pancakes."

"My mouth is watering." Hedda smacked her lips.

"You'll be rewarded for your work, my girl."

"What about me? Thorsten asked. "I vacuumed my room."

"It doesn't count. We expect you to clean your room. You must vacuum the whole house to get extra points."

When Malena had left, Svenung cleaned up in the kitchen. After he had read the newspaper and listened to the evening news, he called Toby.

"So, you're home, Svenung. What do you think about the latest development?"

"I was surprised but happy about the shipments from the United States."

"We're all surprised, but mobilization is a slow process. The army doesn't have enough trucks for the troops, and private vehicles had to be recruited."

"NATO should have offered trucks."

"Where do you think the troops are going?"

"From southeastern Sweden, it will probably be Gotland and Öland. The rest will be stationed along the eastern coastline."

"I expect the same. But how can they be shipped to Gotland when there are no ferries from the mainland anymore?"

"I heard that Estonia is making ferries available."

"That would work. Sweden received many refugees from Estonia during the war."

"Finns and Norwegians have made a difference in Norrland."

"And the Danes helped Sweden in Malmö."

"Yes, it's good to hear that the neighboring countries show solidarity. How's the work going on the electric grid in Sweden?"

"Alex says that the only cities with power are Gothenburg and Trollhättan. Norway made that a reality."

"I'm off duty now, but when I begin to fly again, it will probably be over southern Sweden. Then I'll be able to see if more cities are lit up. It would be good if Stockholm had electricity. I've heard that the Finns are over there working on it."

"Yeah, they must know how to do it since they managed to light up Finland." Toby felt guilty about having fled to Norway and wished he could help Sweden somehow but didn't know how. His brothers had the needed skills, but he felt useless.

The hacker: *Toby is unhappy because he is unable to help Sweden and also because he and Ella have marriage problems. She is working the nightshift and is always tired. Toby is restless and wants sex, so there is a situation that isn't easily solved. Svenung and Malena seem to be happy though.*

Chapter 32

Norway celebrated its Independence Day on May 17, and although the Swedes had seen it on TV in the past, they were still surprised to see how engaged the Norwegians were in the celebration. They dressed up in their provincial costumes and participated in a huge parade in every city, waving their flags. There was music, singing, speeches, and a sea of red, white and blue flags all over Oslo. Sweden hadn't caught on to the Norwegian way of celebrating, and now it had nothing to celebrate.

In Oslo, the days were getting longer with each passing day. The sun didn't set until 11 p.m. and rose at 3 a.m. Children played outside until late because it was still light. It was the most beautiful time of the year. Alex and Mia made plans to have their son baptized when Kurt could join them. Toby and Ella agreed to be godparents.

"Mamma and Pappa will be delighted. We could gather here after church and make it festive. I'll talk to Mamma about it," Alex said.

As soon as Lena heard, she offered to bake a cake and make sandwiches. Mia said that a strawberry cream cake would be great, small sandwiches, and finger food. Lena readily agreed. To her, the main thing was that her grandson would be baptized, and she looked forward to the ceremony in the church. Everyone thought the third Sunday in June would be perfect. Mia took out a calendar and checked the date. It would be Sunday before Midsummer. I hope it will be a beautiful summer day with the lilacs still in bloom."

Alex welcomed Kurt at the airport. After they had chatted for a while, he said, "You're staying with us. We have plenty of room."

"I'm so glad that Pappa and Mamma are here and not in Sweden anymore," Kurt said.

"Me too. We always worried about them when they lived on the farm."

The baptism took place before the service at the same church that hosted the Swedish Club, and Lena was happy to see some of her new friends in the pews. The baptismal service reminded her of the times her own children were baptized at home in Sweden. They had baptized four children, and she wondered what it would have been like if their daughter had lived. Would she be here today? Would she have children of her own? It would have made their family more complete, but God had other plans. She felt tears pooling behind her eyelids when she thought about it, but now she was thankful for another grandchild, the first since Lynn was born.

All the young cousins were dressed up in their best clothes—the girls in colorful summer dresses and the boys in suits. The baby wore a traditional baptismal dress, white with a blue ribbon, to signify he was a boy. Lena couldn't have been prouder of them all. Cameras clicked to preserve the memories.

"I hope we will have more grandchildren," she said after the service.

Ella said she and Toby were done, so Lena's eyes turned to Alex.

"I'd like to have another child, but when I saw how hard the birth was on Mia, she has to decide."

"The first time is the hardest, but it's already forgotten," Mia said. Lena agreed, adding, "That's what's all mothers say." Kurt said he was in no hurry to have a family.

The men and the boys gathered outside to listen to Svenung talk about his flyovers in the north.

"Northern Norway is beautiful from the air," he said. "I flew over the coastline to Svalbard and the Arctic Circle. The sun never sets in the summer. I saw the midnight sun."

"Did you see any polar bears, Uncle Svenung?" Emil asked.

"I saw some when I came in low."

"Is there enough ice for them?" Emil wanted to know because climate change had been discussed in his class.

"I saw much more open water than before. The polar bears might become extinct. The ice is melting because the temperature of the ocean is rising."

"What does Sweden look like from the air?" Emil wasn't done with his questions.

"Sweden is the prettiest along the Norwegian border and the rivers."

"Did you see any Russians?" Emil asked tongue in cheek.

"We always look for troop movements, but I didn't see any Russians. I'm glad they are gone."

Svenung asked Anders and Lena if they wanted to return to Sweden after the country had recovered. "Lena wants her last resting place to be in the cemetery at home, but we don't have anything else to move back to anymore," Anders said.

"And what about you, Alex? Could you imagine moving back?"

"I can imagine it, but Mia and I like it here."

Toby said he and his family definitely would not return to Sweden. "We will go there on vacation when Gothenburg is restored, but the children are established in their schools now, and they don't want to move again. Children adapt fast. Ask Emil."

"In the beginning, I missed Sweden and my friends, but now I have new friends here. I can't wait for our summer break, so we can see more of Norway."

"We have made plans," Toby said. "Ella and I want to use some of our vacation to drive around the coast to Stavanger. We won't have time for a cruise to Lofoten, but we could take a shorter cruise on the fjords."

Hedda and Lynn came walking with the baby pram. "Now, I've got a question for you, Lynn," Svenung said. "Would you like to move back to Sweden?"

"Not really, but if everything becomes normal again, I might want to attend the university in Gothenburg like Pappa did. It would be cool. I know Swedish. But I'm only 14 and I might change my mind. This summer, I'd like to come here and learn to take care of Andy. I also want to help Mamma so she can sleep during the day. Mia taught me to cook."

"You sound very smart for being so young. Then it's only Kurt left who might return to Sweden to live, or what do you say, Kurt?"

Kurt shook his head. "I don't know. My last visit to Uppsala was rather unpleasant. I found out that my roommate had died for a lack of insulin and the university would have to close for lack of funds. My memory of Stockholm isn't good either."

The threat of the Russians and the mobilization in Sweden were on everyone's mind and dampened their good mood. Toby talked about Sweden's past wars with Russia and how Charles XII had been successful until the Swedish troops encountered the Russian winter.

"And then Charles XII was killed here in Norway when he tried to invade us," Svenung reminded Toby.

"Yes, I agree he made some mistakes, but he was very young. We called him the boy king."

Emil listened, and had a question for Svenung. "So, why did your ancestors raid western Sweden in the 18th century?"

"Ugh, I have to think. It was probably because the Danish king told us to do it. We belonged to Denmark at that time. Our constitution was adopted on May 17, 1814. Did you like our celebrations, Emil?"

"It was great. I never saw anything like it. But Norway was united with Sweden until 1905, so it was not really free until then."

"Yeah, that was unfortunate, but we still had our own constitution."

"Sweden has been a nation since the 16th century, and now it's threatened by the Russians."

"Let's hope it is just a threat, Emil."

The hacker: *Svenung must know that we are not "just a threat" to them. The Swedes were brave in the past wars against our country, but that was centuries ago, and now they have no experience of warfare. Toby might get a chance to help Sweden after all.*

Chapter 33

Toby had a meeting with his boss and finally found out what the company would do with the building in Gothenburg.

"Tobias, we're wondering if you would be interested in managing a food distribution center we're opening in Gothenburg? Now that the power is restored to the city, we can finally utilize the property we bought the way we intended."

It took Toby by surprise, but he was delighted to hear the building would be used for charity.

"You would get extra pay and compensation for being away from home. You can live in a small apartment in the same building. Most of the space will be used for storage of food and distribution. You would be responsible for hiring personnel and management. We think you're the perfect man for the position. It will be a temporary job, but we hope you're interested."

While his boss talked, Toby had time to think. He had wanted to help Sweden somehow, and now he had the chance, but it would mean they had to delay their vacation, and Ella needed time off from her work.

"How long are we talking about? I promised my family a vacation this summer."

"A few weeks until you can get it going."

"I would be happy to help my fellow Swedes. So, if my family has no objection, I'd like to hear more about it."

"Good, we have noticed that you have leadership skills and are a good organizer. The job could very well lead to a higher position in our company."

"Alright, I'll get back to you as soon as I talk to my wife."

"You can take the rest of the day off and do just that."

Since Ella worked nights, she would be asleep, but Toby hoped she would wake up so he could tell her the big news. He made noise in the kitchen on purpose as he prepared lunch, and it wasn't long until Ella appeared in the doorway.

"Thank God, it's you," she said falling into his embrace. "I thought it was an intruder. What are you doing home in the middle of the day?"

"Sit down, honey, and I'll tell you." He grabbed a chair opposite her and explained the offer he had received to start up a food center in Gothenburg. "I'm sorry it will delay our vacation. I just have to get everything setup and started, then we can leave."

Ella rubbed her eyes. "As long as we can take our vacation later in the summer before the children go back to school, I won't object. If Malena can manage without her husband while working the nightshift, so can I. I like the idea of helping people in our hometown. They really need it."

"It's ironic that I will be in Sweden now that my parents are here, but I can come home on weekends."

"That's great. I think it will be good for our marriage. I will be more rested when I can sleep undisturbed," she said with a wink and a smile. He knew what she meant because sometimes he had tried to wake her up early in the morning when he missed their intimacy.

"So, it's settled then. I'll tell my boss tomorrow. Now, how about a tuna sandwich?"

They enjoyed having lunch together, and afterward Toby joined Ella in bed for an unexpected, undisturbed, and wonderful afternoon.

"Do you remember when we left Sweden, Ella? You said we must always stay together."

"Yes, I remember, and we will. Our only problem is that I work nights. I wonder how other couples manage because many men work nights in factories."

"If they work nights all the time, they probably adapt," Toby said. "My work in Gothenburg might last for a few weeks, but as long as I know I can come home to you, it will be fine. We came here for the sake of our children so they could attend school."

"Yes, and I said I hoped we could return to our home."

"It doesn't look like that will happen. Who would have thought that Sweden would be in so much trouble? Finland has managed much better."

"I know, and I'm glad we're safe here, but I worry about our house at home."

Toby didn't say anything about what he had seen because he didn't want to upset Ella. Instead, he said, "I will check on the house while I'm in Gothenburg."

"I want to go there too."

"I hope we can all go while I'm there."

"It was awful what happened in Stockholm and Norrland. Gothenburg is a strategic port city, so it might be next."

"I think Norway will step in if anything should happen there."

When the children came home from school, Toby told them about his job in Gothenburg for the next few weeks. Emil and Lynn were excited about it and said they would like to volunteer.

"But not until I had a chance to start up the operation. Then perhaps you can come with me and spend a week there." Toby called his parents and told them the news, and they were also excited about it. "We're so proud of you," they both said.

Toby left on Sunday, so that he could start to work early on Monday morning. He was glad to see that the streets downtown had been cleaned up. Now, he had to hire staff. He began by calling his former colleagues at the university asking if anyone was interested. The result overwhelmed him. If they couldn't do it themselves, they knew someone who could, and many began to show up the same afternoon ready to work. Men, women, and teenagers were happy to have something worthwhile to do and be paid at the same time. They cleaned the building from top to bottom, and when the supply trucks from Norway arrived, they were met by staff eager to move everything inside. Toby scurried from room to room and marveled at how well the new employees worked together. He went over the inventory and showed the distribution workers how to keep it current. New products had to be ordered when the supplies became low.

Scraggly-looking hungry people lined up outside every day, sometimes in pouring rain. Once inside, they ogled the large selection of military rations, oatmeal, powdered milk, water, hardtack, jams, canned fish, soup, fruit and vegetables. The hygiene products were in high demand. Toby recognized some of his former college buddies and students standing in line. One woman said she had taken a class from him and asked if he could give her a job. Toby felt sorry for her and asked what she could do.

"I'll do anything for a meal. My children are hungry." Toby could see her ribs through her top.

"You don't have to work to get food here, but if you want a job, come back tomorrow morning and I'll see what I can do. For now, help yourself to what you need." The next day, he hired her to unpack supplies.

Toby was tired at the end of the week, but as he took the ferry home, he realized that he had never been as happy about a job. After a weekend at home in Oslo, Emil and Lynn came with him to Gothenburg. They brought their sleeping bags and spread them out on the floor in his apartment. Toby placed them in the distribution department and noticed how eager they were to hand out supplies. At the end of the day, they both told him they hadn't realized how serious the situation was in Sweden.

Toby had a feeling that Emil and Lynn would never again complain about anything trivial. He called Ella and said his temporary job was the best thing that could have happened. Having noticed that many of the visitors walked barefoot or had worn-out shoes, he said, "I want Norway to collect shoes to be ferried over."

The shoes arrived and were soon gone. When people asked for school clothes for their children and warm jackets for the coming winter, Toby had to refer them to the Salvation Army. Many had lost their homes and all belongings. Some lived in tents. Others lived in railroad cars. Now that the trains would be moving again, they had to find other shelter.

Toby talked to his boss and said he needed a vacation before the children went back to school.

"Of course, just select someone to take your place while you're gone."

The hacker: *Norwegian electricians have restored the power to Gothenburg, and Toby is happy for the opportunity to feed starving people in his hometown. He no longer feels useless in that respect. I am not supposed to check on any of my victims, and if my government finds out, I will be fired, but now I really have to see if Sweden will defend its strategic islands in the Baltic Sea.*

Chapter 34

Swedish journalists with battery-operated recorders embedded with the troops sent their reports via ham radio to Stockholm. Anders and Lena could watch the war on the islands from their home in Oslo, but Lena said it was too scary to watch. "It's frightening," Anders said, "but as long as the Swedes are winning, I don't mind."

The Navy had transported troops and supplies from the closest provinces on ferries headed for Gotland, Sweden's largest island. Once they reached the city of Visby, the troops set up camp by the ancient wall. Curious locals watched from a distance as the troops dug latrines and set up generators for cooking. It was late in the evening but still light when the hungry soldiers lined up for grub.

The sun rose at 3:00 a.m., and with no time to waste the bugle call rang through the air, waking the sleepy soldiers. Following the morning routine, the order came for one battalion to march east across the island, a distance of 350 kilometers. New boots chafed the soldiers' feet. As the battalion approached the sandy beach, the level land slanted toward the sea. The gulls swooped down and shrieked at the intrusion. Guards equipped with binoculars scanned the waters from the church towers for any enemy activity, subs in particular.

The recruits enjoyed the scenery. "This is like a vacation, and not far from home either," said Johansson from Oskarshamn. "I'm happy to have enough to eat. In civilian life, there isn't much food."

"It can be a matter of life and death if we have to fight the Russians," said Lindgren, a fellow from Linköping.

"Let them come, and we'll show them what they are up against. If nothing happens it could be boring," Johansson said.

"So, it's a big adventure to you?"

"Yes, why not? It's like camping. I ripped off the patch that said U.S. Army."

"Your name patch is not straight, Johansson."

"So, Lindgren, what are you going to do about it?" Johansson wiped sweat from his forehead. "What does it matter? We have to be ready to fight at any time."

"Attention! Line up," the sergeant barked.

Johansson didn't like the idea of exercising in loose sand and pebbles. "Isn't there any grass around here?"

"Maybe, but the officers want to make it as damn difficult as they can for us. You have to get used to it." Lindgren knew what to expect.

After the exercises, their fatigues were drenched in sweat, and they wished they could go swimming, but, of course, it was impossible with the weapons. After dark, Johansson crept down to the beach and let the water wash over his naked body. He pulled on his pants as soon as he was back on land but was still wet when he heard the scary word, "Halt."

"I'm a Swedish soldier," he said, stretching his arms up in the air.

"You've escaped the camp and disobeyed orders to stay there. Name and number?"

"Johansson, but ... but, I forgot my number."

"That's another offense. Where are you from?"

"Oskarshamn."

"Oh well, then I'll let it pass, but don't do it again and always remember your number."

"Yes, sir." Johansson's shaking legs relaxed as he walked back to camp.

The troops had exercised for one week when the alarm went off at midnight. A submarine had been sighted along the coast. The sun had set, but the last light still lingered on the surface of the water.

"Attention! Line up!" The sergeant barked worse than ever.

"What the hell! They can't expect me to line up in my underwear," Johansson said.

"Get dressed and hurry up!" Lindgren murmured.

In various stages of dress, the soldiers lined up for inspection. Thanks to the darkness, the officers didn't see what they looked like.

"Attention!" The men stood at attention for at least two minutes until they were told to relax. It had been a false alarm. The sub was Swedish. The sergeant sounded relieved when he ordered more guards posted along the coast to be on the lookout for intruders.

Anders who had done his obligatory service in the Army recognized the light side of military life. He was only sorry that this time it could turn into something deadly serious. The next time, he turned on the television, he saw that the situation was about the same on the island of Öland as on Gotland. The soldiers had marched over the long bridge from the mainland to the ancient fort of Borgholm, or rather the ruins that were left of it, and made camp for the night. The next morning, they marched 20 kilometers east until they reached the Baltic Sea. Most of the recruits were from Småland, and they had driven across the six-kilometer-long bridge from the mainland many times. Runestones carved by the Vikings weren't new to them. They had seen them in Småland, too.

"It would have been fun to see something other than Öland," said a red-haired fellow, named Göransson. "I've seen plenty of windmills. I'd rather be stationed in Stockholm. There, I could see the castle, City Hall, and all the other great buildings."

"It's not that grand anymore. Stockholm has no electricity either. There has been much destruction," said Bergius next to him. "Öland has probably managed better than other provinces without power. The farmers can use the windmills to grind their grains and they know how to butcher sheep. The weather is not always as pleasant as today. The wind can be awfully strong and cold."

"But they can cover themselves with sheepskins."

"Remember that we are here to protect Öland from the Ruskey. He'll be scared to death when he sees us," Bergius joked.

"Where did the name Bergius come from? It sounds almost like nobility."

"It's not. It used to be Berg. At one time, there was a minister in the family and he latinized the name."

"I wonder how long we'll be here. If the Ruskey doesn't come before winter sets in, I hope we can go home."

Just as they were about to go to sleep, they heard gunfire. The troops hurried to lace up their boots and get hold of their M-4 carbines. No line-up, only a run toward the sound of the shooting. When they came to the stone wall, they had built the day before, the sergeant barked, "Halt."

The Russians had nowhere to hide, and the evening sun blinded them. Fresh soldiers could hit their target. The result was a bloodbath on the beach. Göransson turned around and vomited in the sand. Bergius's face was white as a sheet. "Dear God, this is worse than in Syria," he said.

"We won the battle," the sergeant declared. "We'll take care of the dead in the morning, but we're staying here with all the guards in place."

The night seemed endless as the soldiers tried to process what they had experienced. Sweden had not been in a war for more than 200 years. Farmers' sons and factory workers who had instantly become soldiers were in shock. Göransson vomited again, but he wasn't the only one. It would be worse in the morning when the result of the night's attack became visible.

"Don't just stand there. We must dig a mass grave, the captain commanded. Spades had been delivered. The men began to dig but hit limestone.

"It's impossible to dig with spades here," a corporal told the sergeant. "Öland rests on limestone. We need a bulldozer."

"We don't have any. The only thing we can do is burn the bodies."

"But we don't have any firewood, and there are no forests around here."

"We'll pour gasoline on the dead. It's the fastest way. Order the men to pile the bodies together, and I'll get the gasoline." The officers almost sounded like human beings.

"But some of them might still be alive," the corporal protested.

"They look dead to me."

"Dear God," cried Bergius. "Lord, forgive us our sins." He grabbed arms that were still warm and pulled. "They look like us," he said. He closed his eyes to avoid seeing all the blood. Göransson was on his knees still vomiting.

"I can't stand up," he gasped.

"Why do you hurt so much. I best take a look," a corporal said. "Ah, you have a bullet hole in your stomach. No wonder it hurts. I'll get a medic," he said just as Göransson fainted.

A medic stopped the bleeding in Göransson's stomach by inserting something in the bullet hole.

"Ambulance," he yelled. Göransson was unconscious when loaded into the ambulance that drove at top speed to the hospital in Borgholm.

Bergius heard the fire take hold and cracked open his eyes. He saw the flames burn the hair and clothes of the dead. The cremation was soon over. No funeral service was held.

"It's not a victory to celebrate," the sergeant said.

The military had equipped the hospital in Borgholm with new generators. The surgeon removed the bullet in Göransson's stomach, closed the wound, and prescribed antibiotics.

"Watch him carefully and report any symptoms to me, he said to the nurse. Göransson didn't wake up until the next day. He was in critical condition.

The hacker: *I am surprised that the Swedes won this fight on Öland, but I doubt it will happen when it comes to Gotland.*

Chapter 35

"Finally, we're getting good news from Stockholm and Öland," Lena said. "I'm glad it's in Swedish."

"I can hardly believe what they are saying," Anders said. "Then the government can return."

The good news report was aired once more:

Finnish and Swedish troops have forced the Russians out of Stockholm. Some Russian soldiers tried to escape by jumping into the water but were shot. A few made it to their sub before it was sunk by the Viby. The castle and the parliament are secure. Swedish soldiers are back guarding the buildings.

Anders remained in front of the TV a while longer. When Lena had left the room to get coffee, the broadcast came from Stockholm:

Since the power has been restored here in central Stockholm, we can report directly that Swedish troops have decimated the Russians who tried to invade Öland. Only one Swedish soldier was wounded.

"Come back here," Anders called out to Lena. "There's more good news. Bring your coffee cup."

Reports from Stockholm and Finland repeated the news several times. Norwegian analyzers predicted that the Swedish government would return and begin negotiations with Russia.

"It's not going to be as easy as they think," Alex said. "It depends on what happens in Gotland. But now I must leave if I'm going to catch the bus."

News about the Swedish victory on Öland reached the United States. The American president said it was thanks to the equipment he had sent to Sweden.

Anders didn't understand English, but Mia translated for him.

"It's what one could expect him to say," Anders said.

Gotland

In Gotland, the situation became serious for the Swedes. The Russians attacked the city of Visby during the night. The Swedish officers had not expected an attack on the western side of the island. There were many casualties and the hospital in Visby was full.

For the Russians, the island was open toward the west where they surprised the Swedes by attacking them in the back. In Gotland, it was the Russians who burned Swedish bodies. While the invaders triumphantly marched back across the island, they ravaged Swedish homes for food. In Visby, they broke into the state-owned liquor store and hauled as many bottles as they could to their submarines. Locals said they had witnessed Russians opening bottles, drinking, celebrating, and singing in their language until they were out of sight and hearing.

The Russian victors sent their jubilant reports to Russia from their subs. The reports were translated in Finland, and the news about the Swedish defeat on Gotland reached Stockholm. The Swedish families with sons who had been sent to the islands demonstrated and demanded the names of the killed and injured, but it took a long time for the military to sort out which soldiers had been sent to Gotland. The only survivors were those at the hospital in Visby.

Reports of Sweden's defeat in Gotland slowly trickled out to the mainland. The Swedes were stunned as they were dealt a blow beyond comprehension. In Oskarshamn, the ferries from Gotland were filled with people who had fled the island, and they told the awful story about the burning of the Swedish soldiers' bodies. Many of the families in Oskarshamn had sons who had been sent to either Gotland or Öland, but they didn't know which island. Anxiety overtook them until they could find out. People in Småland and Östergötland had no working televisions or radios. They didn't know until the newspapers finally reached them.

In Oslo, all the Swedes sat glued to their television sets. The churches offered prayers for the Swedish victims.

"This is too awful to be true," Anders said. "Gotland became the pawn in the war against our arch enemy."

"If NATO had helped us, this would not have happened," Lena said. "The small American contribution wasn't enough. I hope my nephews weren't among those killed."

Anders and Lena felt deflated when they shut off the TV. Anders worked off his distress in the yard. Lena cooked and baked, while Mia took care of her baby, but all they could think of was the bad news.

The Swedish defeat was the subject of a lesson in Emil's class.

"Sweden doesn't have to give up more than Gotland, right?" Emil asked.

The teacher took a quick poll, asking, "How many believe that Sweden has to surrender Gotland?"

Almost all hands went up.

"We'll see. The United Nations will probably start negotiations. Do you think Sweden will decide on mandatory military service?" Almost all hands went up.

"Do you think Norway should make military service mandatory? It's voluntary now."

A convincing "yeah" rang out from the class.

"My uncle flies for NATO," Emil said. "I want to join the Air Force and learn to fly."

"Do you all know that you can get an education through the military?"

Most of the students didn't know. History and current events had become the most popular subject in school. The students brought newspapers to class and cut out the news articles and pinned them to a wall.

Norwegian reporters went to Sweden to find out if the opinion about membership in NATO had changed. It had. Now, the Swedes were united in the importance of joining the alliance. In Stockholm, people demonstrated with cardboard signs saying, "WE MUST JOIN NATO." The parents of the killed soldiers blamed the politicians who had said that Sweden didn't need to join NATO because the country had such strong technology. That technology had proven to be as worthless as Sweden's defense. The leftist party had a hard time defending its previous friendly views of Russia. Immigrants and native Swedes alike had lost family members in the defense of Sweden.

"Our sons were immigrants and died defending Sweden," said the Muslims. Solidarity and unity became the new motto.

Memorial services for the dead soldiers were held on Gotland and the mainland, especially in Östergötland and Småland. To calm the country, the Swedish prime minister declared that all the state offices would open so pensions and other benefits could be paid. Electricity would be restored to all parts of the country as soon as possible, but he said nothing about how this would be accomplished. "But where is he?" Anders asked. "We still don't know where the government is."

Construction companies counted on making money on restoring buildings in Stockholm and Gothenburg. Gasoline was once again imported but it would take a long time before it became available to the general population.

In western Dalsland and Värmland, the residents often had relatives in Norway who provided them with coffee, sugar, and flour, but farther inland the pantries were empty. Many people were still hungry. Cars that had run out of gas littered the roadside without wheels and other parts that had been stolen. The distances had grown wider. Most people couldn't walk more than 10 kilometers. Someone with a bicycle could move about a little more freely. The few existing horses were needed on the farms. Busses that ran on gengas could take people to the nearest town but no farther. The schools were still closed.

The electric trains were stalled on the tracks. Commuter trains running on diesel had no diesel. The airports were closed. If Swedish planes and ships happened to be in other countries when the cyber attack occurred, they had to stay there. No country could function without electricity in the modern world. City people were weakened by hunger and most had no strength to protest.

The Norwegians had restored the power to Gothenburg and Trollhättan but the interior remained in the dark.

"How long is it going to take?" Anders asked Alex.

"Olafssen is working on it."

"I'm guessing there is no longer a threat of ransom."

"No, I think Putin is waiting for a bigger price. He always wanted Gotland, and after this victory, he might have it."

The hacker: *The situation has escalated beyond what I intended. The Swedes are getting angrier because the lives of so many of their soldiers have been lost. This is going to affect Lena deeply. Anders and Alex fear that Sweden has lost Gotland. Olafssen is trying to restore power in a small area.*

Chapter 36

In Trollhättan, Ole Olafssen worked hard at restoring the power to the regional grid, but he needed more help. Most of the personnel at the power plant had fled to other countries. He turned to his employer in Oslo and asked that Alex Almåker be sent to Trollhättan for six weeks. When Alex was asked about it, he said, he was willing to do what he could, but he had to talk to Mia first. He was glad that his parents lived with them so Mia wouldn't be alone with the baby.

"I'll miss you, but I know how important it is to have electricity," Mia said. "Of course, you should go."

"Thanks, honey, you're always so understanding. The company will give me a car to use, so you can keep ours."

"When are you leaving?"

"As soon as I have packed and told my parents."

Lena was hesitant because she was still afraid of the Russians.

"The more of Sweden we can electrify, the less the risk, Mamma."

"The region powered by Trollhättan includes our farm," Anders said.

"Then I hope you can restore the power there," Lena said to Alex. "If not, the farm might deteriorate and I don't want that to happen."

It was still difficult for Alex to leave Mia and little Andy.

"I'll be back in six weeks," he said.

"Andy will probably know how to roll over by then."

Alex drove E-6 from Oslo until outside Uddevalla where he turned toward Trollhättan. Ole Olafssen welcomed him with a firm handshake.

"We need you here. Come with me to my office, and I'll show you a map."

The office was located in an old brick house that had been restored before the power outage. Alex could hear the familiar rush of water from the roller dam.

"You can have a room at my house," Ole said.

"Thanks. What is it that you think I can do here?"

Pointing to the map on the wall, Ole said, "Here's the entire region. The city of Trollhättan has power, but the rest of the region is still in the dark." Ole continued his technical description, saying they had to drive from one transformer station to another and search for switches they could bypass to establish a new grid circuit.

"I understand."

"Great. Now, it's time for you to meet your colleagues."

Alex was surprised to meet two of his friends from the university, Henrik and Hanna. After a few minutes of reminiscing, it was time to get down to business.

"Henrik will be your second man in the field," Ole said. "Hanna will accompany you in the beginning and help you with the computer part of the work. You'll get a company truck that has all the equipment you need, strong batteries, a driver, and an electrician. The truck runs on biodiesel. There's food and water on board. You'll get overalls and rubber boots."

"Sounds good."

"This will not be office work like you are used to, but I think you're the right man for the job and you're familiar with the area."

"I look forward to doing fieldwork for a change."

"See you later. Hanna will show you to the computer room."

Alex followed her and admired her figure dressed in pants. Her long, blonde hair hung down her back. In the computer room, Alex stood behind her while she showed him how to start the program.

"I'll enter your name here, and you can add your ID, username, and password, but you must remember them. Do not write them down anywhere. There are security questions you have to answer." She went to the side, while Alex sat down at the computer. When he was done, he got a compliment from Hanna. "Ole has employed you because he says he can depend on you." Hanna looked up at him when she said it.

"That he can."

"The salary is fantastic."

"Oh, I haven't asked."

It was evening, and Alex walked with Ole to the director's villa on top of the hill, where Ole himself showed Alex to his room on the second floor.

"Make yourself at home," he said. "When you have unpacked, you can come downstairs and we'll have supper."

Alex hung his suit in the closet. He didn't think he would get to use it, but Mia had said it was best to be prepared. He found a hook for his jacket by the door. The rest of his things could go in drawers. He felt relaxed and satisfied. His former boss was hospitable and treated him almost like his equal. He called Mia and told her he had settled in. Then he called Toby's cell phone number.

"How's is it going bro? We are both in Sweden right now."

"Yes, but it's only temporary, and our families are looking after our parents. I'm up to my ears in work and love it. Hope we can get together, but you'd have to come here, because I can't get away during the week. I'll be working most of next weekend, but I'll make time for you if you would like to come."

"It would have to be on Sunday."

The next day at the office Hanna said they should prioritize the area between Trollhättan and Gothenburg. The power needed to be restored to the train tracks. "But first we'll drive to the plant in Vargön."

On the way to Vargön, Alex asked what it had looked like in Trollhättan while the power was gone.

"It was awfully dirty with a lot of trash in the streets and on the sidewalks," said Bengt, the driver. "The food stores were empty. Store windows and doors were broken by the looters."

"Is commerce restored now?"

"All the stores are not open yet, but the food stores are," said David, the electrician. "People are coming from the countryside to shop and fill their gas tanks. They bring their gas cans and fill them, but old gasoline makes the cars difficult to start."

"Yes, old gas can be a problem. Do people use cash or can they use debit cards and credit cards?"

"There isn't much cash in circulation, but we can use plastic as long as we have money in our accounts."

"I don't have any Swedish money and I need to find an ATM."

"We will show you where the ATMs are."

Alex looked forward to seeing the food distribution center where Toby worked. He also wanted to drive by his old place to pick up some of his and Mia's stuff. He had brought the key.

The hacker: *Alex thinks his apartment is still there. He also thinks he can restore the power to the local grid, but I could stop him if I wanted to. I will let him do all that work so he can feel better, and then I can undo it.*

Chapter 37

David, the electrician, described the power sources along the river Göta Älv.

"The river has four hydroelectric plants. The two plants in Trollhättan are already working. Vargön is important because that's where the water level in Lake Vänern is regulated."

"That's interesting. I know there are industries in Vargön," Alex said.

"Yes, there's a foundry, but it's closed for now," David said. "Normally, it provides heat to all of Vänersborg and Trollhättan in the form of hot water from the foundry."

"That's great. What did they do with the hot water earlier?"

"It was let out in the river."

"Then we must turn on the power so that the foundry can deliver hot water and heat to the cities again."

It took a couple of days. With the work accomplished, Hanna said, "Lilla Edet, next. There is a hydroelectric plant there and a factory that makes toilet paper. By restoring power, we can get toilet paper again."

"We are also going to restore power to the railroad so the trains can run," Alex said.

While they drove south on E-45, Alex asked Hanna how she had coped while the power was out.

"My sister and I sat on the couch covered with blankets and comforters to stay warm. Except for daylight through the windows, our only light came from lit candles on the table. We didn't dare to drink the water from the canal like some desperate people did because it would mean diarrhea. When we ran out of food and liquids, we put our clothes in backpacks and biked to Dalsland. Our parents have a farm there, it's where we were raised."

"My wife and I went to my parents' farm and lived with them for about a month," Alex said. "They had kept an old wood-fired kitchen stove in case the power went out, and it came to good use. They had clean water in a well, so we were luckier than most."

All four compared their experiences of living without modern conveniences until they arrived in Lilla Edet. As required, they had to check the power plant for damage. Then Alex issued lengthy instructions for how they would modify the output transformer to a voltage that the newly constructed grid could handle. Alex said it was like testing a string of Christmas lights. It didn't light up until the missing link was found. David did the work, and Alex reminded him of the automatic breakers that had to be installed on the lines so they would not fail when the power was restored by remote control. When they had finished their work in Lilla Edet, the production of toilet paper could resume.

The next day, they went to all the railroad stations between Trollhättan and Gothenburg and switched on the power to the tracks.

Olafssen was satisfied and issued new orders: "Tomorrow, you'll be working in the area north of Trollhättan so the trains can run as far as possible to the north. Eventually, we want the railroad to be functional to the Norwegian border. If you continue at the same rate, the work will be finished sooner than expected."

In the evening, Alex listened to the local news, but heard only a short report announcing that the staff at the hydroelectric plant in Trollhättan worked on restoring power to the railroad. He called Toby in Gothenburg again and told him he would come to see him on Sunday.

"Great, I'm free on Sunday morning, so see you then."

On Alex's third workday, Hanna said they would drive to Vänersborg first. When they came to a large intersection, she pointed to the apartment houses across the road.

"I lived in one of those buildings when the cyber attack happened. It was before we moved out to the farm. There's still no power here, so I prefer to live with my boyfriend in Trollhättan."

"Didn't you feel like going out to demonstrate against the government's inaction?"

"Yes, we did, but we had to preserve our energy."

After they had worked on all the transformers and switches for the railroad, a large area in Västergötland and Dalsland had power.

"It will make my parents very happy," Hanna said.

"Are they living far from Mellerud?" Alex asked.

"They live along a smaller road on the way to Vänersborg. Almost all the farms around here grow grain, and the farmers work in town, but my parents still have some cows and chickens, so we were lucky to have milk and eggs. We didn't have to starve like many city folk. I don't think there are any obese people left in Sweden."

Bengt wanted to drive to Vänersborg to look at the restored lights. "I went to school there," he said. He parked the truck in the town square where the farmers' market had closed for the day. A man came running, yelling, "The power is back."

Alex looked up at the largest building called Residenset, beside the town square, where most of the windows were lit up. Someone said the lights must have been on when the outage happened.

"The governor doesn't live here anymore, does he?" Alex asked.

"No, the governor resides in Gothenburg, but there are many county offices in the building," Hanna said.

After a while, a large group of people gathered around the truck that had the company name on the side.

"Are you the ones who restored the power?" Alex and his crew took a bow. Everyone laughed, talked, and was happy.

"It feels great. I love my job," Alex said.

"Yay, I have lights in my apartment," Hanna said with her arms in the air. "I love my job, too, but it's thanks to you, Alex, that we got this done."

"I had good help."

"Mission accomplished for the day," Bengt said and started the truck.

Olafssen met Alex at the entrance to the office building and congratulated him on the day's work. "But we aren't done yet. Gothenburg wants Landvetter Airport up and running. I have promised to make my team available."

"Then I'll need electrical blueprints showing how the airport is wired," Alex said.

"We have worked on it today, and the details are now on your computers. Good luck."

Alex realized the airport was important but didn't have much time to prepare for the work. After dinner, he opened his laptop and began to study the new document. It was midnight before he felt he was adequately prepared.

On the way to Landvetter, he told his coworkers how they would proceed. They worked methodically with the lines for several hours before they closed in on the terminal. The guards welcomed the team from Trollhättan. Alex showed his credentials and got full access.

"We have to work on the internal circuits before we can switch on the power," he said. He didn't know that a television crew was on the way to film the event. The reporters had to wait a long time.

Back in Trollhättan, Alex called Mia and told her that he and his team had restored power to Landvetter and that he had been interviewed by TV West. "It might be aired tomorrow," he said.

The hacker: *I just found out how clever the Swedes can be. It is great that they can divert hot water from a plant to heat two cities. It is a lot more productive than what I do. I am anxious to see if Alex can restore the power to the entire region.*

Chapter 38

Alex decided to visit his childhood home on Saturday to prepare the farm for power restoration on Monday. The town where he had sold farm products with his parents looked deserted. Driving into the farmyard, he was met by a man and a dog. Alex recognized the dog that his mother had named Bruno, and as soon as he got out of his car, he scratched him behind the ears, and Bruno wagged his tail.

The man introduced himself as Martin Gustafsson, the tenant farmer.

"I'm Alex Almåker, the former owner's son."

"What can I do for you, Alex?"

"I work for the power plant, and we are restoring the electricity around here. I need to prepare for it."

"Fantastic! Are we going to get the power back?"

"Yes, on Monday. I want to make sure the circuit breakers didn't get damaged during the shutdown."

"Then you'll need the ladder."

Martin walked ahead of him. If he hadn't moved the ladder, Alex knew exactly where it was. Gustafsson raised the ladder against the barn wall where the fuse box was located and Alex climbed up.

"I can see the cows in the meadow from here," he said. "Do you have the same cows we had?"

"The cows are the same, but there are more calves."

"I helped Pappa with the milking before we got the milking machine to work."

"So, you set up the generator?"

"Yes, I bought it at an auction. It was broken, but I was able to fix it. I hope it works."

"It works just fine."

"I built the windmill, too. It's very primitive," he said with a laugh.

"You must be an expert if you can do that much electrical work."

"I have the education for it."

When Alex had finished the inspection of the circuit breakers, he said he could remove the temporary lines from the windmill.

"But they might be good to have if we lose power again. You can just disconnect them from the windmill and in the house."

"It's not necessary to disconnect them either."

"So, you're done then. Everything will happen automatically on Monday."

"Yes."

"Do you charge anything for coming out?"

"No, nothing at all." Alex smiled with satisfaction.

When Mrs. Gustafsson came outside, Martin told her the good news and that Alex was raised on the farm. She stretched her arms in the air at the prospect of getting the power back.

"I'm Monika. Is it true that the power will be back on Monday?"

"Yes, it's true. I'll see to it myself. I know what it's like to be without power, so I can imagine it will be welcome."

"I can hardly believe it. Won't you come inside and have fika (refreshments) with us? I like to hear how your parents are doing in Norway." Alex had nothing else planned and accepted the invitation.

"The kitchen looks exactly the way I remember it," he said.

"Yes, we still have all your furniture. We haven't changed anything."

Martin washed his hands.

"Fika is ready, but it's not coffee because we don't have any coffee beans. Instead, we drink milk," Monika said. "We have plenty of milk, and we dunk the rusks that I made of graham flour from the gristmill."

"Thanks, it sounds good." Alex thought about how his mother had complained about the coarse rye flour, but graham flour was made from wheat.

"Are you separating the milk?"

"Yes, we do, and we churn butter with the churn that someone had made of an old spinning wheel."

"That was me," Alex laughed. "I'm glad it's useful."

"It's great. I can sit and knit while I turn the wheel with my feet."

"But when the power comes back the dairy will open again," said Martin. "We have lived here three months now and we haven't had any income. The grain farmers buy milk from us, and I'm sure they'll pay later, but we can't count on the city folk paying."

"I know because my wife and I lived here for a while before we moved to Norway. My parents sold firewood, potatoes, milk, and butter in town. In the beginning, people had cash, but it soon dried up."

"It will be great to have power again," Monika said. "We have carried tons of water into the house, not to mention firewood. I can't wait to use an electric stove again, and the toilet, and the bathtub, of course," she added. "How is it in Norway? We are curious."

"It's good. We like it."

"If you live in Norway, why are you working here?" Martin asked.

"I'm here temporarily."

"How're your parents? It must have been hard for them to adjust?"

"I don't think so. They live with us. Pappa takes care of the orchard and the yard and Mamma cooks. My wife and I have a baby, so it's good to have help."

"Please say hello to them."

"I certainly will."

Alex turned to Martin and asked how he had managed the spring planting.

"Thanks to the horse and diesel for the tractor, I was finished before my neighbors." Martin said with pride in his voice.

"But how could you do all that work by yourself?"

"Two men from the city came out and worked for food and a place to sleep. I don't need any help now until harvest time."

Alex thanked Mrs. Gustafsson for the treat and drove back to Trollhättan. He was happy about what he had accomplished and hoped to do more.

Hanna had invited the crew to her place to celebrate their achievements and Alex had accepted. He got to use his suit after all. They had a pleasant evening together and enjoyed meeting Hanna's boyfriend, Håkan. Henrik had brought a bottle of wine that they finished along with a deep-dish pie that Hanna had made with chanterelles she had picked in the woods.

On Sunday morning, Alex drove to Gothenburg to visit Toby. He saw stalled cars on the side of the road, and a few bike riders. The weather was sunny, but clouds emerged from the west. First, he drove passed Chalmers, his Alma Mater. Plywood covered the windows, and the homeless had pitched tents between the buildings. When Alex approached the distribution center, he saw people waiting in line. He entered the building from the back as Toby had said.

Toby took his brother through the center and proudly showed him what he had accomplished in the short time he had been there. "This is amazing," Alex said. "I'm impressed."

"It's thanks to my company's generosity that I can do all this, and I can tell you that it's much needed and appreciated. I'm so glad I got the opportunity to set up the operation."

After a while, Alex said he wanted to drive over to his apartment. "Can you come along? Mia wants me to pick up our wedding pictures and some other mementos."

Toby looked up and then away, feeling uncomfortable, "No, I've got to check on things here. "When you come back, I'll make coffee and we'll have lunch."

Alex could hardly believe what he saw. There was only a skeleton of iron beams left of the upper floors where he and Mia had lived. He took out his phone and snapped pictures.

I'm not showing these to Mia, but I might need pictures to show the insurance company. The windows on the lower floors were broken and he guessed that those apartments had been ransacked. The falling rain made it even grayer and more dismal. He didn't see any people around. He thought about the last time he and Toby had met in the parking lot after they had lost power and what they had decided.

How could all this destruction have happened, and why didn't Toby tell me about it?

He had no use for his key and threw it in the rubble.

"You knew what it looked like, didn't you, bro?" he said as he confronted Toby

"Yes, I am very sorry."

"Why didn't you tell us?"

"I didn't want to upset Mia, but I should have told you. Now that you're here, I thought you should see it for yourself."

"We have lost everything we had in Sweden, and I feel terrible."

"Yes, but you are alive. I don't know what happened to the other people who lived there, if they perished in the fire or not. I don't know what my house looks like today."

"I saw it and it looks good from the outside."

When Alex had calmed down, he realized that he and Mia were lucky. They had a new life, and what they had lost was only stuff that could be replaced.

"I'll make coffee and we'll talk about happier times," Toby said. "I don't know what awaits me when I open the door to my house, but that's for another day. We have been through a lot, but we are young and we have time to recover. It's harder for our parents. Mamma is not taking it well."

The hacker: *I am sorry to learn that Lena is having a hard time. Toby and Alex are both in Sweden, and she misses them.*

Chapter 39

Stockholm enjoyed electricity again, mostly thanks to Finnish assistance, but Arlanda International Airport, the largest in Sweden, remained closed. Stockholm businesses demanded a functional airport like the one in Gothenburg, and the power company serving Stockholm contacted Ole Olafssen in Trollhättan.

"The Stockholmers feel slighted and want Arlanda opened for business," Ole said. "They want you, Alex, to take care of it, and you can set your price."

"Really?" Alex looked surprised. "But I promised to stay here six weeks."

"We'll have to rethink the situation. Your assistants can continue here, but you can choose one man to take with you to Stockholm."

"Then I'll choose Henrik."

"I think you should accept the offer. It's important. We must train more people because you can't be everywhere."

"Hanna's boyfriend, Håkan, is an electrical engineer. He works for the railroad, but perhaps he can be persuaded to do this until he gets his railroad work back. I'll talk to Hanna."

Håkan declined the offer, saying, "I can't risk a permanent position with a state pension for a temporary job in Stockholm."

Alex advised Olafssen to contact the university about hiring last year's graduates, who were most likely still unemployed. A week later, two engineers and one computer programmer had applied for the jobs, but they had to be trained before going out into the field.

"Now we can make an important contribution to the re-electrification of Arlanda and the Stockholm suburbs," Ole said.

Alex agreed to move temporarily to Stockholm, but first, he asked for and was granted time off to go home to Oslo and tell Mia about his next assignment.

Everyone at home welcomed him with open arms. Alex delighted in his son's smiles, his growth, and efforts to roll over on a blanket that Mia placed on the floor. Alex carried the baby around until Mia told him he would spoil him. When Mia had put Andy down for the night, they gathered in the living room. Alex told his family about his work so far, and that he was expected to restore power to Arlanda, which required him to move to Stockholm.

"It will be very favorable to me economically and if I'm successful, it will give me excellent references for the future," he said with one arm around Mia.

"How long will you be gone?"

"I don't know, honey, but you and Andy can come with me. We can move into a furnished flat in Stockholm."

"What a nice surprise. Can I travel by train from here to Stockholm?"

"No, no yet, but it's possible to drive. As soon as I've fixed the power to Arlanda, you can fly."

Anders wrung his hands. "Can we stay here if Mia moves?" he asked.

"Olafssen said you can stay and take care of the place."

Mia had another question. "Are the hospitals open in Stockholm? I'm thinking of Andy."

"Yes, the hospitals accept patients, and most stores are open."

"But I'm afraid the Russians will be back," Lena said.

Alex looked at his mother and shook his head. "Please, Mamma, don't frighten Mia. I want my family with me."

Anders thought it would be best if Alex went to Stockholm first to find out what services were available.

"I think so, too," Mia said.

After a wonderful night with Alex, Mia agreed to the temporary move provided that Alex went to Stockholm first and planned for their arrival.

"It will be fun to come back to Sweden, but best of all, we can be together. I want you to see how Andy grows and develops. I don't want you to miss his first year. It's the only time Andy will double in weight. He'll learn to sit, crawl, and perhaps take his first steps."

"I look forward to coming home to you and Andy every evening," Alex said.

"We must bring the baby carriage with us, and baby food and diapers in case the stores in Stockholm haven't restocked yet."

"I'll find out and let you know before you leave."

When Mia said she wanted to go to Gothenburg and pick up lots of their things, Alex had to tell her it was all gone. "I filed an insurance claim, and you can replace it with new purchases."

"Is it really gone?" she asked. "Was it stolen?" Does someone else have it now?"

"You don't have to worry about that because it all burned in a fire."

Mia drew in a long breath and blew it out. "I wish I had our wedding pictures, but it's okay. Maybe we can order new ones. I'm thinking about the soldiers who died in Gotland. I have you and Andy and a new life." She wiped away a few tears, and then she smiled. "We're going to Stockholm, and I'll be fine."

Alex called Toby in Sweden the next day and told him about the opportunity in Stockholm.

"I'll be working for the company that is responsible for the power in Stockholm and the surrounding area, but I don't get the work specs until I get there. I will have two engineers with me, so I don't have to do any dangerous work myself. I can't think of a more rewarding job than restoring power to people who have been deprived of it for a long time."

"I understand," Toby said, "because I feel the same way about the work I'm doing right now. "But what does Mia say about you going to Stockholm?"

"She has agreed to move to Stockholm temporarily."

"It's good that you don't have children in school. I hope you'll be well paid."

"You bet. I don't think I will ever make that much money again."

"Do you think you'll come back to Norway?"

"I'm sure, but we want to see you and Ella before we leave."

"Of course. We have a lot to talk about it." Toby said.

They agreed that what had happened in Gotland was awful. The people on the mainland can hardly believe it.

"The mass killings will be part of Sweden's history for all time," Alex said.

"And Sweden could lose Gotland," Toby commented. "Svenung told me that Estonia is ferrying fleeing Gotlanders to the mainland."

The hacker: *If Alex can restore the power to Arlanda Airport, passenger planes can take off and land. Will that lead to more Swedes leaving the country? Will foreign journalist land there and report to the whole world about what goes on in Sweden? What would it mean for my work? Do I need to take precautions? Will Lena be able to take any more bad news from Sweden?*

Chapter 40

Anders couldn't believe his eyes when he saw Johanssen on TV and heard the report.

We have learned that the Norwegian A. Johanssen has made illegal purchases of farms in western Sweden. He said he was an investor and signed the contracts himself. But in reality, he was buying the farms for a league in Russia. The contracts will probably be annulled because he neglected to register the purchases in Sweden. Johanssen defends himself by saying the Swedish offices were closed. He has been arrested by Norwegian police. Johanssen has obtained operators for the farms and collected the rent. Likely, he has also earned a commission from Russia. Our television station would like to come in contact with the sellers to get their side of the story.

"What does all this mean?" Anders asked himself. "Come here, Lena. The investor is in prison! The sale might be annulled."

"What are you saying? I thought he looked trustworthy, and he gave me coffee bread. How are we going to take the farm back and how can we return the money when it's invested?"

"I don't know, Lena. This is something we must talk to Toby about, but he is Gothenburg. He arranged for the man to come to our farm." Toby had seen the report in Sweden and called as soon as he could.

"I'm sorry, but I didn't know Johansson was a crook."

"We know you didn't. But it's hard to accept that we may have sold our farm to the Russian mafia. Just think, Alex was there and turned on the power for them."

"This must be investigated. I'll be a witness in court if needed."

"If we get the farm back, we could probably sell it for a much higher price now that the power is back," Anders said.

Toby cautioned his father about talking to journalists. "The reporter said the station wanted to come in contact with the sellers, but you need an attorney before you say anything."

"I'm not going to talk to any reporters," Anders said.

"You can probably demand compensation."

"Who would pay? I don't think the Russians will."

"Still, you'll need an attorney to protect your interest. If Johanssen has profited, he should pay. I'm sorry, but I really believed it would be best for you to move to Norway. I'm sorry I recommended him."

"You couldn't know he was a crook. Not Alex either. Mamma and I signed the contract, so we are responsible."

"It would have been better to keep the farm," Lena said. "If we had known that the power would be restored in a few months, we would have stayed, don't you think, Anders?"

"It's easy to say now."

"You need to drive to Sweden and consult an attorney there."

"But Mia is moving to Stockholm, and Olafssen wants us to take care of his house."

"I'm not moving yet, so you have time to go to Sweden," said Mia, who had heard what Anders just said. After he had hung up the phone, he turned to Lena, saying, "But where can we stay? It feels strange not to have a home there."

Lena couldn't sleep at all during the night. "We were so happy with our new life and now this." She could not be comforted. Having held back her tears earlier, she let them flow freely. As soon as she had wiped them away, new ones ran down her cheeks.

"So, so, Lena. I can understand you are upset but everything will be alright."

"That's what you always say."

"Alex said that the man who leases the farm is a responsible man and the harvest looked good."

"But the man didn't know he was leasing the farm from Russians. When he finds out, he might leave."

"We can talk to him when we get there."

"I'm not going. I'm staying here with Mia." Lena had decided. She said it would break her heart to see the farm again, knowing that they had sold it to Russians.

"Lennart and Lisa also sold their farm to Johanssen. They were going to move to Halden. I wish I could talk to them," Anders said. Mia promised to look up their number.

After a sleepless night, Anders and Lena got up when they heard their grandchild cry in the next room. "How're you feeling this morning?" Mia asked.

"I haven't slept a wink," Lena said. "It's even worse now when I've thought about it. I don't want to go home. Seeing the farm again would make everything worse."

Mia phoned Alex in Stockholm and told him about Lena's decision.

"I can't leave your mother now. She's upset, and Anders said she cried all night. She's not going to Sweden."

"I can't say that I blame her. I'm shocked, too, about what happened. Of course, you can't leave her. You and Andy can come later."

"Yes, we will, sweetheart."

"It's a shame what happened with the farm. The power company I'm working for has attorneys, and I can talk to one of them and ask what he thinks. I feel like I have to do something. Everyone has heard about the swindle."

"Then you don't have to pay for a consultation?"

"No, he works for the company. Pappa should get an attorney in our hometown. Perhaps the sale can be voided."

"How do you like your new job?"

"The job is fine. All of us guys sleep in my apartment, but sometimes we work too far away to go home in the evening."

"Then I don't want to come. I just want to be together with you, not strangers."

"But the apartment is large enough. There are separate rooms for us."

"I think it's easier for you to visit us…."

"You're probably right. If we can restore the power to Arlanda I can fly home."

The hacker: *What happened to the farm confuses me. I did not know the buyer represented people in my country. Poor Lena is devastated. I wonder what can be done about it.*

Chapter 41

Mia searched for Lennart Andersson's phone number online and found it. She punched the number into Anders's phone and handed it to him.

"Hello, may I speak to Lennart?"

"He can't come to the phone at the moment. This is Lisa Andersson. May I help you?"

"Hej, Lisa. Anders Almåker calling."

"Hej, Anders. Lennart is getting ready to go to Sweden. How's it going in Oslo?"

"We're doing fine, thanks, but I wonder if you've heard what happened to our farms?"

"Yes, we saw it on TV. It's awful how we were fooled."

"Lena is heartbroken. I need to go to Sweden, too. I wonder if Lennart and I could go together? Toby and Alex are both in Sweden and Lena doesn't want to come with me."

"I'll let you talk to Lennart."

The two former neighbors talked for a while and decided that Anders would drive to Halden and Lennart would drive from there.

"Are you and Lena willing to take the farm back?" Lennart asked.

"We haven't decided."

"I just don't want the Russians to have it."

"We feel the same way."

"Hope we can straighten it out."

Anders left early Sunday morning. Once he had reached Halden and was seated in Lennart's car, the two men talked about the Swedish laws concerning purchases of farms.

Looking at Lennart, who concentrated on the driving, Anders said, "I thought it was strange that I never received a stamped copy of the contract, but I thought the process was delayed because everything was closed. I knew the sale had to be registered and the deed to the farm had to be transferred. Then I got so busy with the move and I forgot about it. I also thought it was strange that the investor signed his name 'A. Johanssen.' It would be impossible to trace a name like that. Did you get his address, Lennart?"

"No, I never got his address."

"He lied and said that Toby had read the contract. If I had known that, I wouldn't have signed."

"I searched the internet for a copy of the Swedish Land Law. It says that foreigners can buy real estate after permission from the government and sometimes the county administration. But the law is old and it has been amended many times. I know that Norwegians and Germans have bought summer houses in Sweden, but I believe it's harder for foreigners to buy farms," Lennart said.

"Yes. The neighboring farmers have to be consulted because they would have the first choice to buy."

"That's true. It's because smaller farms should be combined whenever possible."

"Mia showed me on the internet that there's a special law from 1925 about decoy buying. If the buyer has not followed all the stipulations, the court can arrange for a forced sale. There are many stipulations. The court or county administration can prevent that anything is removed from the property. But the law must have been changed since then."

"We have to consult an attorney," Lennart said.

"I haven't needed an attorney until now, but I know our pastor's son is an attorney, and his practice is next to the bank. We can look him up."

"That was my plan, too. Since Johanssen is in prison, he has lost his chance to register the purchase," Lennart said, as he drove across the border to Sweden. "Would you be interested in taking the farm back, Anders?"

"I'd rather not, but if it should be necessary, I would. We could sell it later and get a better price. Lena is so upset about what has happened."

Lennart turned on the radio, and they listened to music and news in Swedish until they stopped at a restaurant for lunch.

"It's nice to hear Swedish spoken," Lennart said.

"And see that the businesses are open."

"Yes, it's a big difference from when we left."

After another hour on the road, Anders directed Lennart to Toby's summer house where they would stay overnight. They turned onto the narrow road leading to the red painted stuga. Anders had always liked the idyllic location. They parked and looked around. At first, Anders thought it was undisturbed, but then he saw that someone had used the grill. The lid stood open and the grill hadn't been cleaned.

The door was locked and Anders fetched the key from its usual hiding place, put it in the lock, and turned it. The trespassers had locked up after they left.

"Come in, Lennart and bring your bag. We'll let the door stay open for a while to air out the place."

Anders did a quick inspection. "Someone has used the propane stove, and there are paper plates in the wastebasket, but the intruders have washed the dishes."

He became suspicious and looked in the beds. "They have slept here and the sheets are dirty." He began to take off the pillowcases.

"Here," he said to Lennart. "Stuff them in a trash bag."

They brought in their sleeping bags from the cars and spread them out on the beds.

"I want coffee in the morning," Lennart said.

"There should be groceries here if the trespassers haven't consumed it all." Anders looked in the pantry and unscrewed the lid to the coffee jar. "There's a little bit left, enough for one cup each in the morning. I'll go to the well and get water."

On the way to town to have supper they passed their former farms.

"The crops look pretty good," Anders said.

Outside the restaurant, Anders got a signal on his cell phone and called Ella. "People have lived in the summerhouse," he said.

"I expected that. Is it awful?"

"No, it's not too bad. Do you want the sheets they used?"

"No, they were old sheets. You can toss them."

The hacker: *It was brave of Anders to drive himself to Halden. It will be interesting to see what happens at the attorney's office.*

Chapter 42

On Monday morning, Lennart dropped off Anders at the attorney's office while he went on another errand. Anders introduced himself to the jurist and explained his problem.

"I'm familiar with the case," the jurist said. "Did you bring the contract?"

"Yes." Anders took it out of his briefcase and handed it to the jurist.

"I see that there were no witnesses to the transaction. Please sit down while I check something online."

Anders felt like a schoolboy as he waited. He had neglected to call in witnesses. Why didn't he think of that? He could have called Lennart and Lisa. The attorney copied something into the computer and waited.

"This will take a while," he said. Anders squirmed.

The jurist finally looked satisfied. "This is good news," he said, "You and your wife still own the farm."

"Is it true?"

"Yes, Johanssen didn't obtain the deed to the farm."

"Well, I thought it was strange that I never heard anything about that."

"He should have paid 1.5 percent of the sales price, plus other fees to legalize the sale. Since he didn't do that, there is no evidence of his ownership."

"So, it's true then that my wife and I still own it?"

"Yes, as of today, that's correct, and since Johanssen is in prison he can't rectify his mistake."

"Do we have to return the money then?" Anders looked worried.

"It's a complicated issue, and I'm not familiar with Norwegian law. It would be best for you to consult a Norwegian attorney. Mr. Johanssen is in trouble, and you acted in good faith and trusted him."

"But what about the lease money. Should it be paid to us then?"

"Yes, you should inform the tenant farmer about the change."

"May I have a statement that says we still own the farm?"

"Of course." The jurist began to type something, and after a few minutes, the printer spit out a paper. "I'm just going to sign it and stamp it," he said.

Anders eagerly reached for the paper and read it. "How much do I owe you for the consultation?"

"For a former parishioner, 500 crowns."

Anders, who had just been to the ATM to withdraw cash, took up his wallet and handed the jurist a crisp 500 kronor bill. "May I have a receipt?"

"Of course." The jurist wrote the receipt in longhand and gave it to Anders.

"How do you like it in Oslo?" he asked.

"We like it just fine, but when we heard what Johanssen had done, we became very worried about the farm."

"It's understandable."

Anders thanked the jurist once again before leaving. As soon as he was outside, he remembered he didn't have his car and had to wait for Lennart. He looked around at the familiar buildings and thought they looked old. When he was in town every week, he hadn't noticed. At the same moment, he saw Lennart walking toward him.

"How did it go?"

"It turned out well. You have nothing to worry about. Lena and I still own our farm, and it will be the same for you. I'll go and have something to eat while you see the attorney. Meet me at the cafeteria when you're done."

Anders decided to call Lena and tell her the good news.

"Have you been to the attorney?" she asked.

"Yes, it went well." Anders smiled broadly as he gripped the phone tighter.

"Let's hear it."

"We still own the farm."

"Is it true?"

"I have it in writing." Anders padded his briefcase.

"Does it have to do with the deed?"

"Exactly. Johanssen had neglected to transfer the deed, and according to Swedish law, we still own the farm."

"I'm so relieved, but do we have to return the money?"

"I don't know. We'll have to consult a Norwegian attorney about that. Martin Gustafsson needs to know he has to pay the lease to us, so when Lennart comes back from the attorney, I'll ask him to drive me there."

Anders had just started to eat when Lennart came up to him. "That went fast," he said.

"My case was the same as yours and I got the same answer."

"Then we have reason to be satisfied with our trip."

"We really do, but we still have to go to our farms and make sure we will be paid for our leases."

Anders got more excited as they came closer to his farm. "I haven't been here since we moved."

Martin Gustafsson came to meet them as they drove into the farmyard. Lennart waited in the car.

"Goddag, we have met." Anders said his name while offering his hand.

"Yes, nice to see you again, Anders."

"I'm here to tell you that my wife and I still own the farm."

"Really? That's great. We were afraid the Russians owned it."

"I consulted an attorney in town, and he said you should pay the rent to us next time it's due. It can be paid directly to our account at the bank in town."

"That's good. Otherwise, I had planned to cancel the lease, but now I'll probably stay on unless you want to take the farm back?"

"No, I hope you will stay. Perhaps you can finally make some money. It looks like the harvest will be good."

"Yes, I believe so. It won't be long until I can thresh the oats. It was nice to see you again, Anders." The two men shook hands and Anders walked back to his friend's car.

"Now, I need to go and see the man who's renting my farm," Lennart said.

"Yes, of course. Did you call Lisa about the good news?"

"Yes, I did. She was happy to hear it."

"So was Lena. She can stop crying now."

As they headed back to Norway, Anders said, "I'm glad it worked out so well."

The hacker: *Anders and Lennart were lucky. I understand that two more farmers in their neighborhood sold their farms to Johanssen. They could go together and file a lawsuit against him. I think I have gotten too involved, but now I want to see how Toby is doing in his mission to help the Swedes.*

Chapter 43

Having worked all day at the distribution center, Toby drove to his former home on Påskgatan. He remembered what the yard had looked like last year when he went there on his way to the ferry and expected it to be worse. But he was pleasantly surprised when he saw it had been cleaned up and assumed it had been done by the sanitation department. The grass was long, so he went to the garage to take out the lawnmower. It started but stalled. He unscrewed the gas cap and saw that the tank was empty. He had to go to the gas station.

As soon as he opened the door to the house, he saw how dirty it was. He went to the closet and took out a mop and a pail. Looking into the living room, he saw that most of the furniture was missing. Obviously, it had been burned to keep the occupants warm during the winter. He turned on the faucet in the sink, but there was no water. Remembering that he had shut it off before they left, he went down to the basement to turn it on.

The water began to run from the faucet, and he let it run clean while he inspected the kitchen. He was afraid to look in the bathroom. Ugh, the toilet has to be removed.

He ran up the stairs two steps at a time to check the bedrooms. All the mattresses and bedding had to go to the dump. He had a lot of work to do. First, he called Ella.

"Hej, I'm at our house."

"What does it look like?"

"No doubt, we have had trespassers. It's dirty, and I've got to get rid of a lot of junk."

"But should we keep the house?"

"We can't sell it the way it looks now."

"I want to come and pick up our porcelain."

"It's still in the cabinet."

"Did you look in the closets upstairs? Hope our good clothes are still there. I don't think the squatters had any use for party clothes."

"I'll check."

"Are the neighbors back?"

"I saw cars parked outside. I'll go and talk to them."

"Do that, and call me later."

Toby went over to his next-door neighbor and rang the doorbell. He remembered Peter Ström with a large belly that used to hang over his belt, but now he was surprisingly slim.

"Hi Toby," Peter said. "Did you come back to stay?"

"No, it's only me. I'm here temporarily. We live in Oslo. I need to know how you managed to make the house livable again. Mine looks terrible."

"Come in and I'll give you a name and phone number to a guy who can help you."

"It's just what I need. You have done wonders with your house in a short time. It's beautiful."

"When the stores opened their doors again, we bought new furniture and rugs. Took all the old stuff to the dump. I can recommend a man by the name of Ronny Danielsson. He lives in the area and he can dispose of junk. Perhaps he can come over, so you can show him what needs to be done."

Peter wrote down Danielsson's number on a slip of paper and handed it to Toby. "I put plywood on your broken window," he said.

"Oh, thanks a lot. I'll pay you for it."

"No need. I had the plywood already."

"Thank you very much. I felt so bad about forgetting to give you a spare key and tell you where we were going."

"It didn't matter much because we couldn't stay here either. We went to our summer house in the country. I'd like to see you again before I leave. Where are you staying?"

"I have a temporary job in the center of the city, but I have to come back tomorrow because there is a lot of work to do in the house."

When Toby called Danielsson, he agreed to come over the next evening. The kitchen needed Toby's attention. He opened the doors to the refrigerator and freezer and saw mildew.

"Ugh." He was sure he had left the doors open. Now they were ruined.

He poured water in a pail and added soap, and worked out his frustration on the stove, the sink, and the counter. He wiped the soiled table and the chairs with a wet rag and hung the chairs upside down on the table. He poured more soap and water in the pail, grabbed the mop, and scrubbed the floor tiles in the kitchen and the foyer. When he threw the water behind the garage and saw how black the water was, he decided to mop the floors a second time.

With that accomplished, he went upstairs to clean the bathroom. He sprayed a cleaner in the tub and the sinks and opened the window before scrubbing the tub with a brush. No one could have used the tub when there was no water, but he felt like he had to scrub away everything that reminded him of the strangers who had occupied his home. He had helped Ella clean many times, but now he had to do it alone. When he cleaned the toilet, the fumes from the cleaner made him turn his head. He wiped all the surfaces before going down on his knees to scrub the floor. When he was done, it smelled clean. He checked the closets and ran the vacuum cleaner before he closed the window and left. Later in the evening, he called Ella and said that the clothes they had left were still there.

When he came back the next evening, Danielsson's truck was parked outside. Together they walked through the house while Toby pointed to the things that had to go to the dump and the appliances that would go to recycling.

They agreed on a price, and Danielsson backed up his truck to the door.

"I'm doing this kind of work to support my family until I can get my job back," he said.

Peter came and asked if he could give them a hand.

"We could use an extra man to move the fridge and the freezer," Toby said. The three men loaded everything in no time at all.

"Are you planning to sell the house, Toby?" Peter asked.

"I can't see how we can keep it. How is the housing market?"

"The prices are low. Everyone is bargaining."

"Is it because of what happened in Gotland?"

"Partly, but also because so many want to move to Norway or England. How do you like it in Oslo?"

"It's expensive, but we like it just fine. The salaries are higher and there's plenty of work."

"The building industry is depressed here now, but I have enough to do just to repair houses."

"What do you think about the fact that Sweden stayed out of NATO?"

"I wish we had been members. The Russians wouldn't have dared to attack a NATO country."

"I agree with you."

Danielsson offered Toby a receipt, so he could be reimbursed by his insurer.

"I'm glad you mentioned it. I have to call the insurance company."

The three men shook hands, and Toby got in his car and drove away. He thought about how he and Ella had saved money for the down payment of the house, and how happy they had been when they moved in. And now their dream home had to be sold. But first he would bring Ella and the children to the house one more time.

The hacker: *I hope that Ella will remember their wedding pictures when she comes. If they were smart, they should keep the house a little longer until the prices go up again, but they probably want to buy a house in Oslo and then they will need cash for the down payment.*

Chapter 44

Two weeks later, Toby met Ella and the children at the ferry. They would use the weekend to visit their home at Påskgatan and get it ready to place it on the market.

As soon as Toby had stopped the company truck outside, Emil and Lynn jumped out.

"Who has the key? Is the garage locked?" Emil asked.

"Wait, and I'll open it," Toby said.

"My hockey clubs are here," Emil said, "but I don't see anything else that's mine. Oh, wait, here's my bike and my football. It needs more air," he said, pressing down on the ball. "The bicycle tires also need air," he said as he sat down on it.

Together they walked into the house. "Usch," Ella said. "It's so bare and empty, and look at all the dust."

"Sorry, I didn't have time to dust. It was a lot worse before I cleaned the floors," Toby said.

Emil and Lynn went to their rooms. "I don't like that those strangers have lived here," Lynn said. Emil looked in his closet and found more of his things.

"It feels so strange to be here," Ella said. "I think I'm more at home in Oslo now." She looked at what was left in the bookcase. "What happened to our books?"

"They were burned in the yard last winter," Toby said. "Like I told you, they burned our furniture to keep warm."

Ella and Lynn checked what was in the clothes closets. "Oh, here's the box I packed with our wedding pictures, studio photos of you kids when you were small, and the portraits of your grandparents," Ella said. "They are irreplaceable. All the other pictures are in digital files on our computers."

"This dress doesn't fit me anymore," Lynn said, holding up a dress. "And not this one either."

"Put them in one of the empty boxes and we can donate them to the distribution center."

"Our friends Anton and Olivia are coming over."

"Then you can be outside," Toby said. "Mamma and I are going to pack the glass and porcelain."

"We mustn't forget the pictures on the walls," Ella said to Toby.

"I'll take them down right now. Do you have anything to wrap them in?"

"You can use the sheets in the linen closet."

"Good idea." He put most of the wall decorations in pillowcases, but wrapped the larger pictures in bed sheets.

Olivia and Anton came on their bikes, looking smaller and thinner than Emil and Lynn. The four friends sat down on the front steps to talk.

"It's so good to see you again," said Lynn. How have you been?"

"Oh, we were out in the boonies," Anton said. "It was boring."

"It wasn't bad. We had clean water and hot food," Olivia said. "Grandma cooked on a wood burning stove and Grandpa brought in firewood and well water. I hadn't realized how important electricity was until I saw that the appliances didn't work and we didn't have running water. We slept in the kitchen where it was the warmest and covered ourselves with sheepskins. We bathed in a washtub."

Anton continued to complain. "It was so dark. We had only candles and kerosene lamps. We could hardly read in the bad light. No TV and no radio. There was no gasoline and no buses. We only had a couple of old bikes to ride."

Olivia had a more positive view of their experiences. "I learned to milk cows. The calves were so cute. It was much worse for our friends who had to stay in the city. They had nothing to eat, and their parents had to go out to the farms and beg for food. Many beggars came to us, and Grandma felt sorry for them and always gave them something. Have you heard of the famine in the late 1860s?"

Emil and Lynn shook their heads. "At that time, hordes of people went begging in the countryside. That's when many Swedes immigrated to America. It's what Grandpa said. And now people are starving again and have to go begging for food."

"We moved to Norway, so we didn't have to starve," Emil said.

"Did you guys go to school?" Lynn asked.

"We were only there to get our homework because the school had no heat," Anton said. "We had to wear jackets. When we came back here, our flat was in bad shape."

"Our house is not too bad, but it was dirty. Pappa was here and cleaned a couple of weeks ago," Emil said. "A lot of our stuff went to the dump. We live in a nice flat in Oslo."

"We missed you so much," Lynn said. "Are you caught up in school yet?"

"No, we studied over the summer, but our teachers say everyone has to repeat one year. We hate it. Not all the teachers and students have returned yet, and some may never return. I wish we had moved to Norway right away when we lost power. You don't have to repeat a year, do you?"

"No, we learned to read and write Norwegian pretty fast. But I want to know how you reacted when all those Swedish soldiers were killed in Gotland?"

"It was like a nightmare, and it's still hard to believe," Olivia said.

Anton shrugged his shoulders. "But Gotland is far from here, and we don't know anyone there. The Swedes killed as many Russians on Öland as the Russians killed Swedes on Gotland, so I think we're even."

Lynn wrinkled her nose at Anton's comment. "I'll ask Mamma if I can make some tea. We brought sweet rolls and cookies from Oslo."

She told her mother what Anton had said. "It's a harsh comment considering the serious situation, but it's probably just to cover up his emotions," Ella said. "Don't let it bother you." Lynn felt better after a hug from Mamma.

"Everything is on the table, teabags too. Pappa and I want coffee. Please start the coffee maker. Just press the button. Please, wash the dishes before you put them on the table."

Lynn asked Olivia to come and help her in the kitchen. Emil had found a bicycle pump and inflated the football first and then his bike tires. He and Anton went on a bicycle ride in the neighborhood and when they met some other boys, they invited them to an improvised soccer game in the school yard.

Olivia and Lynn went into the house. "It looks good here," Olivia said, "but the fridge is gone."

"Yeah, Pappa said it had mildew inside." Lynn started the coffee maker and rinsed out a teapot for the hot water. When she began to wash the dishes, Olivia offered to dry them. "Here's a clean towel."

"How long are you staying in town?"

"Just over the weekend." Lynn told Olivia about the place where her father worked to help hungry Swedes. "Cool," Olivia said.

When the refreshments were ready, the boys were back. Lynn called her parents and they all sat down around the kitchen table.

"This is almost like old times," Toby said. "What are your parents doing now? Have they gone back to their jobs?"

"Mamma is unemployed," Olivia said, "She worked in elder care, and there are hardly any old people left in town. Many have died or moved away. Pappa went back to his job, but he hasn't been paid yet."

"We don't get any allowance. Our clothes are too small, and we have nothing to wear," Anton said.

"Maybe we have something that will fit you," Ella said. "Emil and Lynn have outgrown what they wore last year."

"We heard that many babies died," Toby said.

"Yes, we have friends who lost little brothers and sisters," said Olivia. It's so sad. Children are not supposed to die. I would like to move away from here."

When they were finished at the table, the children went upstairs, and Olivia and Anton tried on clothes.

"These pants will fit me," Anton said.

"I would like to try on these dresses, but I don't have much use for them," said Olivia. "Aren't there any jeans for me?"

"Try these," said Lynn, holding up a pair.

Ella went down to the basement and came back with a basket of freshly laundered linen that she put in a suitcase while thinking about Anton and Olivia's situation. They weren't the only children in Sweden who were poor these days. She had seen the lines at the Distribution Center.

"Lynn, would you please do some dusting? You should use a damp cloth. I'm ready to mop the hardwood floors."

"Sure, Olivia can help me."

The realtor came and went from room to room with Toby to see how much the house could be worth.

"You won't get more than half of what it was worth before the cyber attack. But this is a very nice home. The balcony and patio are a plus," she said.

Toby looked shocked. "How much is half?"

"Probably two million. Buyers have problems getting mortgages. The commission and closing costs are deducted. Do you still want to sell?"

"What do you think, Ella?" Toby asked. "We have no use for it, and it just costs money to keep it. I think we should sell. We can't keep coming back here to check on it."

"I suppose the house is mortgaged?" the realtor said.

"We have about a million left on the loan," Toby said.

"Some sellers are 'underwater,' so you're lucky. If you sign the contract and give me a key, I can show the house a week from now. Will all the inventory be included?"

"Yes, and there is lawn furniture in the garage. We can take the bikes with us."

"Okay, but we'll ask 2.5. My neighbor said that people like to bargain."

Toby and Ella thought about how they had saved and sacrificed to be able to build their home, and now it would be sold. But more importantly, the proceeds would help them buy another home in Oslo.

The hacker: *It was interesting to hear Anton and Olivia's comments. At least they still have both parents. I'm glad Ella remembered their wedding pictures. Now, I want to check on Alex.*

Chapter 45

Alex usually stood at a safe distance from all electric powerlines, but this time he didn't see the danger. He got an electric shock and hit the ground. Henrik saw that his friend had a burn on his right arm where the power had entered his body and a hole in his shoe where it had exited and called for an ambulance at once.

"Electric shock! A man is down. Come at once."

The minutes passed slowly until help arrived. Alex was unconscious when he was carried into the ambulance. The ambulance drove at high speed with blasting sirens to Danderyd Hospital with Henrik at Alex's side. At the hospital, Henrik told the doctors that Alex had been hit by a power arc.

The doctors said that Alex's heart rhythm was affected and ordered an EKG. Henrik waited anxiously to hear about Alex's prognosis. The attending physician said the risk was small for lasting damage. When Alex's heart rhythm had stabilized, Henrik called Mia.

"This is your husband's colleague, Henrik. I'm sitting with him at Danderyd Hospital in Stockholm. I'm sorry to tell you, but he got an electric shock at work and has a burn on one arm He can't come home to Oslo for a while."

"Oh, how awful. May I speak to him?"

"He's asleep right now, but he'll call you as soon as he can. The doctors say he'll recover."

"Tell him I'll come to him as soon as I can."

She called out to Lena and Anders, "Alex is injured. I must go and see him."

"Injured. How?"

Mia repeated what Henrik had said. Her voice shook.

"Was it an electric shock?" Anders knew his son's work was dangerous.

"Yes, I've always been afraid of that," Mia said.

"Then he'll probably be in the hospital for a long time."

"Oh, my poor Alex," Lena said. "But you're nursing, Mia, and can't leave Andy. I can come with you and watch him while you visit Alex."

"Do you want to do that? I know how afraid you are of flying."

Lena's voice quivered. "For Alex's sake, I'll do it. I want to see Alex, too." She had been depressed by the bad news from Sweden and about their farm, but she would do anything for Alex.

"We can't decide until Alex has called. I'm so nervous," Mia said.

Anders called Toby in Sweden because it always felt better to share a worry.

Toby's first reaction was, "I hope he hasn't sustained lasting damage."

"I pray he hasn't," Anders said. "I didn't think Alex had to do any dangerous work himself."

"I didn't think so either."

Mia thought about what she would have to bring for Andy. Lena said she was afraid that the Russians would come back to Stockholm. Anders and Mia ignored her. Lena was always afraid of the Russians.

Everyone jumped when the phone rang. Mia answered while holding Andy on her arm. Alex's voice was weak and he talked slowly. Mia listened and said, "We've been so worried about you since

Henrik called. How do you feel?"

"I'm tired. Getting oxygen. I don't remember what happened, but I'm sure I didn't touch anything. Henrik said it was an arc."

"Lena and I are thinking about taking Andy with us and fly to Stockholm."

"It would be wonderful to see you, but I think you should wait until I get stronger. We can call each other every day. Don't buy any tickets yet. Tell Mamma to stay home." Alex sounded like a robot.

"We can wait, but is it okay for us to stay in your apartment when we come, or is it too far from the hospital?"

"No, it's not far. I've asked Henrik to clean the apartment. He or another colleague will come and visit me every evening."

"Are they able to work without you?"

"Yes, they're working. I don't think I'll be doing that kind of work again."

"I hope not."

"Olafssen called and said I'm insured. I'll be reimbursed for everything. The next time I call, I want to speak with Pappa. Tell him and Mamma not to worry. I'll get through this."

"Andy wants to listen. You can hear him babbling." But Andy got quiet when he heard his daddy's voice and just smiled.

After two weeks in the hospital, Alex was told he could return to his apartment provided he had someone to look after him. It was the good news they had waited for. Henrik said the team must move because they worked too far from Stockholm to live there. Alex and Mia could have the apartment to themselves. The rent was paid.

Alex called Mia at once and said she could book the flight. "Mamma doesn't have to come."

"Lena likes it best when she can stay home. How will I get from the airport to the hospital?"

"You can take a cab."

"I'll let you know when I'm coming as soon as I have booked the flight," Mia said.

"I miss you and Andy so much."

"I miss you, too, honey."

A week later, Anders drove Mia and Andy to the airport. "Say hello to Alex and wish him a speedy recovery," he said as he waved goodbye.

The reunion with Alex was both happy and emotional. He walked with the help of a crutch. Mia thought he looked pale. His wide shoulders seemed to have shrunk. His dark blue eyes met Mia's light blue, and they felt the love between them. Alex said Mia was more beautiful than ever. Her face reminded him of a pink flower. Her pantsuit fit her slim body perfectly. She wore a white blouse that did not quite close over her high chest.

"Do you want to hold your son?"

"Yes, but I have to sit down."

Mia placed Andy on Alex's knees but held on to him. Father and son smiled at each other. Andy waved his arms and babbled.

"He's a cute little guy. I'm so glad that both of you are here. You'll meet one of my doctors before I'm released."

"So, this is your family, Alex?" A doctor in a white coat stood before them and extended his hand to Mia.

"I've heard about you and little Andy. He's a beautiful child. How was the flight?"

"Fine, thanks." Mia put Andy in his carriage.

"Please come with me. I have some papers for you."

The hacker: *It was an idyllic scene, but I expect some problems before Alex is well.*

Chapter 46

The doctor led the way to another room where they could talk in private. Mia listened.

"You have to have patience with Alex. He still has a limp. His burn has healed, but there might be some clinical changes to his nerves from the shock. He can be easily irritated. He can have pain and be overly sensitive to warm and cold temperatures. I have explained to him that other functions could have been affected. A physical therapist will come to your home and work with him every other day. Nerves will heal on their own but it takes time. The neurologist here at the hospital says that Alex has a good chance to recover completely. The therapist will report to us, so you can let him know if something unusual happens. Do you have any questions?"

"How soon can I bring Alex back to Oslo?"

"Perhaps in about three weeks depending on his progress, but he has to be checked at the hospital in Oslo after you get home. Here are some papers that you might want to read."

A nurse took Alex to the exit in a wheelchair where a cab waited. Mia secured Andy in the backseat while Alex sat down in the front seat. When they were on their way, she looked out the window and saw building after building pass by, signs she didn't have time to read, no grass, only trees, and buildings. Factories looked like they were closed. No smoke from the chimneys and no cars in the parking lot. Many storefronts were still covered with plywood.

The doorman recognized Alex, who said, "I've been in the hospital and I'm not very strong. This is my wife and son. Could you please help us with the suitcase?"

"Of course, welcome back."

Mia pushed the baby carriage into the elevator, and they passed many floors before it stopped. Alex had his arm in a sling, but unlocked the door with his free hand, switched on the light, and let Mia pass with the baby.

"Thanks for your help with the suitcase," Alex said to the doorman and gave him a tip.

"Isn't it a little unusual with a doorman?" Mia said. "I've seen them only at large hotels."

"The keypad was ripped out. Doormen make the building safer than a keypad."

"And they can carry luggage."

"Here's our home for the next few weeks, sweetheart." Mia went from room to room. "We've lots of space here," she said.

"We don't have to use all the rooms, but Andy can have his own. There's no crib for him."

"Andy can sleep in his carriage in our room," Mia said.

"This was my room before the accident. My clothes are here."

"Then it will be our room now. It's close to the bathroom."

"Feel at home, honey. You're the boss."

Mia thought it felt strange. She wasn't used to being the strongest of them. She went to the kitchen and opened the refrigerator. "I'm glad there is some food here because I don't feel like going shopping right away," she said.

Alex limped into the living room. "Come and sit down here beside me. The guys have cleaned the place. It didn't look this good when we camped out here."

Mia sat down beside him, and he put his good arm around her.

"To start with, it's not going to be like before. I'd like to have both arms around you, but I can't."

"I understand. But we can be together and it's more important." She offered him her lips and he kissed her.

"This, I can do," he said and kissed her thoroughly. Mia kissed him back.

"Wonderful. You're wonderful. I'm so glad you came. I can't get enough of looking at you. You're so beautiful, and I've missed you very much." He stroked her blonde hair. "Have you been to the hairdresser? You look so modern."

"Yes, I wanted to look my best when I met you. I've missed you so much, and I can hug you even if you can't hug me." Alex smiled and his eyes looked happier than before.

"Hug as much as you want. I feel better already." Mia got a glimpse of her husband as he used to be. But then Andy woke up and let them know he was hungry. Mia stood up.

"I'll call home and tell my parents how happy I am that you and Andy are here with me, Alex said.

Mia picked up Andy and the diaper bag. "You need food and a dry diaper, my little one. Then we'll return to your daddy."

In the evening, when they had gone to bed, Alex began to fondle his wife. Their lips met in hot kisses. He kissed her breasts and long body.

"Please help me." Alex took her hand and showed her what to do. Mia stroked, but nothing happened. Alex caressed her nipples. Milk began to run. "Stop, please, I'm getting wet." She grabbed a towel she used for nursing and held it against her breasts.

Alex rose from the bed, took his crutch, and went to the bathroom. At once, Mia understood what the doctor had meant about certain functions that might take time to heal. She heard the crutch moving toward the living room. The baby slept. She flung on her robe and hurried to her husband. Dressed in his bathrobe, Alex swore as he kept hitting the pillows on the sofa with his crutch.

"Alex, it's okay. The doctor said that the nerves will heal."

"It's my fault," he cried. I knew better than risking a shock. Can you ever forgive me?"

"Accidents happen. You must forgive yourself."

"I'm only 32 and useless as a man."

"No, you can't give up." His tears dropped on her naked breasts until they fell asleep in each other's arms on the sofa. Mia woke up first and let Alex sleep while she went to the bedroom to check on the baby. Andy was awake so she decided to feed and diaper him. It gave her much needed comfort.

When she returned to the living room, Alex was awake and they looked at each other, both a little embarrassed. They didn't speak about what had happened. Mia said she had to go shopping.

"Where is the nearest store?"

"There's a convenience store around the corner. It has milk, bread, and some dry and frozen food."

"Can you watch Andy while I'm gone? He's sleeping."

"Of course, but I don't dare to lift him up. If he wakes, I can sit and entertain him. Do you have any storybooks with you?"

"You can make up stories, or you can sing to him. He likes to listen and doesn't care what you say or read."

"How much does he sleep now?"

"As a rule, he goes to sleep after I've changed him and nursed him. But he can stay awake if you play with him. He'll play with his toes and feet. Babies are so flexible."

Mia put the dishes in the dishwasher. "Where's the washing machine?" she asked

"In the basement. I'll show you later."

"Even though I don't have to wash diapers, there's always something that has to be washed when you have a baby."

"I'll turn on the TV and look at the news. There're books on the shelf that I would like to read."

When Mia was ready to leave, Alex asked her to buy a newspaper. "I'm sorry," he said. "I forgot to give you money. Or do you want to use my Swedish card?"

"I have my own. We can use yours when we go to the supermarket. I'll go now, but I'll hurry back."

The doorman greeted her with a cheerful, "Good Morning." She looked around and wasn't sure which way to turn.

"May I help you?"

"Which way to the nearest store?"

"That way," the doorman said and pointed. "It's on the left corner."

When Mia had crossed the street, she turned around and memorized the house number. All the high-rises looked the same. She met people who looked thin and worn. Walking faster, she tucked her purse tighter under her arm. Perhaps she was too well dressed. In the store, she selected as little as possible, or it would be too heavy to carry.

The doorman saw her coming with a plastic bag in each hand.

"If you need help, just ask?"

"Thanks, but I can manage." He pushed the elevator button for her. She had forgotten to bring a key and had to ring the doorbell. It took a while before Alex came to open the door.

"I was in the bathroom. Next time, bring your key, honey." He sounded a bit irritated.

The hacker: *I feel sorry for Alex. I have been married, but with my job, it is impossible to be married so we got divorced. I am thinking about Kurt and hope to see him again soon.*

Chapter 47

The first thing Mia asked when she came back to the apartment was, "Is Andy asleep?"

"Yes, he is. I've been sitting and looking at him the whole time. He looks like you, and I love that."

"But I thought he looks like you. Here's the morning paper, Dagens Nyheter, is that okay?"

"Sure, thank you so much."

While Mia unpacked the groceries, Alex sat down at the kitchen table to read the paper.

"Do you see anything interesting? I read the posters outside the store and they're awful."

Alex browsed the headlines. "Another mass shooting in America. A knife murder in Stockholm. Just the usual."

"Nothing about the negotiations with Russia?"

"No, I don't see anything about that. My therapist is coming today. His name is Adrian. It's his job to train my muscles." Alex winked and smiled while pouring another cup of coffee.

Andy let them know he was awake. To entertain Alex, Mia placed a blanket on the floor and put Andy down on it. "Andy can roll over now," she said. He curled up until he was round as a ball and then began to roll sideways. He continued until he was at the end of the blanket when Mia made him roll the other way.

"That's my boy," Alex said "I wish I could go down on my knees like you do, Mia." Alex tried to lean on his good knee, but it looked clumsy. "Adrian will have to train me to do that."

"I think I'll go for a walk with Andy while Adrian is here," Mia said. "Is there a playground here where we can see other children play?"

"I've seen a playground behind one of the buildings. Next time, you go there, I'd like to come with you. My doctor said I should walk to get stronger."

Adrian arrived just as Mia left with the baby in the carriage.

After the treatment, Alex was tired. "I'm sure I'll be very sore from today's workout," he said. "Did you enjoy the park?"

"Yes, I met another mother with a baby, and we talked for a while. Her name is Lisbeth, and she lives on the second floor of this house, so I'm sure we'll meet again. She has a little girl the same age as Andy, but she also has a son and he played in the sandbox."

Mia was just about to say that the next time she wished for a girl when she realized that another child might be impossible. She didn't mention what Lisbeth had told her about the awful things that had happened in their building before the power was restored. Many occupants had died, and their bodies had been stored on a separate floor. That floor was now closed. The elevator didn't stop there. People had been afflicted with lice because they couldn't keep themselves clean. Many of them either starved to death or died of disease. Mia felt bad when she passed the "morgue floor" in the elevator. Alex's problems seemed small in comparison.

"I don't know how I'll be able to stand the winter because I'm cold now," Alex said, "even though I'm wearing a Norwegian sweater. It's best to be outside as much as possible while I still can."

After the next therapy session, Adrian met Mia outside the elevator and she decided to tell him about Alex's outburst. Adrian said that Alex had already told him about it, so she didn't have to. "Don't worry, you just have to be patient. He'll recover."

When bedtime came, Mia placed Andy between them. Alex and the baby fell asleep at the same time, while Mia lay awake thinking about Alex's injury.

Adrian had left a muscle strengthener for Alex to use on his own, and Mia looked on as Alex placed it between his knees and tried to push it together. In the beginning, he could only do it halfway. He trained his leg muscles several times each day until he could push his thighs together.

"Feel this," he said to Mia. "I'm beginning to get strong muscles in my thighs again."

Mia tried to use the muscle strengthener but was disappointed when she wasn't as strong as she thought. Alex was stronger, and that gave him confidence. The therapist didn't have to come as often. Alex could train at home by himself. He put away his crutch and walked without. He could push Andy in the carriage.

His erectile problem decreased, and he didn't have to go to the toilet as often as before. Mia helped him as much as she could without embarrassing him. Much patience was needed because Alex's nerve signals were still healing.

"You're my best therapist, sweetheart," he said.

"It's in my interest. Your mood has improved. You aren't as easily irritated and you haven't had any more episodes."

"I'm very sorry about that. How could you stand me?"

"You couldn't help it. It was the electric shock that hindered you."

Mia met Lisbeth on the playground again and asked her if she had stayed in Stockholm the whole time when the power was out. "We did," she said, but it was awful. The people on the other floors tried to force their way into our apartment, so they didn't have to walk to the top. My husband works in the wholesale food industry and brought home food and water, but he was robbed several times. I was on maternity leave but of course I didn't get my compensation. I still don't."

Mia and Alex slowly established a schedule that suited them. They took the bus to the fish market and the supermarket. The bus lifted the baby carriage up and down and it was easier than taking a cab. They visited City Hall, which Mia always had wanted to see. She was surprised to learn that the blue room, where the Nobel festivities were held each year, wasn't blue but covered with red brick. The architect had planned to paint it blue and that's why it was called the blue room. Nothing else of interest was open. With Andy in the carriage, they walked around the parliament building and the castle, both of which the Russians had temporarily occupied. Mia wished she could see the Vasa Museum, but it was closed.

"Next time we come here you can see the old Vasa Warship," Alex said. "It's worth seeing."

He called Ole Olafssen, saying he felt strong enough to fly home to Oslo. Alex asked how the team was doing in restoring the power to the east coast.

"It's going well. They are almost done with their project. Now we might be able to keep the Russians at bay. Will you go back to work at the plant?"

"I hope so."

"I'm glad you're well again, but you will be missed here."

Before Alex and Mia left Stockholm, Kurt came to visit them. The distance between them would be greater when they were back in Oslo. Kurt told them about the Cyber Defense Center in Tallinn and that he had been there at a conference.

"I was impressed," he said. "The Center was founded in 2008 on the initiative of Estonia and five other nations, Germany, Italy, Lithuania, Slovakia, and Spain. The organization now has 21 member countries, NATO countries, and others. Estonia joined NATO in

2004. Sweden planned to join the Cyber Defense Center when the attack happened."

"If we had been members, the attack might have been prevented," Alex said.

"It's possible, but Finland was a member, and it was still attacked. It could have had something to do with Finland being on the same grid as us."

"How's the Defense Center financed?"

"It's financed by the member countries but is not included in NATO's military defense. It has the world's largest and most complex annual exercises in cyber defense."

"It sounds like a good place for you to work, Kurt," Mia said.

"Actually, I filled out an application for a position. It has directors who are specialized in various topics, but unless someone retires or resigns there won't be any openings."

When Alex went for a checkup at the Danderyd Hospital, the doctors were pleased with his progress.

"It's thanks to my wife, I can be a dad again." Mia reddened. Everyone smiled.

"You've gained weight without getting fat. I can write a remittance to the hospital in Oslo, but I don't think you'll need it," the doctor said.

The hacker: *There will probably be a happy family reunion in Oslo when Alex and his family return. But more bad news from Sweden can be expected.*

Chapter 48

Alex and Mia heard yet another awful TV report from Sweden.

A Swedish fighter plane, Gripen, has destroyed the 300-year-old ship Vasa that has been under restoration since 1961 when it was lifted from the bottom of the bay. At this time, we can't say whether there were any causalities on the ground, and we don't know if the plane crashed due to a technical problem or if it was intentional.

"A Swedish pilot could not have done this," Alex said. "It might be a copycat attack of what happened in New York in September 2011."

The report continued:

There will be an investigation as soon as the fire has died down. The Swedish Airforce has not identified the pilot. The fighter is presumed to have taken off from F-17 in Ronneby for a training exercise, and this is also being investigated.

Large crowds of protestors have gathered at Djurgården, loudly demanding the return of the government. It looks like they have been heard because the prime minister and the rest of the administration are finally on their way to Stockholm after a long absence. The invasion of the castle and the parliament building could not get them out of the shelter, but the destruction of Vasa did.

If it can be confirmed that an unauthorized pilot hi-jacked the fighter that destroyed the Vasa Museum, it will have serious consequences.

Alex and Mia were stunned by the news.

"It's ironic that Gustav Adolf's warship should play a role in the fight for power today," Alex said.

Mia called Anders and Lena to the living room. "The Vasa Museum wasn't open when I was in Stockholm and now it's destroyed."

"What do you mean? How can it be destroyed?"

"Come and see. It's unbelievable. I'm so sorry I never got to see the restored ship."

The special news report played over and over and confirmed that the government had returned to Stockholm. Norwegian TV continued with a brief history of the ship:

"At the beginning of the 1620s, Sweden found itself in a dangerous war situation. Gustavus II Adolphus had been king for 10 years and was in a war with Russia and Poland. Control of the Baltic Sea was necessary if Sweden was to become a great power in Europe. But the Swedish Navy was badly prepared and consisted mostly of older and poorly equipped ships. To strengthen his position in the region the king decided to upgrade Sweden's naval capability.

"In 1956, Anders Franzén located a large wooden object in the water almost parallel to Beckholmen. The location of the ship received considerable attention, even if the identification of the ship could not be determined without closer investigation. Soon after the announcement of the find, plans were underway to determine how to excavate and raise the wreck, which was believed to be the Vasa Warship.

"Divers spent two years digging six tunnels under the ship for steel cable slings, which were taken to a pair of lifting pontoons at the surface. The final lift began on April 8, 1961, and on the morning of April 24, Vasa was ready to return to the surface of the brackish water for the first time in 333 years. Press from all over the world, television cameras, 400 guests on barges and boats, and thousands of spectators on shore watched as the first timbers became visible.

The ship was then emptied of water and mud and towed to a drydock at Beckholmen, where it was floated on its keel onto a concrete pontoon.

"Although Vasa was in surprisingly good condition after 333 years at the bottom of the sea, it would have quickly deteriorated if the hull had been simply allowed to dry. The large bulk of Vasa, over 600 cubic meters (21,000 cubic feet) of oak timber, constituted an unprecedented conservation problem. After some debate on how to best preserve the ship, conservation was carried out by impregnation with polyethylene glycol (PEG), a method that has since become the standard treatment for large, waterlogged wooden objects. Vasa was sprayed with PEG for 17 years, followed by a long period of slow drying.

"From the end of 1961 to December 1988, Vasa was housed in a temporary facility called Vasavarvet (The Vasa Shipyard), which included exhibit space. The ship was constantly sprayed with water. A building was erected over the ship on its pontoon, but it was very cramped, making conservation work awkward. Visitors could view the ship from just two levels. In 1981, the Swedish government decided that a permanent building was to be constructed. The winning design called for a large hall over the ship in a polygonal, industrial style. The ground was broken in 1987, and Vasa was towed into the half-finished Vasa Museum in December 1988. The museum was officially opened to the public in 1990.

"One problem was that the old oak, of which the ship is built, had lost a substantial amount of its original strength. To deal with the problem of the inevitable deterioration of the ship, the main hall of the Vasa Museum was kept at a temperature of 18–20 °C (64–68 °F) and a humidity level of 53%.

"The once mighty ship carried 64 bronze cannons, 48 of them extra heavy with 24-pound cannonballs on deck. The ship was 69 meters long, 12 meters wide, and a good 52 meters high from the keel to the top of the mast. The ship carried 145 seamen and other crew, as well as 300 soldiers ready to fight. It had 10 sails. Sculptures, gilded in blue and gold, adorned the stern that rose 20 meters above the water."

Alex had seen the Vasa and said that it attracted more than a million visitors yearly from all over the world. "What has happened is not only a loss of a natural treasure, it's also a considerable financial loss to Sweden. Buildings can be repaired but the Vasa ship can never be replaced. It was the pride and joy of Stockholmers and everyone who saw it stood in awe at the sight of the beautiful ship."

"The fighter plane Gripen can be replaced, but I've heard it cost one million crowns to build just one," Anders said.

It was just too much for Lena to process. "I can't stand it anymore," she said and went to bed. The family left her alone.

That night she told Anders she hated what was happening to their beloved Sweden and asked him if he didn't feel the same way.

"Of course, I do. Even though we have moved here and are safe, we'll always love Sweden and care deeply about it, my dear. There might be more bad news about Gotland, and there is nothing we can do about that either."

The hacker: *I knew nothing about the ancient Vasa ship. Too bad I did not get to see it. Toby and Alex have already turned their attention to the northern part of Sweden.*

Chapter 49

Most of Sweden was still in the dark from the cyber attack, and Alex feared that the Russians would promise Sweden electricity if they gave up the mines in northern Sweden. He discussed the possibility with Toby.

"Airports and train stations must open so that all the elected members of parliament can come to Stockholm before the government makes more concessions," Alex said. It would be good if the hydroelectric plants in Norrland could be restarted. The highest waterfalls are almost 100 meters highs. They can create tremendous power."

"Do you think it could be done?"

"That and much more. We could activate all domestic trains and the rest of the airports."

Toby's cell phone pinged. The call came from Sweden.

"Hi Peter, what's going on?" Toby put the cellphone on speaker, and Alex heard what was said.

"Sit down. I have bad news," Peter said.

"What?"

"Your house has burned down."

"Oh, no. How, why?"

"The fire chief said they had tried to save a man, but the upper floor collapsed on him. It must have been a homeless person, and he probably caused the fire."

"Is there nothing left? Didn't the fire truck come in time?"

"There's only the basement left. When we came home, the flames engulfed your house. Someone had called the fire department, but it was too late. All they could do was prevent the fire from spreading."

"That's horrible. We had the house for sale. Ella will be terribly upset." Toby's face had turned red.

"I took a video, and I can send it to you. I hope you have fire insurance."

"Yes, of course. Thanks for letting me know."

Toby turned to Alex. "As you heard, our house has burned down. Now, all we have left in Sweden is the summer house."

"I'm so sorry, bro. I remember how happy you and Ella were the day you moved in."

"We still own the family farm, but I wonder for how long." Toby closed his eyes and sank down in his chair.

After what had happened to their dear Vasa ship, the people's anger rose. They said, "We might as well take what we can before the Russians take everything." Swedish television reporters with battery operated cameras filmed how former warehouse workers used axes to cut up the plywood that covered the entrance to a large warehouse. The city's name was not mentioned but it had to be located somewhere in the interior where there was no power.

At first, they stole everything that could be eaten without being cooked. But when they found a room full of charcoal, they wheeled out as much coal as they could on warehouse carts. With charcoal they could cook meat, they said and raided the meat lockers next. More people came and helped themselves to charcoal, meat, and potatoes. Everything they needed was right before their eyes.

Someone soon found the state liquor storage facility. They hacked their way in and carted out boxes filled with bottles. Just as they were leaving, they heard police sirens and hid in the bushes. Through the greenery, they saw the police officers entering with raised clubs. When they came out, they carried heavy boxes and placed them in the trunk of their squad car before driving away. In the morning, a poster board on the squad car said in large letters, "Did you enjoy the booze you stole?" The poster board remained all day while the hungover policemen slept. The private citizens, who didn't have much to be happy about, laughed.

Anders reacted by saying. "We have seen looting in America, but I never thought I would see it in Sweden."

Lena coughed and coughed. "I can't say that I blame the hungry, but I don't think the police should be stealing," she said.

"I'm going out to get some cough medicine for you," Anders said.

The medicine helped some for the cough, but then Lena got a fever and had to stay in bed. Mia called Ella for advice.

"Colds are common these days, but Lena's symptoms sound like she has bronchitis. She needs to see a doctor and get medicine."

"That's what I was afraid of. Anders can take her."

"Bronchitis is contagious, so keep Andy away from her. You've got to be careful, Mia, until Lena has taken antibiotics for a few days."

Lena protested when both Mia and Anders said she had to see a doctor. I'll get better in a few days," she said. But when Mia said that Andy might catch her cold, she agreed to go to a clinic. They were on their way to the clinic when Anders heard her labored breathing and drove to the hospital instead. A physician listened to her lungs.

"You have pneumonia," he said. "We need to admit you for observation."

"Is it that serious?"

"It can be."

After a week in the hospital, Lena came home but was still weak. On Saturday, Toby and Ella came to visit and everyone gathered around the coffee table. Toby had been relieved of his work in Gothenburg and had come back home to stay.

"It's good to see you're on your feet again, Mamma," he said.

"I can't be up for long. I get so tired."

"It's normal after pneumonia," Ella assured her.

Anders turned to Toby saying, "It was sad to hear that your house burned down. Will the insurance pay?"

"Yes, we'll be compensated, but it might take a long time because our agent said there have been many fires in Gothenburg. Some are arson, but they can't blame us for anything like that. We spent all that time cleaning up the house for nothing," he said with a scowl.

Ella had news. "We have been looking for a house, and now we have found one. Our bid was accepted. Toby has been promoted so we can afford it. Best of all, it's in our area. The children don't have to change schools. They refuse to do that."

"Congratulations. Tell us more," Anders said.

"I got the position I always wanted in Research and Development, Toby said. "I'll be working with renewable energy. When I first applied, there was no position available in that department. Now we are happy to be able to afford a house of our own."

Ella told them more about the house and said she would show them pictures later. Andy sat on her lap, smiling and showing two new lower teeth. Lynn had wanted to come, but she didn't have time, Ella said. "The children are so busy these days."

"It means they have adjusted," Mia said.

"Just imagine, we have lived in Oslo for a year now. As we become homeowners, we will be even more established, but I'm sure we will still call Sweden home."

Lena stood up and said she would rest for a while. Her illness and the uncertainty about what would happen with Gotland had deepened her depression. Toby and Alex went for a walk. As usual, they wanted a chance to talk in private. They wore leather jackets and walked with their hands in the pockets.

"Mamma looks tired," Toby said.

"Yes, but just think if she had become ill in Sweden. I'm glad they moved here."

"I thought about that, too."

"Have you heard who the pilot was who crashed the plane on the Vasa Museum?"

"I heard it was a terminally ill pilot who would have died anyway, but no one knows anything for sure. I don't think any Swede could have been convinced to destroy the Vasa. The crash might have been planned for the parliament building."

"Perhaps. It was lucky that the museum was closed, or hundreds of people would have died."

"It's true, but an even bigger catastrophe could happen if Sweden doesn't join NATO."

"I agree with you."

"That's why it's so important to restart Sweden's communications. The entire Riksdag needs to meet. There might be a battle for Norrland, just like there was for Gotland."

"We can't lose Lapland and Norrbotten with all the hydro power, iron ore, gold, and silver mines."

When the guests had left, Anders said he would like to take a job over the winter. "There isn't much for me to do here. The fruit is harvested and I've cleaned up the orchard. I saw in the newspaper that a home improvement store is hiring. I'll ask if they have something for me."

The hacker: *Alex is right. Losing the mines in the north would be much worse than the loss of the old Vasa Warship.*

Chapter 50

Alex studied the hydroelectric powerplants in northern Sweden but wasn't feeling useful at all until he received a phone call from Olafssen in Trollhättan. Without delay, he told Alex about a project he had initiated that was in jeopardy.

"Our work in Lapland has abruptly come to a stop in Gällivare. The project leader quit, and we need you, Alex. You're the only one I know who can replace him."

Alex sat up straighter in his chair and pressed the phone closer to his ear. His muscles tightened. Ready to spring into action, he stood up so fast that his chair overturned.

"You don't have to come close to any powerlines. You'll get a team of several men and all the technical equipment you can imagine, a fully equipped motorhome, smaller vehicles for snowy terrain, scooters, skis, warm clothes, and gasoline from the military."

"I'm listening. How would I get there?"

"We'll fly you to Narvik. From there you'll go by helicopter to Kiruna."

"When?"

"ASAP. You can borrow my bodyguard. He has already landed in Oslo. A plane is on standby for you. Norway is backing the project."

"I'm ready, but I must let Mia and my boss know."

"Your boss already knows, but you need to call your wife right away."

Alex told Mia that he had to fly up to Kiruna. "It's an emergency. Could you please pack a bag for me? We don't have any time to lose."

As always, Mia agreed. Alex knew she would worry about him, but she would not stand in his way."

Alex hurried to the director's office but didn't have to explain anything.

"I know you've received an important phone call, Alex," he said. "If you want to take on the job, you'll get time off. The nature of the project will be kept secret for the time being."

"Understood, but I must get home and say goodbye to my family.

"A driver is ready to take you there." The director grabbed his coat. "Where's your jacket, Alex?"

"In my office." Alex ran there, shut down his computer, and bagged it before wriggling into his jacket. The other employees in the office looked on as Alex and his boss ran toward the exit.

The director pointed to the car that stood waiting with the engine running. "There's your get-away. Godspeed."

When the car came to a shrieking stop outside their home, Mia held the front door open for him.

"I have already packed your bag," she said.

"I'm sorry I have to rush, sweetheart." He took her in his arms and covered her face with kisses. "Thank you for not opposing this. It means a lot to me. Where's Andy?"

His parents came toward him with Lena holding Andy on her arm. Alex went up to them and embraced them all at the same time. Lena cried.

"Don't worry, Mamma. I'll be fine." Alex took a last look at his son and hugged Mia once more, picked up his bag, and ran to the waiting car.

He felt like everything had happened in a dream, but at the same time, he felt more alive than in a long time. He smiled when he thought about how fast it had all happened. This project appeared to be much more urgent than the one in Stockholm. Alex recognized the bodyguard, Joakim, who met him at the plane that would take them to Narvik. Alex suspected that the Russians would not appreciate their project and that was the reason for the bodyguard.

"I got urgent orders to fly to Oslo," Joakim said. "I understand we are on the way to Kiruna. I'm born and raised there and familiar with the area. What are you going to do that's so important?"

Alex explained his mission while the private plane flew them north. The setting sun shone on the glaciers. It was dark when they landed in Narvik. A car took them to a hotel for the night. Alex saw the opportunity to call Kurt in Tallinn and tell him he would be out of calling distance for a while but didn't say why.

Kurt told him he was ready to ferry over to Helsinki and meet with the Finns who had restored the power to Finland. "I can learn a lot from them," he said.

A helicopter stood waiting for Alex and Joakim the next morning. The Norwegian pilot saluted them as they boarded. The chopper lifted and flew east toward Sweden. Alex saw the snow-covered top of Kebnekajse, Sweden's highest mountain. The mining town of Kiruna was lit up, and they landed safely. Alex and Joakim ran from the helicopter while the wings still whirled. Light snow blew in their faces.

Engineer Rune Brorsson took Alex and Joakim to a room with large maps on the walls, showing the large regional power grid of the hydroelectric power plants with all the transformer stations, and Alex studied them.

"You don't have to memorize them, because we will bring paper maps, and they will also be available in our battery-operated computer system," Rune said. "You have probably heard that the cities of Kiruna and Malmberget will be moved?" Alex nodded. "There's a risk of cave-ins where we're going. Due to all the mining tunnels, the buildings are no longer standing on safe ground. This is how large the area is," Rune said, pointing to a map.

Alex understood the enormity and urgency of the project but had other questions.

"Is there snow on the ground everywhere? What kind of weather can we expect?"

"The snow cover is thin, and the ground is frozen."

"I understand that the equipment is topnotch."

"Of course. We'll sleep in a heated motorhome that is equipped with a shower and toilet. Here are your sleeping bags and another bag with warm clothes. You should change here. We got your size in advance."

"Where is the rest of the team?" Alex asked.

"In Gällivare, about 700 kilometers from here. It will take more than an hour to drive there."

Once they were there, Alex met the electrician, a computer specialist, the driver, and the cook. Rune introduced Alex Almåker as the chief engineer and project leader. Rune described the work area.

"We're heading for the hydroelectric power plants along the river Stora Luleälv first. Then we'll cover the river, Lilla Luleälv." On the map, he pointed out all 14 plants located along the rivers. When Rune was done with his presentation, it was Alex's turn.

"We will cooperate with the personnel at the power plants. Before we drive to the transformer stations, we'll check the plants for any possible damage that could have occurred during the outage. We'll divide up the work so we don't waste any time. It's a race against time. We cannot allow the enemy to take this vital part of Sweden." Alex paused and let his words sink in.

"We'll do the physical work in daylight, which means that we travel mornings and evenings. We'll reserve eight hours for sleep, but if we can't keep the schedule, we'll sleep less. We'll eat whenever we can. Everyone must drink at least three liters of water a day. Never leave our vehicles without two bottles of water. Everyone must be aware of the risk of electric shock. So far this year, four electricians have been killed. Is this understood?" Everyone nodded. "Any questions?"

"Can we return home after we have finished our work in these areas?"

"After that, I have no orders, but they could come later," Alex said.

He had an important mission ahead of him and was anxious to get started. I must succeed, he told himself.

The hacker: *I must say that I admire Alex for taking on a new dangerous project after what happened to him the last time. Will he succeed? And what can be expected of Kurt when he gets to Helsinki?*

Chapter 51

Alex had studied the geography of Lapland at the office for the last few days. Gällivare had a population of 18,000 and included four Sami villages. Located 100 kilometers north of the polar circle, the city was the last one on the railway named Inlandsbanan. Normally, it was possible to take the night train from there to Stockholm. Lapland's only airport was located in Gällivare, but it wasn't included in the project and neither was the railroad. The power plants, the iron ore mines, and the Boliden copper and gold mines were more important. They could not fall into Russian hands.

The work continued day after day in good weather until a snowstorm stopped all activity. The snow blew and visibility was limited to one meter in all directions. Joakim suggested they park their vehicles in a circle. It reminded Alex of the Conestoga caravans in Western movies.

"We have everything we need here, and no one can go outside the circle," Alex said. Turning to Joakim, he asked, "How long can a storm last in this area?"

"I have seen storms that lasted more than three days. Hope we can play cards?"

"We can," Rune said. "We also have books, both fiction and nonfiction."

Alex put on a Norwegian sweater and selected a book to read. But his thoughts went to Mia, Andy, and his parents. He imagined what they were doing and what the weather was like in Oslo. It was probably mild. He wondered if his father was working in the home improvement store. He opened his laptop and decided to write down everything that had happened so far on his journey and hoped to continue his entries for the rest of the expedition. He wrote letters to Mia, to Toby, and Kurt, although he could not send them until later. It gave him something to do.

His colleagues played cards, laughed when they won, and cussed when they lost. They discussed politics and raised their voices when disagreeing. They ate and slept. Alex worried about losing so much time.

When he woke in the morning of the fourth day, he didn't hear the wind. As he opened the door, he saw deep drifts around their vehicles, but it wasn't snowing anymore. The men brought out the snow shovels. They all took turns clearing away the drifts that were in their way. The food and the coffee tasted much better afterward.

They traveled slowly through the snow. The sun shone and the temperature rose. Alex photographed the colorful group of workers against the majestic background of snow-covered mountains.

Joakim said that Aktra in Jokkmokk was Sweden's most photographed mountain, and Sarek was considered to be Europe's last existing wilderness with alpine heights. "The two rivers, Stora and Lilla Luleälv, flow through Jokkmokk and meet in Vuollerim, where they form Lule Älv, which flows out in the Bothnian Sea," he said.

"There is so much hydropower in these rivers that it could light up all of Sweden, night and day, if we could distribute the power that far," Rune said.

When the driver parked the excursion vehicle at the Porjus powerplant, he noticed that the back wheels began to sink into the ground. Quickly, he jumped into the driver's seat and slowly added more pressure to the gas pedal to ease the vehicle forward. But when the back wheels sank deeper, he gunned the engine and got the entire vehicle on solid ground. The men stood and looked into the deep hole that had opened up. Slowly, they took several steps back.

"The truck could have ended up on the bottom," Alex said, shuddering at the thought. Turning to Rune he asked, "Do we have any maps that show where the mine tunnels are?"

"Yes, but they are only approximate. When we come to such an area, it's best to sound the terrain."

Rune saw the opportunity to educate the crew about the area. "The first hydroelectric power plant in Porjus was built 1910-1915 to electrify Riksgränsbanan, the railway that transports the iron ore from Kiruna across the border to Narvik," he said. "The old power plant is now a museum, and the new hydroelectric plant is the third largest in Sweden."

When the team came to the largest power source, Harsprånget, Alex told his men that a 700-mile high-voltage line runs south to Hallsberg in Närke. It was finished in 1952 and delivered power to the middle of Sweden and parts of southern Sweden until the cyber attack put a stop to it. "Harsprånget is Sweden's largest hydroelectric power plant," he said. Alex assured the men they were not going to work on the line going south. "We have enough to do up here."

The men would never forget the scene that met them at Messaure, where another large hydroelectric power plant was located. When they woke up, their motorhome was surrounded by hundreds of reindeer.

"It's too bad it's not Christmas Eve," Joakim said. He snapped pictures of the animals as they licked the snow and frost off the windows on their vehicle. "My children will love these photos," he said.

Alex smiled while he photographed the reindeer. "They aren't afraid of us. I've heard that they invade people's yards and do damage."

"We've made camp in Sweden's largest winter feeding area for reindeer. It's called Sirgis," Joakim said. "The reindeer scrape away the snow with their hoofs and eat the lava (moss) underneath. We have invaded their feeding area and should leave right away."

About the Laxed hydroelectric power plant, Joakim said that because Lule Älv was used for floating timber, a 122-meter-long canal had to be built for the timber to pass. Between 10,000 and 24,000 logs were floated through the canal every hour.

The last hydro plant on Alex's list was the one in Boden. It was located at the site where Ljusnan's old sawmill had once stood. The first power plant was built in 1905 when few Swedes could imagine having electricity in their homes. Boden was not only known for its copper and gold mines; it was also known for its fine salmon and trout fishing just below the falls and only a few minutes from the city center. The men wanted to stay and fish. Rune said it would be a small reward for the important work they had done. "We're at Sweden's best fishing spot. Can't we set aside half a day?" he asked.

"But what would we do with the fish?" Alex didn't want the vehicles smelling of fish when they were returned. "Also, you have to have a permit to fish here."

"Well then, all we can do is to stand here and watch the lucky fishermen pull up one big salmon after the other while we can only photograph them," Rune said with resignation in his voice.

While they drove back to Kiruna, they were happy to see the villages and ski slopes lit up. Everyone used their cell phones to call their families. Alex checked his emails and sent the ones he had written earlier.

He had received a text from Kurt saying he was at the University of Helsinki. "We're making progress," it said. Alex texted back that he was finished with his project in Norrland. He texted the same message to Toby but called Mia to hear her voice. He could hear her draw in her breath before saying that she was relieved he was safe and coming home.

Back home again, Alex told a story he had heard in Luleå. "About 40 years ago, when Sweden had suffered a countrywide power outage that didn't have anything to do with cyber, someone had forgotten to restart the power plant in Boden. When an off-duty employee took a walk, he saw water rushing down the dam and felt the ground shaking. He opened the gates and saved the city of Luleå from disaster. The episode was hushed up, but the story leaked out in the Boden area."

"We can't always depend on remote control from Stockholm," Alex mused.

Lena was glad to see Alex, but her disposition had not improved. She did not want to watch television. Instead, she went to bed and stayed there. She had lost interest in cooking and baking, and not even Andy could make her smile. She complained a lot about everything that had happened in Sweden and also regretted they had left the farm. Anders said they could go back to the farm if it would make her happy, but she said it was too late. She feared the Russians would come and take it.

When Lena complained about pain in her stomach and back, Mia took her to a doctor who prescribed pills and told Mia that that her mother-in-law suffered from depression.

Mia understood why. It was always more difficult for older people to move to another country, and with all the dramatic changes in Sweden, Lena risked losing her foothold there. Anders had a calmer disposition and a job to concentrate that kept him busy.

The hacker: *I am saddened by Lena's depression. I'm not supposed to care about the family but I do. I think I'll check in on Kurt.*

Chapter 52

Kurt had met many beautiful girls in Tallinn without falling in love with any of them. But when he came to Helsinki University and was introduced to Elsa Stenlund from Turku, he was smitten. Elsa was a Finnish Swede with naturally blonde hair, light blue eyes, and curves in all the right places, as Kurt phrased it.

Everything about her attracted him. Besides her physical attributes, she was super smart and one of the experts who had restored power to Finland after the cyber attack. Kurt could not resist the magnetic power she had on him. Surely, she could have any man she wanted, and he feared she already had someone special in her life. He was prepared to be disappointed when he asked her to have a cup of coffee with him. With a glint in her eyes, she said yes, and it gave him hope.

Elsa told him she had studied at Uppsala University one semester while being enrolled at a University in Turku. Kurt could not take his eyes from her lips as she spoke Swedish in her sing-song Finnish accent. She said she hoped to contribute to the restoration of electric power to all of Sweden.

Kurt told her how he had come to Tallinn on the day of the cyber attack, and how his brother Alex had worked to manually restore the power to the local grids.

"He must be a very brave man. I would love to meet him."

"Alex is married and has a child, so there you don't have a chance, but I happen to be single in case I could stand in for Alex."

Elsa reddened. "Of course, I was only interested in Alex's work."

Kurt felt even more tenderness for her when she looked embarrassed. Perhaps he had a chance, after all, so he asked, "Do you want to go out with me tonight?"

"What do you have in mind?"

"I thought we could go out to eat, just the two of us."

"I would like that." Kurt could hardly believe his luck.

"May I pick you up at 7 o'clock?"

It was November, and it got dark outside at about 3 p.m. They usually left the university at 5 p.m. Kurt walked Elsa to her building. She gave him a warm smile that showed the dimples in her cheeks. "See you tonight," she said. He stood and looked at her until she gave him another smile and went inside.

He hardly knew which way to turn. He was dazed. His legs felt weak as he began to walk to his building. It was like being 18 and in love for the first time.

He sweated as he sank down on his couch. All his nerves were high-wired. How would he be able to concentrate on his work with a distraction like Elsa close by? He rubbed his chin, and at once he knew he had to shave off his beard because he wanted to feel Elsa's skin against his own. He got out a clean shirt and his favorite tie. But the clock had hardly moved. He grabbed his jacket again and went out to look for a suitable restaurant where he and Elsa could have a quiet table. When he had found one, he reserved a table for two.

At exactly 7 p.m. he knocked on Elsa's door, clean-shaven. He wore a warm jacket over his suit because it was cold outside. When Elsa opened her door, she stood before him in a dusty pink sweater, jeans, and long, high-heeled boots that made her taller. The top of her hair reached his nose, and he could breathe in her lovely aroma while he helped her with her coat. He stood and looked at her while she pulled on her gloves and hung her purse over her shoulder.

"We're ready to go," she said and stuck her arm under his. Kurt felt like the world had stopped.

"I found a nice restaurant not far from here. Do you mind walking?"

"No, I don't mind," she said, as she cast a sideways look at him. "I see that you shaved off your beard."

"Do you miss it?"

"No, not at all."

When they were seated at the table, he asked if she wanted a glass of wine and what kind.

"White wine, please."

They said "cheers" and looked into each other's eyes. Kurt was speechless. After a while, Elsa asked him how long he planned to stay in Tallinn. He had thought about how it would feel to kiss her and didn't hear what she said.

"Sorry, what did you say?"

Elsa repeated her question, and Kurt straightened up.

"Until I'm done with my dissertation."

"I'm also writing my dissertation. It's about the hacking of the grid in Finland, and how it could have been avoided and also rectified."

"I'm writing about the cyber attack on Sweden. "

"We must meet and compare so we don't have the same hypothesis."

Kurt was glad she was the one suggesting it. Their conversation changed to their upbringing. Elsa was born and raised in Swedish-speaking Turku, formerly Åbo. Kurt knew that the area had remained culturally Swedish much longer than the rest of Finland.

Elsa had earned her bachelor's degree at Åbo University, which had a Swedish department for migration research but also a department for computer science. For her post-graduate studies, she had chosen Helsinki University.

"My whole family tree is Swedish," she said. "I thought about majoring in history, but selected computer science."

Kurt told Elsa about growing up on the family farm, his brothers, and parents, who now lived in Oslo, and said he would join them for Christmas.

While Elsa went to the ladies' room, he paid for their meal. He didn't even remember what the food had tasted like. Elsa came back and said she would have been glad to pay half.

"I was pleased you could join me, so it was my pleasure to pay. We must do this again. If you like, we could go to a place where we can dance."

"It would be fun."

He helped her with her coat and squeezed her gloved hand while tucking it under his arm. When they said goodnight outside her door, he wanted to feel her lips against his but was happy to brush his face against her soft cheek. There would be other chances because they would work together every day while he was in Helsinki.

Kurt wanted another date with Elsa and asked Johannes if he could recommend a nice place for eating and dancing.

Leaving the center together that night, Kurt asked Elsa if she felt like going with him to a grill and cocktail bar called Svenska Teatern that had music and dancing.

"Of course," she said with a smile.

"As you know, people here in Helsinki go out rather late. How would it be if I pick you up at 7 o'clock?"

Elsa agreed. Kurt couldn't remember when he had felt so happy about a date. As soon as he was back in his room, he texted Alex, saying he had met a Finnish woman who broke all records. "We'll be working together while I'm here in Helsinki. Then I'll come and visit you."

"Can't wait to hear more about your work and dating, bro," Alex said.

When Kurt picked up Elsa for their date, he put his arms around her waist, pulled her close, and kissed her on her forehead. His face was lit up in a big smile and so was hers.

They heard the music from Svenska Teatern as they approached. Kurt hung up Elsa's coat and admired her narrow skirt that showed off her beautifully shaped body. She took a pair of high heels from a bag and put them on instead of her boots. "I can't dance in boots," she said.

The most popular drink appeared to be a locally produced beer that they enjoyed. They heard different languages —Swedish, Finnish, Estonian, and English. Elsa said she also heard Russian spoken.

"Do you speak Russian?" he asked. "We have many ethnic Russians in Tallinn."

"I have studied the language, but it's hard. English is so much easier. I already knew Swedish."

After a while at the bar, they got a table and ordered from the impressive menu. They listened to American oldies while they ate. Kurt asked Elsa if she had been to the United States.

"Yes, my sister and I were in New York once."

"I would like to visit America, but it will have to wait until I'm done with my research."

Elsa swayed with the music. A few couples were already dancing.

"Do you want to dance?" Kurt asked.

"Love to." Kurt led Elsa to the dance floor where they soon danced cheek-to-cheek.

"I'm so glad I met you," Kurt said. Looking into her eyes, he felt like he floated.

When the beat quickened, the couples on the dance floor began to rock and sing along with the lyric that went perfectly with Kurt's feelings. "I think I love you," was repeated over and over. It was an old song, sung by David Cassidy, but the feeling in Kurt's heart was new.

"I'm so glad we could do this," he said.

"I'm glad, too." Kurt hoped for goodnight kisses and was thrilled when his wishes came true.

Back in his room, Kurt opened his laptop and saw an encrypted message. He assumed it had something to do with his current work. It could be from the hacker and it could be a threat....

It was an unpleasant disruption to his happy state of mind. He decided not to open it right away and instead he wrote an email to Alex telling him about his date with Elsa.

The hacker: *Kurt is in love, and I know how to get his attention, and then I think he will open my message.*

Chapter 53

The next morning, Elsa didn't show up at Data Central. Kurt thought she had overslept and called her cell phone. It rang a few times before it said, "The number you are calling is not valid. Please check your number and try again." Kurt did with the same result.

"I'm going to check on Elsa," he told Johannes and grabbed his jacket. He ran out of Data Central, raced to Elsa's apartment building and bolted up the stairs, three steps at the time. When he stood outside her door, he paused to catch his breath before ringing the doorbell. He pressed it several times while calling Elsa's name, but there was no answer. With his back against the wall, he slowly sank to the floor. Sitting with his hands around his knees, he just knew that Elsa's disappearance had something to do with the encrypted message he had received. A man passed him in the corridor. "Have you seen Elsa Stenlund today?" Kurt was grasping at straws. "No, not today. I saw her yesterday."

Kurt opened the encrypted message and turned cold. He stared out in the air. One thought raced through his mind. I have to find Elsa, and that means I have to do what the message says.

Kurt answered with an encrypted message and agreed to meet with the messenger in Tallinn. Solving the hacker's code at Data Central had to wait. Elsa's disappearance had turned into a rescue mission. He called Johannes and told him he was still looking for Elsa, but didn't say anything about his forced contact with a suspicious person.

"I hope you find her," Johannes said.

Kurt went to his room and quickly packed what he had brought to Helsinki. While he was on board the ferry to Tallinn, he was in touch with Igor, the messenger, via encrypted messages. He was told how he were to identify himself. As Kurt walked into the terminal, he spotted the man who met Igor's description. He was dressed in black from top to toe and carried a black briefcase.

"Hello," Kurt said and added the phrase he had been instructed to say. The man gestured to him to follow him. He took Kurt to one of the boxlike buildings from the Stalin era, and they walked up to the third floor, their steps echoing through the stairwell. Igor took up a key and opened a grey door that looked like all the other doors except it had no number. Kurt got a sense of a trap but had no choice but to enter.

The room had two narrow beds and no other furniture. It was obvious to Kurt that Igor checked the lamp attached to the wall for bugs before he turned it on.

"Okay, Kurt, we can talk here," Igor said in a Russian accent. They were the first words Kurt had heard him say. By now, Kurt suspected that the man was responsible for what had happened to Elsa.

"What have you done with Elsa Stenlund?" Kurt demanded to know in a stern voice.

"Elsa is safe. You'll see her again after you have gotten me into your country."

"Why can't you get there without my help? I'm sure you can falsify passports and everything else."

"I need you to verify that you know me and can vouch for my character, so I can get what I need. My boss will be looking for me, and I have to cover my tracks. I will need a Swedish valid ID. This is not the way I usually look. I have already changed my appearance."

Kurt stared at the man's hair, beard, and dark eyebrows. The eyebrows showed signs of having been blackened. His glasses seemed to bother him and he took them off. The only prominent feature he couldn't have changed was his unusually tall and husky frame.

"We are taking the ferry to Stockholm tomorrow morning, and you are paying for my ticket. You will also get me some Swedish currency," Igor said. He pronounced every word and didn't use any contractions.

"What about tonight?" Kurt asked, looking with disgust at the dirty mattresses.

"We will sleep here. You might as well make yourself comfortable."

Kurt stepped into the bathroom and saw a rusty shower and equally rusty handbasin. He turned the faucet to see if there was any hot water, but it was cold. He peed in the dirty toilet and flushed. He had an apartment in Tallinn, but he had no choice but to stay with Igor if he wanted to see Elsa again, and more than anything else, he wanted her to be safe and sound. She must have been taken hostage, and it scared Kurt to think about what she may have to endure.

"We are going to go through everything you need to know about me," Igor said.

"If you can remember your lies, I can."

"It will not help you to be sarcastic."

The man spoke good English, but Kurt was not surprised. All hackers and scammers knew English, more or less. Kurt hung his coat on a hook behind the door. They sat on the side of their beds facing each other while they went through everything Kurt had to learn about Igor Oblonsky. Supposedly, they had met at TalTek, where Igor claimed he had studied Computer Science. He had an ID that said he had graduated from TalTek.

Kurt memorized Igor's birthday and the names of his parents. He imagined they would check out somehow. Igor must be the hacker who had shut down the power grid, and there were no limits to what he could do. He already knew everything about Kurt.

Both men lay down fully dressed. When Igor had turned off the bed lamp, Kurt listened to the sounds from the city and thought about the terms of Elsa's possible release. There was something that didn't make sense. He set up and asked, "How can I be sure you will release Elsa when she's in Helsinki, and you will be in Sweden?"

"I was not the one who kidnapped Elsa. A buddy of mine did that, and he will release her when I say so."

"Then I'll need the name and contact information of your buddy."

"I will give it to you later."

"No, I need it now, or I won't do what you're telling me." Kurt sat up in bed and turned on the lamp.

"Alright, his name is Ivan Romanov, and he works as a cook at a bar and grill in Helsinki. I'll write down his mobile number in the morning."

"No, you will give it to me now."

Igor told him the number from memory.

"Wait a minute, I have to write it down." Kurt didn't want to depend solely on his memory with something this important.

"Alright," Igor repeated the number and Kurt made sure he had it right as he jotted it down.

"Are you happy now?"

"I won't be happy until I see Elsa again. And if I don't, I have your new identity and I will report you."

Kurt couldn't relax. He was in the worst situation of his life. The thought about holding Elsa in his arms finally lulled him to sleep.

He woke with a start when he heard a toilet flush. Where am I? Oh, this hellish place! He rubbed his face, his eyes, and shook himself awake. Igor came out from the bathroom.

"It is time to go the ferry," he said.

Kurt entered the bathroom, splashed cold water on his face, and finger-combed his hair. There was no mirror, but Kurt didn't care. He rubbed the stubble on his chin.

Kurt bought tickets for them to the ferry and used the ATM to withdraw the Swedish money Igor had demanded. They ate breakfast on board and didn't talk more than necessary. Most of the passengers were Swedes who had been to Tallinn to shop for groceries, wine, and vodka. Kurt recognized the store names printed on their bags, and he listened to their chats about how empty the stores were in Stockholm.

While they went through the passport control in Stockholm, Kurt saw that Igor carried an Estonian passport that was immediately accepted. It must have been a good fake.

Kurt heard a Swedish man talking to a woman who was either his wife or girlfriend because she leaned into him all the time. They spoke Swedish, and the woman had a marked Russian accent.

Igor stopped the couple and asked the woman a question in Russian. She smiled and nodded. Then she took up a card from her purse and gave it to him while speaking his language. Igor accepted the card and thanked her with a bow. The tall, white-faced Swedish man began to pull his wife away. Kurt whispered something to him in Swedish, and the man tightened his grip on the woman, and they hurried away.

Igor held up the card and said, "This is where we are going. Do you know how to get there?"

Kurt took one look at the card that gave the address to the Russian Club.

"Yes, we can take the bus there," he said.

The hacker: *It is going well so far. I am in Stockholm to begin my new life. I will play a part in Kurt's life a little longer, but my career as a hacker is over.*

Chapter 54

At the Russian Club, people played cards and took lessons in Russian dancing. Kurt smelled food, and Igor said they would stay for lunch. The bar just opened and Igor said, "Come and have a beer."

Igor and the bartender talked in Russian while Kurt sipped his beer and studied the bulletin board that announced various activities. He was surprised to see a card with a picture of the Russian woman they had met on the ferry. It said in Swedish and Russian that she taught a children's classes in ballet at the club. She had a Swedish last name, and Kurt guessed she was married to the tall man.

A Russian-Swedish dictionary lay on the bar disk, and Kurt picked it up and studied it because he had nothing else to do. Absentmindedly, he listened to Swedish spoken by younger Russians who must have been born in Sweden because they spoke without an accent. They should be at work or in school, but although Stockholm had power, jobs were scarce, and the schools may not have enough funding to be in session. Kurt wondered if the Russian Club received financial assistance from Russia for its cultural activities.

Igor excused himself and went to a room behind the bar together with another man. When they finally emerged, Igor said. "Meet my roommate, Sergei." Sergei stretched out his hand for a shake, and Kurt offered his fingertips.

"It is time for lunch. Thanks for paying for the meal," Igor said to

Kurt.

While Igor and Sergei ate Russian black soup, Kurt ate a sandwich. Igor said their next stop would be at a bank. He had already secured a job at the club as a record keeper. The man was a go-getter, but it suited Kurt fine. The sooner he could get back to Helsinki, the better.

At the bank, Kurt had to lie to win Elsa's freedom. If he was apprehended for it, he would claim extortion. But, of course, he had heard of the Russian mafia that killed without mercy. Sergei acted as Igor's second character witness. Igor was photographed and got his Swedish ID. He also opened an account with the cash he had received from Kurt and got a debit card. How could it happen so fast? Kurt could hardly believe it.

Once they were out on the street, Kurt said to Igor, "Now you must call Ivan Romanov and tell him to release Elsa." Igor took up his cell phone, clicked on it, and said, "It does not work here."

"You need to buy a Swedish sim card, and you should know that. You can do it with your new debit card."

"Guess I have to use it to get a good credit report."

Igor bought a sim card, opened his phone, and inserted it. Many people around them talked on their phones, and no one paid attention to them when Igor made the call.

"You can go back to Helsinki now, Kurt, and meet Elsa," Igor said before closing the phone.

"I want to hear Ivan saying it." Igor gave his phone to Kurt.

"Hello, Ivan, this is Kurt. Where can I meet Elsa?"

"At her building. I will drop her outside the entrance." Ivan had the same accent as Igor.

"If you don't, I'll report Igor for fraud."

"Kurt gave the phone back to Igor.

"Have a good trip," Igor said with a smile.

Kurt turned on his heel and hurried to the bus stop. He had lost a lot of money, but Elsa was the prize. He took the first available ferry back to Tallinn, and then the last ferry for the day to Helsinki. An hour later, he hailed a cab and gave Elsa's address to the driver.

It was late and Kurt hoped she was still awake. Inside the door, he pressed the button beside her name, and when she answered, he blew out the breath he had been holding. "It's Kurt," he said, while digging for a breath mint in his pocket.

"Come on up, Kurt."

He took three steps at the time, still carrying his suitcase. Elsa stood in the doorway, and they fell into each other's arms.

"I've been expecting you," she said. "That awful man, who captured me, told me you were on your way."

"He didn't hurt you, did he?" Kurt held her shoulders while looking into her eyes.

"No, but I was so scared. Come and sit down, and I'll tell you," she said.

Kurt let her talk.

"I was blindfolded and locked in a room. There was no bathroom, only a can. I thought I would be killed or transported to Russia to reveal everything I knew about codes. I didn't think I would ever see you and my family again. I thought I had lost you forever and wondered if you, too, had been kidnapped. I cried and cried. "

"I'm so sorry, Elsa. When you didn't come to Data Central in the morning, I rushed here to look for you." Kurt told her everything he had been through in the last two days, the longest in his life. "But we're safe now, sweety. I love you, and I want to spend the rest of my life with you."

"I love you, too, Kurt," Elsa confirmed it with a hiccup and a smile. Kurt took her face in his hands and kissed her tenderly.

"I have lied to the Swedish authorities to see that smile again," Kurt said. "Our hacker is now in Stockholm. First, he had defected from Russia to Tallinn, then I had to help him get to Sweden. He had a fake Estonian passport, a new name, and now he has a Swedish identification card, a bank account, a debit card, and a job at the Russian Club."

"You did all that for my sake?"

"Yes, and I think I could have killed Igor if necessary. He said he had to get away from his boss."

"That's good, but can we believe it?"

"We need to change all our passwords, and get even more internet security."

Exhausted but happy, Kurt said goodnight to Elsa and walked to his apartment, where he took off his clothes and showered away the bad feeling of having been held hostage by Igor. He still worried about Elsa. She could have been traumatized.

The next morning at Data Central, they both updated their internet security.

"I think Igor has snooped on us ever since the cyber attack," Kurt said. "Then when he saw how much you meant to me, he decided to kidnap you, knowing that I would do anything to get you released."

"I'm very glad you did. Do you think he will stop the hacking now?"

"I hope so, but we can never be sure."

Kurt and Elsa spent long days on their computers except for a quick lunch. Their work required concentration, but most of all, patience. Elsa doubled her effort to get back at the hacker. They continued their work long into the night and found that they complemented each other. Still, they were up early the next morning to check what their programs had accomplished during the night. If there was no progress, they had to start over again.

Kurt had discovered that the hacker had begun his destructive work by infiltrating smaller companies and copying their contacts. Then he had hacked the contacts' contacts, and so on until he found correspondence with a power plant, the regional grid, and the main grid. Kurt applied his "mile-long" code and waited for the result.

"Bingo!" The happy expression came from Kurt. It was not a data word, but Elsa understood what it meant.

"Congratulations," she said and jumped up from her chair. Kurt embraced her and danced around with her.

"We did it! We have conquered the hacker's destructive work. What a wonderful feeling! Kurt pumped his fists in the air, sat Elsa on his knee, holding one arm around her while calling Johannes.

Johannes came, took a look at the screen, and said, "Good job, but please don't contact television because then the hackers can attack us again with even worse codes. You can tell your families. When people have power again, everyone will be so happy that no one asks how it was done. But it's not going to happen at once."

The satisfaction of having succeeded was what mattered the most to Kurt and Elsa.

"You can write about it in your dissertations. I'm sure they will be approved. You'll be able to pick and choose among teaching positions." Johannes shook their hands and thanked them. When he left, he turned and said "Congratulations! Sweden owes you a large debt of gratitude."

Kurt and Elsa couldn't resist the temptation of calling their families. Johannes had said it was okay. As soon as Alex answered, Kurt told him the good news and asked why the entire country couldn't be lit up at once.

"Because there could be faulty wires. Hopefully, most of them can be repaired by remote control, but if not, electricians have to be sent out to work on the lines. That's why it doesn't happen all at once."

"Elsa was done with her call to her parents. Her cheeks were rosy and her eyes danced with excitement when Kurt embraced her.

"Let's go out and celebrate with champagne. Where do you want to go?"

"To the place you took me the first time."

With their arms around each other, they walked out of the building, tired but happy. Kurt was already planning for their future together.

"I wish you could come with me to Turku," Elsa said. "I'm nervous about traveling alone."

Kurt looked at her pleading eyes and said, "If you're afraid, I can change my schedule. As you know, I had planned to visit my family in Oslo, but I also need to go to Uppsala and check on my apartment there. How about this? I cancel my ticket to Oslo, then I come with you to Turku for a couple of days, and after that, you come with me to Uppsala?"

"Great, I'd love to go to Uppsala with you now that the power is back."

"I don't know what my apartment looks like. My roommate with diabetes might be dead, and then I have bills to pay."

"You have too many apartments, one in Uppsala, one in Tallinn, and a temporary one in Helsinki."

"I know, and I have to cancel the one in Uppsala. But first I have to go to Tallinn to get some more clothes. Then I'll come back here and we'll take the train to Turku."

"Oh, Kurt, you make me so happy, and my parents will love to meet you, but your family in Oslo will be disappointed if you aren't with them on Christmas Eve."

"They have each other, and they won't miss me too much. I can call them right now." As expected, they understood and asked him to bring Elsa the next time he came to Oslo.

That evening, Elsa treated Kurt to dinner with champagne. "It's the least I can do. Without you, I might still be a captive," she said.

In Tallinn, Kurt repacked his suitcase, bought a Christmas gift for Elsa, and wine and chocolates for the family. Satisfied with his choices, he returned to Helsinki. Being in love with Elsa, he could have gone to the end of the world for her.

The hacker: *Kurt is a good man, but he is taking credit for breaking the code. Of course, he is not aware of my assistance. The view he has of me is not good, but it was the last time I acted as a hacker, although I will not stop spying on him and the rest of his family, not just yet.*

Chapter 55

In the morning of Christmas Eve, Kurt and Elsa sat on the train to Turku, Elsa looked at all the male passengers as a potential threat to her. She was paranoid but with good reason. She still had nightmares about being a prisoner in a small room for two days and not knowing what would come next. Kurt understood because he had nightmares himself about Igor. He called his parents from the train, talked to everyone, and wished them God Jul (Merry Christmas).

They arrived in Turku two hours later and were met by Elsa's parents. "This is Kurt," Elsa said, and here are my parents, Oliver and Anna." Kurt thought they both looked very Swedish, which they were although they lived in Finland.

"Pleased to meet you, Kurt, and welcome to Turku," Oliver said.

"Thanks, it's the first time I'm here."

"We heard about your success in restoring power to Sweden. It was quite an accomplishment."

"Elsa and I both did the necessary work, but there were some problems along the way."

"We heard about it from Elsa," Anna said, and we appreciate everything you did for her. We're glad you decided to accompany her here." To Elsa, she said, "Now that you're home, I hope you can relax."

"I think so. I can't wait to see Annika and her family."

As soon as Oliver had parked outside their ranch-style home, the front door flew open. "Welcome, welcome, Kurt and Elsa," Annika said. The two sisters hugged first.

Kurt put down his suitcase inside the door and handed a bag with three wine bottles to Oliver with the words, "I hope you like the assortment."

"I'm sure we will. Thank you very much. I'll take them to the kitchen."

Kurt took off his coat, and Annika's husband, Steve, hung it in the hall closet. As soon as Kurt stepped into the living room, he saw the welcoming sight of the lit Christmas tree and smelled the enticing aroma of food coming from the kitchen. Steve, speaking British-English, asked Kurt to sit down while the rest of the family whirred around them speaking Swedish. Steve was a computer specialist and professor at Turku University. He spoke English because he said his Swedish was only elementary.

"I see that my children have torn themselves away from the television," he said. "Kai and Jasmin, come and say hello to Elsa's boyfriend, Kurt. He's staying with us for a couple of days." The two tow-headed children came forward with Kai bowing his head and Jasmin bobbing one knee.

"Your children are very polite," Kurt said.

"Annika has taught them."

The two men talked about the cyber attack and Kurt's work to counteract the attack. "I'm still not sure how Finland restored our power. It seems like it was a combination of know-how and luck," Steve said. Elsa came and sat down at Kurt's side, and he took her hand in his. "Sorry for interrupting, she said, but it looks like you'll be sleeping here in the living room. The bedrooms are full, and the kids are in my room."

"It's alright, sweety."

"Dinner is ready, please get seated," Anna said.

During dinner, which was very much like Christmas Eve dinner at the Almåker farm, Kurt had to tell the family about the ordeal his folks had faced in Sweden. Everyone in the room knew what it was like to be without power caused by the cyber attack, everyone except Kurt, who had only experienced short power outages caused by the weather. He told the story of his brother's efforts to make life on the farm more bearable, and Elsa encouraged him to relate how the farm was sold and later returned to the family.

It was late when they opened their Christmas gifts. Kurt had selected his gift to Elsa with care, and he looked at her as she opened it. "Oh, a bracelet, and it's beautiful, Kurt. Can you help me fasten it?"

"With pleasure," Kurt said. "Amber is supposed to fight infections, but it's not scientifically proven."

"It doesn't matter. I like it because you gave it to me." She let the bracelet glide back and forth on her wrist while showing it to her family.

"We have amber in Finland, too," Anna said. "It comes from the sea."

"Yes, I learned it's a fossil formed from coniferous trees and it's most common in the Baltic Sea," Kurt said. "The clumps are dull when they wash up on the beach and must be polished to get their luster. But it can't be called amber if it's younger than 20 million years. It's a gem."

"Twenty million years! My bracelet has an amazing history," Elsa exclaimed.

Her gift to Kurt was a book. When he unwrapped it, he saw that it was about cyber terrorism.

There was only one gift left underneath the Christmas tree, and it was the large box of chocolates that Kurt had brought. Anna opened it and passed it around, while Oliver opened a bottle of dessert wine and served it to the adults. The children played with their new video games. Anna collected all the wrapping paper that Oliver took outside. He said it had started to snow. "It's beginning to look like Christmas," Steve said while glancing out the window. Everyone rushed to the window to see, and the children went outside to catch snowflakes on their tongues. After a while, Kurt and Elsa were alone in the living room.

"Thank you for giving me a private moment with you. I enjoyed your family, but you're the one I like best." He kissed her on the nose, the lips, the neck, and the arms, all the way to her fingertips.

Elsa made up the sofa bed for him, yawned, and said she was tired. After a tender goodnight, she went to her room and Kurt turned off the lights. He hadn't slept very long when he heard Elsa talking in her sleep. "No, no," she cried out. Then she burst into the living room and threw her arms around Kurt.

"So, so, did you have a bad dream?"

"I probably woke up the entire house, but I dreamed about that awful room with the bucket."

"But you're here with me now, and nothing bad will happen."

"I want to sleep with you," she said and made herself comfortable beside him."

"Your parents will think we are in an intimate relationship."

"I'll move before they wake up. I just want to cuddle and feel safe."

When the family gathered for breakfast, the grounds were covered with snow that had fallen during the night. The children got excited and wanted to go outside and play.

"We're going to church first; then you can play in the snow as much as you want," their grandmother said.

They walked the short distance to the white Lutheran church where the candlelight service, including the music, lasted only 20 minutes. They sang the familiar Swedish Christmas hymns, and Kurt thought it was almost like being at home in Sweden. As they walked out, Elsa introduced Kurt to friends she met.

"Let's go sledding," Kai said. Oliver got an old toboggan out of the garage, and Kurt borrowed boots. At the sledding hill, the adults watched as the kids and many of their friends, all dressed in colorful jackets, went down the hill, shrieking with laughter.

"Come on, Mom and Dad," Kai said. "There's room for you, too." Steve and Annika went first, and then they urged Kurt and Elsa to do the same. "It's invigorating," Annika said. Kurt declined, pointing to his clothes, but Elsa went on a run with the kids and laughed heartily when the sled speeded up. Having pulled the sled back uphill, her cheeks were red and she wanted to go down again.

"It's good medicine for you," Kurt said.

In the afternoon, Elsa took Kurt to the university grounds and showed him the outside of the buildings where she had earned her bachelor's degree. The snow kept coming down. They walked with their arms around each other and enjoyed being by themselves for a while.

The kids wanted to go home to ski. Steve said they lived on the other side of town and that it would be best to drive home while it was still light outside. They said goodbye and hoped to see each other soon.

The hacker: *Now that Kurt has been introduced to Elsa's family, we have to wait and see if he will take Elsa to Oslo and introduce her to his family.*

Chapter 56

The next morning, Kurt and Elsa said goodbye to her family and took the train back to Helsinki, where Kurt canceled the temporary apartment that he had used while working at Data Central.

Elsa checked the weather in Tallinn and Uppsala and decided to wear her sheepskin coat that had fur on the inside. They strolled the streets of Tallinn at night, and Kurt showed Elsa where he had been held by Igor. He looked over his shoulder as they took the ferry to Stockholm, Kurt relived the awful morning he had been forced onto the ferry by Igor.

As they arrived in Stockholm, Kurt thought about the occupation of the castle and the parliament. He felt the bile rise in his throat when he remembered that the Vasa Museum was gone. He heard Stockholmers complain about the lack of merchandise. At the railroad terminal, he was glad to see the trains departures to many different locations in Sweden. They rode the train the short distance to Uppsala. The students were gone and the town looked deserted, but it felt comforting to see the ancient cathedral and the university buildings. Kurt had the key to his apartment in his hand and heard the click that opened the door. He was back after more than one year. When he left, he thought it would be for only a weekend. He wondered if his roommate Arnie had survived his diabetes.

Inside the door, they stepped on a lot of mail which meant that Arnie had been absent for a long time. "Come in, sweety," he said to

Elsa. Ignoring the mail, Kurt flipped the light switch, but no lights came on. He went to the kitchenette and turned the water faucet, but there was no water. "The electricity and water have been turned off," he said to Elsa. He opened the refrigerator and it was empty. "We can't stay here," he said.

He looked at the letters and saw that they were bills.

"Please sit down while I make a phone call to my professor."

"I'll keep my coat on because it's cold in here," Elsa said.

Kurt recognized his professor's voice right away. "Doc Harald, this is Kurt Almåker."

"Kurt, how nice of you to call. We heard about you on the news. You're the one who cracked the hacker's code. Congratulations."

"Thanks, but I didn't do it alone. My colleague and I just arrived at my apartment here in Uppsala, and I wonder if you know what happened to my roommate, Arnie?"

"Oh, you don't know! He died when he couldn't get any more insulin. He was very ill toward the end."

"It's sad to hear. I worried about him. If he had come with me to Tallinn as planned, he would be alive today." Kurt looked as unhappy as he felt.

"His brother came and stayed for a while, but I believe he has moved out."

"Yes, I saw all the mail."

"How long are you staying?"

"We can't stay here. The lights and the water are shut off, and there's no heat. We're going back to Tallinn today."

"I wish you could come over for a chat. You know where I live. My wife can probably round up some food. The power has been back here for a while now, thanks to a team from the Trollhättan power plant."

"Thanks, but I need to clear out the apartment. I've got a lot of books here and no car to take them to the library."

"I can come over and do that for you."

"That would be great. I'll carry them downstairs. Kurt gave him the address.

"Alright see you in about 20 minutes."

Kurt turned to Elsa, who had heard everything. "We'll get warm by carrying these books downstairs."

"Do you have suitcases we can pack them in?"

"I do." Twenty minutes later, they stood with two heavy suitcases at the curb as Doc Harald pulled up.

"This is Elsa Stenlund from Finland," Kurt said.

"You're also famous, and I'm honored to meet you." Elsa extended her hand to him.

"I need the suitcases back," Kurt said.

"I brought these crates for the books. I'll donate them to our library in your name. Don't you want to keep any of them?"

"I've already saved a few. How did you survive the power outage?"

"After a while, we went to our vacation home and stayed there; at least we could cook and stay warm."

When Doc Harald had closed the trunk, he said, "Good luck with your dissertations then. I'm sorry I can't offer you a position here. We're running out of funds and will probably have to close. I'm ready to retire anyway. I'm sure you'll receive many offers from other universities. You won't need my recommendation."

"We're already assured of good positions at the University of Helsinki. Thanks for doing this for me, Doc Harald."

"No problem. Let's keep in touch."

Kurt took the empty suitcases upstairs.

"I'm glad the books are out of the way," he said. "Now, let's go out and eat."

He escorted Elsa to his old student hangout, but it was closed. "I'm guessing they couldn't stay in business with the students gone, but something has to be open downtown." Seeing few cars and people around, he began to wonder. Finally, they found a place where they could have coffee and sandwiches.

Kurt packed all the clothes he had left in his closet on that fateful day in October last year and cringed when he thought about the expense he had incurred by replacing them in Tallinn. But if it hadn't been for all that he wouldn't have met Elsa, and he wouldn't have the recognition he had today.

"Don't you want to take the sheets and towels in this cabinet?" Elsa asked.

"Oh yes. It looks like those are mine. There are no sheets on the bed. I wonder what happened to my other bedding? It doesn't matter. I've spent eight of my student years in this town, but I can't wait to leave."

They rolled their suitcases to the train station on the dreary and dark day in late December and didn't look back.

As soon as they had arrived at Kurt's apartment in Tallin, he sat down at his laptop to pay his bills and cancel the Uppsala apartment. He was not in a good mood, and Elsa sensed it. She looked over his shoulders and saw he had his bank account open.

"I'm almost out of money," Kurt confessed. "I had a lot of expenses lately."

"Did you pay a ransom to get me released?" she asked jokingly.

"That's no joke, sweety."

"So, you did?"

"It wasn't called that, but I had to provide Igor with some cash."

"Oh no! I'll reimburse you, of course."

"Let's not talk about that now. Once I get my stipend from TalTek, I'll be alright, but I'm afraid I can't take you out for a New Year's Eve celebration."

"No, problem, it will be my treat. You have done so much for me already. We're supposed to be equal, you know."

"Since you put it that way, I accept." Kurt slumped in his chair.

"Let's call your parents. It will make you feel better."

"It's too late. We can do that tomorrow. I'm too tired and it's been a long day."

Kurt gave his bed to Elsa and slept on the couch. He hadn't gotten over his disappointment with Uppsala and felt very bad about Arnie's death. But there was something else bothering him as well. *Why did I waste a whole summer in Oslo on entertainment when I could have worked on destroying the hacker's code?*

While they strolled the streets of Tallinn in daylight, he said to Elsa, "As you can see, we have old houses here that are reminiscent of Sweden, but also ugly concrete box-like buildings from the Russian period. The newer construction is modern like TalTek, where I spend my days. "Do you want to see it?"

"Yes, if it's open."

"I've got a key."

"Then let's go."

"I want to show you where I spend most of my time. I'll be back in the new year to work on my dissertation," Kurt said, as he unlocked the door. "This is much better than Uppsala."

"I can see why," Elsa said, "You have a beautiful view of the sea. Those large windows let in a lot of light. I wouldn't mind working here."

"The problem is that most universities won't hire both of us."

When they visited the Center for Cyber Defense, Elsa was as impressed as Kurt had been and filled out an application for a position. The directors were not there between Christmas and New Year's, but the clerk assured her that the cyber defense was at work 24/7. He looked from Elsa to Kurt and back to Elsa again. "Hey, I saw your pictures on TV. You're the couple who returned the power to Sweden?"

"Kurt Almåker did most of the work," Elsa said, pointing to him. "He has already applied for a position here."

"This is an honor. I want to shake your hands. I'm sure your applications will get the attention you deserve."

"We'll get our doctorates in the spring, and then we'll see what happens."

"I'll make a note of it. Please come back when the directors are here. They'll be glad to explain the mission of the center."

As they were leaving, Kurt said, "It was nice to finally be recognized for our long hours at the supercomputers. I just hope that the hacker doesn't attack again."

"Me too," Elsa said with conviction.

They celebrated New Year's by going to a fine restaurant. Kurt felt much better and showed his best moves on the dance floor. "You know that I'm in love with you," he said.

"And I'm in love with you."

"I'm sorry I've been so grumpy."

"I understand. I haven't been the best companion either after the kidnapping."

They had one more glass of champagne at midnight. "I've been an idiot—sleeping on the couch," Kurt said.

"Yes, especially since you didn't have to." Elsa looked up at him and smiled invitingly.

"Happy New Year my love," Kurt said while squeezing her a little tighter.

"The same to you. I think it will be a very happy year."

It was difficult to part after their first love night, but they both had to finish writing their dissertations. Elsa said she felt strong enough to return to Helsinki alone, and Kurt promised he would come and see her the following weekend. It wasn't bad to live in two different countries when it took only 45 minutes by ferry to cross the distance between them.

The hacker: *It looks like Kurt and Elsa will be a couple, and I am happy for them. I'm sure they will be interviewed by many TV stations when they return to work.*

Lilly Setterdahl

Epilogue

In the middle of January, the Swedish parliament, Riksdag, convened to vote on admission to NATO. The elected members arrived in Stockholm by air and rail from all corners of Sweden. Alex, Kurt, Elsa, and others who had worked to restore the power and communications were gratified to see the ease of traveling. All Swedes were happy to follow the news on TV.

After the near loss of Gotland, the Riksdag agreed with the government ministers that Sweden should join the NATO alliance. The vote was unanimous. Funds had to be appropriated although no taxes had been collected for the last year. Companies had been forced to close for lack of personnel and supplies. Most of the workers who had lost their jobs had fled to other countries. There were no taxes to collect. On the plus side, the appropriations for the past year had not been spent. Pensions and benefits had to be paid. Hospitals, eldercare, and schools could not start up unless they were financed. All state employees demanded retroactive salaries. Large loans from China with high interest rates had to be approved.

Many unemployed had become homeless and still wandered around the countryside begging for food. Lacking medicine and care, the old and the sick continued to die. The birthrate was at a record low. More and more immigrant families returned to their home countries. Those who remained took any job they could find for cash, but bartering was the most common. Buildings needed repairs, but the banks did not issue loans. Other countries had lost their faith in Sweden's economy, and Sweden could not deliver goods for export. It would take a long time for the nation to get back to where it was before the cyber attack.

Although the restored communications helped, they also hurt because they enabled more Swedes to leave for greener pastures across the borders. Demographically, Sweden was at the breaking point. Significant restrictions were needed. The universities lost all their funding. It was only a matter of time before Uppsala University would close.

Ole Olafssen called Alex and said that he and his wife would be returning to Oslo. Alex and Mia had to find another place to live, and so did Anders and Lena. With all the Swedes moving to Oslo, the city had a housing shortage. Newly-constructed homes were sold before they were finished. Luckily, Alex had saved most of the money he had earned in his high-risk jobs and could buy a house from a Swedish family moving back to their home in Sweden. Just as Alex and Mia had signed the contract, they learned that the apartment they had waited for would be available to them. Now that they didn't need it, they offered it to Anders and Lena, who were happy to move in and once again be independent. Lena's disposition improved when she could select new furniture and pay for them with some of the money they had received for the farm, which they had not yet been told to return. The four couples who had sold their farms to Johanssen had gotten together and filed a lawsuit against him and his company citing his deliberate, unlawful deceit that had caused them extreme anxiety and pain. Anders and Lena had gladly signed the papers.

Alex was afraid he would lose his job when Olafssen returned, but the plant director said he would retire and Olafssen took his place. Alex could keep his job as the second man in charge. Mia said she would like to start a daycare in her home.

Kurt took the ferry to Helsinki to visit Elsa as often as he could and sometimes, she came to visit him. Elsa came to congratulate him when he had earned his PhD in Computer Science from TalTek, and so did Kurt's former professor from Uppsala and his wife. Doc Harald said they would do some shopping in Tallinn at the same time. When Elsa got the same title at Helsinki University, Kurt went there with a temporary engagement ring in his pocket for her. He would replace it with a more appropriate ring, as soon as he could afford it. For now, he just wanted Elsa to promise she would be his wife, and she did.

With that taken care of, Kurt wanted to introduce Elsa to his family in Oslo and ordered plane tickets. Alex met them at Gardermoen Airport, congratulating them both on their new titles and their engagement.

"Here's Elsa Stenlund, my fiancée," Kurt said, placing an arm around her shoulders while looking proud.

"I'm very glad to meet you, Elsa. I've heard so much about you from Kurt."

"And he told me about everything you've done, Alex."

"It wasn't much compared to what you two have done. By the way, you'll stay with us while you're here. Everybody is already at our house waiting for you.

"How do Mamma and Pappa like their new apartment?"

"They love it. It's on the first floor, and they have a patio that Mamma has decorated with flowers. She has recovered from her depression. They're once again active in the Swedish Club and socialize with their many new friends." Kurt was glad to hear it and anxious to visit his parents in their new home.

Alex asked Kurt if he planned to return to Sweden. "Not the way it is now. Higher education has closed down, but both Elsa and I have been offered positions in Helsinki, at TalTek, and several other universities. One of them is the University of Oslo, and we'll go there first. Then we have tickets to fly to London and New York directly from here. We want to look at all the universities that have sent us offers."

"Sounds like you'll have a lot of choices. It would be great to have you here in Oslo. Have you heard from the Center for Cyber Defense in Tallinn?"

"No, not yet. Elsa has also applied for a position there. Now that we have our PhDs, we might have a chance. If not, we have many other opportunities."

"In Sweden, the job situation has deteriorated lately, but it's probably because of all the new restrictions imposed by the government. Before that, there were no rules. People exchanged goods and work and didn't pay any taxes. They thought it would be better once the power was restored but there are no good jobs. The prices of food and clothing have doubled. The best that has happened is that Sweden has joined NATO," Alex said, as he parked the car in front of his new home with the log cabin façade. "It's beautiful," Kurt said. "Congratulations. I can only hope to have a home like that one day."

"We have houses like that in Finland, too," Elsa said.

The family members came outside to welcome and congratulate Kurt and Elsa on their engagement and accomplishments. They stood in front of the house for a long time and enjoyed the warm sunshine. Emil and Lynn spoke mostly Norwegian, especially when they talked to their Norwegian cousins. Little Andy was 13 months old and walked a few steps at the time. Anders and Lena were happy that Elsa could speak Swedish.

"When I was little, I always spoke Swedish at home," she said. "I didn't learn Finnish until I started school."

"We're so glad to meet you, Elsa. "Kurt is lucky to have found you," Lena said.

"He told me how hard you had to work last winter when you lost all your modern conveniences."

"We were healthy and that's more important than anything else," Anders said. "My grandparents survived the Spanish flu when life was much harder. Do you know that 50 million people died of that flu worldwide?"

"No, I didn't know that. It was a pandemic, but something like that will never happen again. Medical science has come too far for that."

"I hope you're right."

The three brothers, Toby, Alex, and Kurt gathered together. Toby had gained weight, but Alex was still slender, and Kurt was as lanky as always. Mia asked them all to come inside for a meal. Alex showed Kurt and Elsa around their new home that Mia had decorated in light colors.

"I love the Scandinavian design," Elsa said.

When Kurt and Elsa were alone and had unpacked their bags, Elsa put her arms around Kurt, and said, "I think you have a wonderful family."

"I think so too. I hope we can see them more often in the future. I also want to show you where I grew up in Sweden. Much has changed in my life the last few years, but a definite improvement is that I now have you, my darling. I can already see that my family likes you."

"I like them too, and I feel welcome. It's a wonderful feeling."

"We don't know what our future holds, but as long as we're together, everything will be alright.

The hacker: *This is where I leave the Swedish family. I like the freedom I have here in Sweden. I live a much better life here than I did before. I do not deserve it, but what I did was necessary to get me to abandon my old ways. You may wonder why I chose Sweden as my new country when I had hurt it so deeply. I wonder about that myself, but it just so happened that I could use Kurt to get me here.*

CPSIA information can be obtained
at www.ICGtesting.com
Printed in the USA
BVHW060310091122
651450BV00012B/459

9 780996 846004